THE TERROR AND THE TORTOISESHELL

John Travis

A Benji Spriteman Mystery

THIS IS AN **ALA "Reading List"** EDITION & IS NOT FOR RETAIL SALE OR DISTRIBUTION

★ "*Animal Farm* meets *The Big Sleep* in this quirky but compelling hard-boiled mystery... Travis packs a lot in, including a twisty whodunit plot, humorous sequences to leaven the grimness... Superior work with a... fully realized imaginary world."
—*Publishers Weekly*, January 11th, 2010

"A novel that's sure to become a classic and will also become a major cinema film. There is no doubt in my mind about that.
"I don't think I've yet made it clear how funny this book is. Since starting it, I've been going round with a smile on my face. That's not to diminish the 'terror' and the poignancy of what the reader feels underlying it all.
"We have here one helluva great novel... I give you my personal guarantee."
— **D.F. Lewis** ('weirdmonger'), April 14th – 18th 2010

THE TERROR
AND THE
TORTOISESHELL

BY
JOHN TRAVIS

ATOMIC
FEZ

METRO VANCOUVER   BRITISH COLUMBIA   DOMINION of CANADA

The Terror and the Tortoiseshell

First Edition Hardback published March 2010
To be reprinted: June 2010 (UNITED KINGDOM), July 2010 (DOMINION OF CANADA)
Trade Hardback: ISBN: 978-0-9811597-3-7
Electronic Book (all file types): ISBN: 978-0-9811597-4-4

The text in this collection is copyright © 2009, John Travis, who asserts his moral right to be established as the owner of this work.

Portions of this work (mostly the prologue) previously appeared as a short story using the same title in *Kimota Magazine*, Issue 15, October 2001 (ISSN 1359-8899).

Cover design by Steve Upham

Typeset in "Sabon" & "Seabird"

The "Atomic Fez Publishing" logo and the molecular headgear colophon is designed by, and copyright © 2009, Martin Butterworth of The Creative Partnership Pty, London, UK (www.CreativePartnership.co.uk).

PUBLISHER'S NOTE:
This is a work of fiction. All characters in this publication are fictitious and any resemblance to any real places, rat-produced newspapers, or persons — living or dead — is purely coincidental.

All rights reserved. No part of this book may be used or reproduced in any manner whatsoever without written permission from the authors, except in the case of brief quotations embodied in critical articles or reviews.

Printed in Canada by Hignell Book Printing in Winnipeg, Manitoba

ATOMIC FEZ PUBLISHING
3766 Moscrop Street
Burnaby, British Columbia, V5G 2C8, CANADA
WWW.ATOMICFEZ.COM

Library and Archives Canada Cataloguing in Publication

```
Travis, John
         The terror and the tortoiseshell / by John Travis.

Also available in electronic format.
ISBN 978-0-9811597-3-7 (bound)

         I. Title.
```

Contents

Dedication	vii
Acknowledgements	viii
Prologue: The Ed Mahoney Incident	1
Part One: What Happened	15
Part Two: Down to Business	75
Part Three: The Country of the Blind	163
Part Four: Last Sappy Standing	245
Epilogue: (Another) New Beginning	279
About the Author	289

THIS IS AN **ALA** "Reading List" EDITION & IS NOT FOR RETAIL SALE OR DISTRIBUTION

Dedication

For my Grandmother, Catherine M^CAuley (1916-1996)

My nephew, Samuel Bloodworth and
my niece, Catherine Bloodworth

Endings and Beginnings

Acknowledgements

A big thank you to the following people: Tim Lebbon, who first told me of a certain Cat-themed anthology which resulted in the short story this novel is based on; Graeme Hurry of *Kimota* for publishing it and Simon Duric for illustrating it so wonderfully, reminding me that Benji might need clothes, and Steve Upham, for creating the wonderful cover for the novel; Peter Cannon, Simon Clark, Tim again and Ted Klein for answering my Machen-based queries; Peter and Margaret M^{C}Auley for their illuminating insights into skunks; and to Mum, Dad, Sharon and Andrew, who have helped me in immeasurable ways. Also, a post-production thank-you to both the late Bob Tanner and Ian Alexander Martin for believing in the novel.

And last but not least, the following animals helped along the way: Cassie, Posy, Toby, Evie, Dog, Patch, a diseased hedgehog, and a certain Capuchin monkey for its rather alarming and urgent information.

Various other animals assisted in this novel, but specifically asked to remain anonymous.

Cats are a mysterious kind of folk. There is more passing in their minds than we are aware of.
— **Sir Walter Scott**

✞ ✞ ✞

The smallest feline is a masterpiece
— **Leonardo da Vinci**

Prologue

The Ed Mahoney Incident

THIS IS AN **ALA** "Reading List" EDITION & IS NOT FOR RETAIL SALE OR DISTRIBUTION

Three weeks after taking over the Spriteman Detective Agency, I was sitting at my office window on the fourth floor watching a Gorilla climbing a rickety wooden ladder propped against the building on the other side of the street. Three weeks in and still without a case to my name, I felt like I could've climbed that building without the ladder.

Lowering his large black mitt into the bucket strapped to the underside of the ladder, the Ape retrieved his shammy leather from it, wrung it out, and slopped it against the nearest window, smearing the grime around a bit before moving on to the next window. At the time it never occurred to me—with ledges *that* wide he could probably have climbed the building himself without the ladder. Perhaps he had a thing about heights, I don't know; once the initial shock of seeing an Ape on a window-cleaning round becomes routine, you tend to ignore the little things. When the world changes overnight for no apparent reason, there are more important things to think about.

Like your company logo, for instance.

Benji Spriteman, Detective
Animal Rights, Human Wrongs.

Roughly licking between my pads, I wondered if all the others out there were as dumb as I was. Why couldn't I have kept the sign as it was, rubbed out Jimmy's name and then added mine? Vanity I suppose; a new start for a new era; forget that the old man was dead, forget what had killed him; live in the present, not in the past.

THE TERROR AND THE TORTOISESHELL

So I'd spent the best part of a day getting the old man's name off the window and scrawling mine in its place. And to be fair, it looked good. Damn good.

Yeah, it looked good. It looked fine; right up to the moment I realised that the only way my handiwork could be appreciated was if you were sitting here in the office with me.

What a sap.

'Survival of the fittest', as someone once said. At this rate I'd starve.

I was jolted out of my thoughts by a loud thud outside. I looked out in time to see a Rhino backing away from a badly parked car, scuffing his hooves or whatever they were back and forth across the sidewalk. Ramming the car again, he took off its other fender. Most of the escapees from the Zoo had calmed down, but you still got the odd hot-head.

I repeat: three weeks without a case. Time was weighing heavily on my fur. I needed excitement, I needed—

From the corner of my eye I saw a shadow pass my frosted glass door. It raised a paw to knock. It knocked.

'Come in.'

She floated into my office like a mirage; tall, elegant, her tail wrapped around her neck like a stole.

'Benji Spriteman?' She purred.

I tried to keep cool. 'S'what it says on the door.'

'But not the window,' she said. 'You've painted it on the wrong way—'

'Yeah yeah. What can I do for you?'

'I didn't know where else to go.' She curled up on a chair, her tail swishing agitatedly in the air near her face. She started to tell me the tale. Outside, I heard squawking. That damned Parrot was doing its loop-the-loop trick on the phone wire again, claws digging into the cable, its brightly coloured body spinning through the air, an excited screech escaping its beak.

PROLOGUE: THE ED MAHONEY INCIDENT

'Hey you, pieces of eight,' I called out to it. 'Keep talking,' I told the Persian. 'Yeah you,' I turned back to the Bird. 'Are you the one who keeps throwing my phone line? Half the time it's on the fritz, and I reckon—*what did you say?*'

One word jumped out at me amongst all the others. Turning back to the Persian, I was all ears.

'Tortoiseshell you say? Tell me more.'

'Well you see, what happened was—'

In between trying not to fall into her baby blues and straining to hear her over the shrieking of the beak outside, I learned that a Tortoiseshell had gone missing. It seemed like fate somehow—not just any Cat, but one of my own. At last I was in business.

I had my spiel memorised for such an eventuality. I delivered it like the pro I so desperately wanted to be.

'My fee is a hundred up front, plus fifty a day plus expenses. If I crack the case I get to take you out for salmon.'

She purred in agreement.

I was about to ask her name when there was a clattering racket outside. Looking down into the street I saw the Gorilla sitting on the pavement rubbing his head, the ladder lying in the middle of the road.

The Parrot had a good laugh at that.

⚜

I wasted no time and headed for Quaffer's, a regular hive of skulduggery. I couldn't think where else to go and you have to start somewhere. Tipping my hat to the Chimp on the door, he scratched an armpit and let me pass.

Despite only being mid-afternoon the club was doing a fair bit of trade, even though they still had the same lousy band as the last time I'd been there. I arrived just in time to see the drummer's tail land on the snare and then get whacked with both sticks. The noise he made wasn't pleasant but it was

THE TERROR AND THE TORTOISESHELL

still more tuneful than the Tabby on bass who had somehow managed to get her whiskers caught up in her strings.

'I'm looking for a missing Tortoiseshell, name of Ed Mahoney, comes in here from time to time,' I told the Tom behind the bar. It was a bluff, but it sounded good.

'Ed Mahoney...' the Tom scratched his whiskers and yawned. 'Nope, doesn't ring a bell. Get you a drink?'

'Tuna oil. On the rocks.'

Suddenly the Chimp on the door shot past me, vaulted two tables, picked up a startled Chihuahua who'd been licking his butt, then shot past me again, throwing the mutt out the door, a full fifteen feet into the street.

'If I catch you doing that in here again, it'll be outta the window next time,' the Chimp said, dusting down his jacket.

The Tom handed me my drink. 'Help yourself to bar snacks.' I took an anchovy from a bowl on the bar.

The anchovies and the tuna oil were making me hungry. I decided to chance the restaurant at the back of the place. I hoped it would be better than the Poodle parlour I'd tried the week before, which charged the earth for a bowl of water that stank of perfume.

'I'm looking for a Tortoiseshell,' I said to the waiter after ordering a rare steak.

The waiter, a longhaired Afghan, looked me up and down. 'Aren't we all sir,' he replied.

'One went missing. I'm trying to find him.'

'*Another one?*' His tone changed. 'Hey Alphonso,' he called towards a back room. 'Here a minute.'

Alphonso appeared through the bead curtain and looked like he'd be happier on two legs. Hobbling over to my table, he panted eagerly. 'Yeah?'

'This fella's looking for a Tortoiseshell too', the Afghan told him.

'No kidding? Jeez, what's wrong with this town lately?'

'What do you mean?' I asked.

PROLOGUE: THE ED MAHONEY INCIDENT

'Well, there's never one around when you want one. Like the Police,' he added, walking away. We appeared to be talking at cross purposes.

My meal arrived, quickly followed by an oversized Toucan who brought me my drink. I found my gaze drawn to a strange-looking guy in the corner hunched over a salad. He had more wrinkles on him than the lettuce he was eating and about half the colour. Something about the guy made me uneasy.

'Who's the wrinkly?' I asked the Tuke when he refilled my glass.

'Oh, *him*. Arnie. Kooky ain't he? Reckons he knows the city like the back of his—' the Tuke struggled for a word. 'He knows the city real good anyway,' he finished, going to another table.

Thankfully Arnie was a slow eater, and we finished our meals at the same time. When he left, I paid my bill and followed him at a discreet distance to a tower block about a quarter of a mile away. At the speed he walked it took us nearly an hour to get there.

It was late afternoon and the streets were coming alive. Offices were emptying, shops were swallowing up new customers. My whiskers began to twitch when I saw Arnie hunched over at the tower block entrance jawing with the doormog. I wondered how a Cat, especially a Persian, could sink so low. If ever there was a mutt's job this was it. When Arnie eventually hobbled through the entrance I went over to the Cat, a grin plastered across my face.

'Hey Bootsy. How's tricks?'

Bootsy's eyes widened when as recognised me. 'Shh!' he licked a paw and began smoothing down the fur that'd just sprung up. 'I'm undercover,' he whispered, eyes darting from side to side. 'Dingus sent me along.'

'Dingus, huh? Must be pretty important.' I'd heard of Dingus. Most cops were Dogs and consequently none too smart. But Dingus... I'd heard things about Dingus.

THE TERROR AND THE TORTOISESHELL

'You know I can't say.' Bootsy said, looking past me to the street.

'Another murder, eh?' I tipped him the wink.

'None of your business,' he snapped.

'Did I just see my old pal Arnie go in there?' Bootsy looked back at me.

'You two know each other?'

'Yeah. What's so funny about that? In fact,' I fished around in my jacket for my office keys, 'I need to return these to him. He left them at my place the other day. The thing is, Bootsy, he didn't say which floor he lived on. I don't suppose…?'

Bootsy, despite his breeding, or perhaps because of it, wasn't the brightest kitty on the block.

'Twelfth floor,' he mumbled, moving aside.

The elevator was one of those old-fashioned cage things. When the door closed, it took me back to the days before The Terror, a memory of Jimmy trying to herd me into a box so a man in a white coat could stick needles in me.

With a jolt, the elevator tossed me out onto a murky hallway with a 12 and an arrow pointing right. To my left was the wall and a window. I could've figured it out myself. If I could've gone left I would have, just to annoy whoever had put the sign up. I padded down the dingy hall.

My guess was that Arnie was the only one living on this floor. Whatever kind of creature Arnie was, his smell was everywhere. Halfway along the corridor one of the lights started flickering on and off like a strobe light for the terminally slow. At the end of the corridor I saw the word MURCHESS on the doorplate full of scratches. ARNIE was written above it. I knocked on the door.

After a few seconds I heard a low wheezing. 'Yeah, just a minute!' he called out irritably, fumbling with the door chains. The door creaked open.

'Yeah, whaddya want?' The green face snapped.

PROLOGUE: THE ED MAHONEY INCIDENT

'Hi Arnie,' I said, showing him the old man's badge. 'I hear you know your way around this fair city.'

'Yeah? Who told you that?' He looked me up and down. 'Who are you? How do you know my name?' He looked at the badge again, shook his wrinkled head. 'That ain't you. I'll ask again. Whaddya want?'

'Relax, Arnie. I just need a bit of information, that's all.' I strode into his apartment before he had a chance to stop me.

'I don't know what you've heard, but I ain't no snout.'

'No,' I said innocently, 'of course you aren't. It's just that you seem pretty clued-in. The kind of fella who'd notice that a Cop was hanging around outside pretending to be a concierge.'

He flopped down onto a sofa, sending a cloud of dust up to his middle.

'They found a dead Sappy on the seventh. You still ain't told me what you want.'

'I'm looking for a Tortoiseshell. Somebody told me you knew your way around so I thought you might be able to help me.'

Arnie's eyes glittered. 'Fancy a change, huh?' he cackled. As I'd no idea what he was talking about, I didn't reply.

'Is that all you want? Really?' Picking up a pen he scribbled an address on the back of an old envelope. 'Go to this place, sometime after midnight. It's near the canal. Big warehouse. You can't miss it.' I could just about read his writing.

'Thanks, Arnie.' Before he had a chance to ask, I took a bill from my wallet and stuck it in his mitt. He nodded, presumably to show that I was doing the right thing, him not being a snitch and all.

*

The path beside the canal was full of sludge. For once, I was glad I was wearing shoes. Something was babbling in

THE TERROR AND THE TORTOISESHELL

the black, syrupy water. I was in no mood to find out what. Behind me, the church bells chimed thirteen. They hadn't got the hang of bell-ringing yet, whoever they were. After ten edgy minutes standing in the darkness listening to the babbling, I decided to make my move.

Climbing the muddy bank, rough corrugated walls suddenly blocked out the stars. At the top of the bank, I flitted across to the nearest warehouse. Peering round the corner, I spotted two odd-looking characters making their way towards the light from an open door. Suddenly the door closed behind them and I was in the dark again. I waited a few minutes more then edged towards the door, grabbed the handle. I left it a minute before opening it. As the door eased open I snuck inside.

What I thought I'd find in there, I don't know. But it certainly wasn't this.

I was in a large metal cave filled with brilliant white light which hurt my eyes. When they adjusted, I was looking at a white wall and several white sinks. I turned to another wall and that was a mass of silver, end-to-end with knives, hooks, nails, wires, hacksaws. *Had this been the* SPCH's *headquarters*, I wondered, *their own little torture chamber? And if it had, what was it now?* My paw gripped the gun in my pocket.

To the right was a smaller room made of glass. Inside were the two oddballs I'd seen earlier, chatting away to two Cats.

As I edged closer I heard their talk: something about chopping and cutting. My blood went from simmer to boil. Was my first case going to result in a corpse? If only I'd listened properly from the start...

But my fur was up. I rushed forward and burst through the door, waving my gun at the assembled group.

'Okay, freeze!' I told them.

PROLOGUE: THE ED MAHONEY INCIDENT

One of the Cats, a Siamese, looked at me in disdain. It's the only way they know how to look. Large red patches of blood were spattered across his white coat.

'What the hell is going on here?' I yelled, facing each one in turn. 'Where are the Tortoiseshells?' The Siamese sniffed the air like I was a bad smell.

'What are you,' I shouted at him, 'the chief butcher?'

'Hey, hang on a second,' he snapped. 'We run a legitimate operation here.'

I looked across at the two weirdoes, who reminded me of Arnie. A rogue thought shot across my mind and I blocked it out, hoping I was wrong.

'So you say. I'm looking for a Tortoiseshell. Ed Mahoney.'

Suddenly the Ginger Tom next to the Siamese opened its mouth.

'A Cop? We told you guys everything last week. Why don't you find out who's taking them and come back then?'

The Siamese grinned. 'He's no Cop. He's a Shamus. Either that or he's our thief.'

I was getting rattled. 'Mahoney—where is he?'

'Who wants to know?'

'My client for one.' I looked at the odd couple again. I had this terrible feeling, but kept going anyway. 'Me for another. He went missing a few days ago.'

'*He?*' the Siamese laughed, followed by the Ginger Tom. When the other two joined in, I waved the gun around a bit.

'You want to tell me what's so funny?'

The Siamese wiped an eye, flicked a claw and beckoned me with it. 'Follow me.'

Even with the piece at his back he was still laughing. With the others following, he led us through a short corridor lined with doors, each with a metal plaque on the front: 'SURGERY', 'DEWCLAW CORRECTION', 'BEAK REDUCTION', 'SPOT REMOVAL'. And every time we passed one I kept wondering: had I really been that dumb?

THE TERROR AND THE TORTOISESHELL

When I saw the plaque marked 'TORTOISESHELLS, A-Z' I knew that I had been.

And there they all were, stacked against the walls like oversized mouldy piecrusts, each slotted in behind the other.

Like Tortoise *shells*.

The Siamese was mumbling to himself as he walked along the row.

'Lemington, Lewis, Mackay, Maddison... ah, here we are! *Mahoney.*' He turned, bowed. He was enjoying this. I didn't blame him. I could hear the others sniggering behind me. Lifting the shell, the Cat placed it in my paws. I knew then that if I cared to walk a little further along the row I'd find Arnie Murchess's too. Maybe even the shells of the two Tortoises giggling away behind me. Even after I left the warehouse I could hear their laughter.

⁂

Outside, it had begun to rain. Using Ed Mahoney's old lodgings as an umbrella, one question kept coming back to me: *What the Hell did she want it for?*

So when I took her out to dinner I asked her.

Since everything had gone crazy, Tortoises, not unreasonably, began to find their shells rather cumbersome, so when a certain place near the canal opened for business, it seemed that hundreds of them crawled over there to get them removed. At some point one of the goons down there had the bright idea of selling the shells on, as 'a relic of a bygone era'.

Surprisingly, the scam took off. The shells became hot property to a certain kind—I won't say what kind—of animal; as ornaments, ashtrays, bedpans, I don't know what else. Of course, when word got round that these things might have some kind of value, then the 'surgery' found that the shells—each of which bore the name of the animal it

PROLOGUE: THE ED MAHONEY INCIDENT

had come from—were starting to go walkies. It certainly explained why I hadn't had a clue what Alphonso and Arnie were talking about; I'd wrongly assumed they knew what breed of Cat I was. In reality, they probably didn't care. To them I was just a Cat.

Besides all this I found out that my first ever client's name was Taki and she was looking for a job.

Over the next few weeks, when things slowly began to pick up, I phoned Taki to ask her if she still needed a job. I knew this guy who needed a receptionist/secretary. She started the next day.

I still don't know what she did with that damned shell.

*

So my first case could've turned out better.

But I was hot to trot if nothing else. Sure, I had a lot to learn, the same as everybody else. And there were big questions to be answered. Me, all I could do was try to figure out the small ones, and leave the *really* Big Question for others, the Question that perplexed each and every one of us.

What on earth had happened?

THIS IS AN **ALA** "Reading List" EDITION & IS NOT FOR RETAIL SALE OR DISTRIBUTION

Part One
–
What Happened

1

ALL I KNOW IS that I fell asleep in the old man's lap just after midnight on Midsummer's Eve and awoke when I heard screaming.

Instead of being in Jimmy's lap I was sprawled across the dusty floor, and *everything* had changed; my sight, hearing and smell were all completely different. I also noticed that I seemed to be taking up a lot more floor space than I was used to.

But initially it was the screaming that bothered me most. Apart from the noise in the office it was going on outside too, and not all of it was human; the air was filled with roars, grunts, howls, even sniggers. But the most disturbing noise was about eight feet away, coming from a bundle in the corner trying desperately to sink into the wall. It seemed to take twice as long as usual for my eyes to adjust to the darkness so I could make out what the bundle was.

Jimmy.

Despite all my apparent changes I wasn't yelling, but I was scared and confused. Suddenly, without thinking about it, I was walking the short distance across the office. I'd barely started when Jimmy screamed even louder. It took me a few seconds to figure out why. And then it hit me—instead of padding across the floor on four paws, I was now doing it on two. I stopped and looked down at myself.

THE TERROR AND THE TORTOISESHELL

I still appeared to be a Cat—I mean I still had the fur, claws, and whiskers to prove it—but I was now about eight times the size I should've been. *And* I was vertical. No wonder Jimmy was yelling. I turned my attention back to him.

He'd squashed himself in a corner, his feet were trying to dig a hole in the floor and he was pushing himself backwards against the wall. His black hair was slick with sweat and plastered to his forehead, his eyes were wild, his suit was creased to Hell. When I took another step towards him he didn't scream, just shuffled around a bit more.

'It's okay Jimmy,' I told him, 'I won't hurt you.'

That did it for both of us. First he screamed, then I did. I'd *spoken*, spoken real *human* words, my voice a cross between Jimmy's and my Cat voice. One of us was going to wake up in a minute and boy, was I pleased about that.

But it wasn't that kind of nightmare, and before I could register what was happening Jimmy got to his feet and shot out through the door into the reception area and then the corridor, yelling like his pants were on fire. The noise was blotted out for a moment as a car horn honked in the street below. Looking out of the window, I saw something incredibly large and white squashed behind the wheel of a sports car, its lights flashing on and off, momentarily highlighting several large, hairy, slavering creatures waddling around in the road on unsteady legs. The car honked its horn one more time before leaving the street on two wheels.

What the Hell was going on? I looked, but saw nothing I recognised as human. There were things down there that didn't seem *right*—and coming from me that was saying something. At that moment a huge dark bulk blocked my view. The blink of an eye later, I was looking at an object the size of Jimmy's potted-plant with wings flying along the street. I discovered later it was an Owl.

Before I had a chance to get my breath back, there was a scream from the street which stiffened my fur. It was followed

PART 1: WHAT HAPPENED

by a cheer, then another scream, another cheer. The noise appeared to be coming from inside a circle comprised of a large group of toffee-coloured creatures with long, sharp teeth. I saw a man trying to crawl through the legs of one of them. His cry for help ended when a paw the size of a shovel full of claws the size of chisels ripped off his face, bringing another cheer from the crowd.

Then I remembered Jimmy darting past me and my blood froze. A split second later, Jimmy appeared on the sidewalk outside the building, standing in a puddle of broken glass. Why had he smashed the door in? Then I realised: because it was either that or return for the keys and face me again. For a second he stood there, looking at the pack of beasts devouring the man who'd yelled for help. He began rubbing his face, his hair, the back of his neck.

A shadow fell across him as another feathery pot-plant with wings arrived on the scene, trying to grab him by the shoulders. Ducking just in time, the Owl kept going. I saw Jimmy open his mouth, but above the other noises in the street I couldn't hear his scream. Evidently the pack devouring the man heard him. They turned and faced him.

I had to get down there and help him. I ran out through the offices and into the corridor, my pads cold against the floor tiles, oversized claws scat-scatting across them, slowing me down, causing me to skid. Cursing my new slowness I took the stairs, at one point going down on all fours, hoping it would be quicker, but it wasn't; it felt strange, *alien* somehow.

By the time I reached the second floor there'd been another explosion of breaking glass, followed by a few more blood-curdling screams. I felt like I was going Hell for leather down the stairs but only getting half the distance I should've been. When I rounded the corner I was standing at the top of the final staircase, looking down at the broken glass of the main door.

THE TERROR AND THE TORTOISESHELL

Out of view something growled, a noise like a rumble of thunder. Slowly, I made my way down to the ground, giving it a few seconds before sticking my face through the door's busted frame.

The toffee-coloured things were padding forward in a semi-circle towards Jimmy. Slaver hung from their jaws. One of the group pinged a lethal looking claw out from a paw when Jimmy began swinging a front bumper around, presumably from the car the joy-riding Mouse had been driving. I discovered that the toffee-coloured things were Lions and, later, that in some small way we were related. It didn't fill me with joy.

'Come here,' one of the Lions' growled, its voice as deep as a mine. Jimmy swung the bumper again. The Lions started widening their circle to close Jimmy in. They hadn't seen me yet. I tried to think of some way to distract them, but my brain was full of ice.

The Lion who'd spoken moved closer, or at least I thought it had. But as the shadow lengthened above it, I realised that it was trying to avoid the swiping of wings which came from a gap between the two office buildings behind it. As the Lion ducked, a few others tried to drag the huge Bird down from the sky, which screeched like a siren as huge claws clipped its wings.

Something moved out of the corner of my eye. I turned to see Jimmy, still with the bumper in his hand racing towards the alley the Bird had come from. He was just about there when one of the Lions turned its attention from the Bird and bounded down the alley after him. Jimmy vanished behind a pile of trash-cans, scattering them wildly about him. I watched in dismay as the Lion vaulted everything put in its path. A few seconds later, the rest of the pack had vanished down the alley after it. Then I heard the screaming and tried to tell myself it wasn't Jimmy. I tried, but it didn't work.

I felt sick. Sick and angry and confused. And scared,

PART 1: WHAT HAPPENED

really scared. Every time I patted my fur down it shot back up again. My head was full of things that shouldn't be in there, my body was doing things it wasn't supposed to be doing.

Somewhere over to my right, another pane of glass shattered but I couldn't see anyone there. Turning, I looked back at the door-frame I'd just walked through. The glass panels on either side of the door were untouched and there was a streetlight directly overhead. I decided to get a good look at myself.

It was an unreal feeling, seeing all that black, white and brown fur, those brown eyes and pointed ears, that dainty little pink nose and those long whiskers on a Cat that was now six feet tall and standing on two legs, its back as straight as any man's back. I looked exactly the same as I always had, only now I was upright. And much bigger. That goes without saying.

I looked back along the street, left and right. Now the Lions were gone, it was pretty quiet. The sudden silence was worse than the noise. The last thing I wanted at that moment was a chance to think. Over towards the city there was plenty of noise, so I headed for that, knowing that I couldn't help Jimmy.

With most of the sidewalk covered in broken glass I moved out onto the road, turning every few seconds to check for cars. I checked the sky too but it was clear. On the top floor of the building opposite the agency, terrified human faces pressed against windows, fingers pointed at me, at things way off in the distance. A few floors below, I saw what looked like Dogs wrecking an office. When one of them pointed a paw at the ceiling the others stopped their ransacking to listen. Then they vanished from view, presumably heading for the staircase next to the office, up towards the people.

Then I was momentarily blinded by a bright flash of light coming from the city, followed by some kind of explosion.

THE TERROR AND THE TORTOISESHELL

From a narrow alley a car sped towards me. I just had time to get off the road as the car, stuffed full of Monkeys, shot past me.

Despite the Monkeys and the explosion, I kept going. Eventually the road broadened out and I had a better view of what was ahead. Straight away I spotted several groups of unfamiliar creatures roaming the main street. Fascinated as to what they might be, I didn't see the pile of rags on the pavement and went sprawling over it. I looked and saw what had once been a man. There was something wrong with him, apart from the obvious. Stepping over his bloody arm fifteen feet further on, I knew what it was.

I knew I was entering what Jimmy had called 'the business district'. When I used to curl up on the window ledge in the office I had a pretty good view of it, and it was usually pretty quiet. But tonight the streets were full.

The first shop I passed was Moe's Coffee Pot. I knew the smell of coffee well enough as Jimmy seemed to live on it. Now where I should've smelled coffee all I could smell was Dogs.

A big black one with sharp pointy ears was standing behind the counter, trying to balance a tray of cups on its paw while a few other mutts egged it on. One of them turned and saw me. He growled at me. I spat at him. He turned away. I kept walking.

I'd expected trouble, but it didn't materialise. Then I realised: we were roughly the same size, possibly I was taller, and in a fight between a Cat and a Dog in the past you'd have put your money on the kitty. Maybe not everything had changed after all.

Two doors along was a shop called Garrett's Tailor's. I looked in the door as something with a long yellow beak emerged from a changing booth in a pin-striped suit. It did a twirl and was wolf-whistled by something white and fluffy wearing a Hawaiian shirt and sporting a top hat. Not for

PART 1: WHAT HAPPENED

the first or last time, I hoped I'd wake up soon so I could pester the old man for dinner.

The ground close to me suddenly began to vibrate. Before I knew what was happening, a group of Human kids ran past me yelling and screaming. As I turned to watch them go something fizzed over my head and landed among them. There was a blinding red flash followed by a noise like a bomb going off. When one of the kids fell down he was immediately set upon by the group of ragged-looking Tomcats that had been chasing them. A scruffy, five-foot high Ginger was running after the rest of the kids, lighting a long thin tube before hurling it among the fleeing group. 'See how you bastards like it!' he yelled before the explosion drowned him out. Seconds later another group of boys ran past, one with a tube hanging out the back of his pants. When the tube finally exploded he stopped screaming.

As another pack of Alley Cats ran by, I saw an older one lagging behind, panting. He pulled up next to me, unable to go on.

'What the Hell's happening?' I said.

'Well,' the old Tom was still bent over, getting its breath, 'those kids have been at us for months. Payback time.' When he grinned he showed a set of uneven yellow fangs.

'I meant in general. What is all this?'

He eyed me up slyly. 'You an insider?'

'A what?' I said above the noise of another explosion, another scream.

'You know, a house-cat. A *pet*.' He spat the word out.

'Kind of,' I said uneasily. 'Why?'

'Oh, this has been building up for quite a while,' he told me. 'It was just a matter of *when*.'

'But why?' I asked again.

'Why?' He grinned. 'Who knows? Who cares? Enjoy it.' Before I had a chance to reply he was half-way along the street, giving the boy who'd been felled a quick kick as he went. The boy didn't even flinch.

23

THE TERROR AND THE TORTOISESHELL

And so it continued the further I went into the city: offices and shops were being smashed, raided, set alight; hardly a minute passed without seeing another Human being hunted down, thrown from windows, ripped to pieces, eaten, shot at (you haven't lived until you've seen a Tiger with a rifle), beaten, run over, stabbed, set alight and generally messed around with. Dogs ran with Cats, Cats ran with Rats, Rats ran with Monkeys. High voices, low voices, grunts, growls, meows, barks, purrs, snarls and roars in a variety of Humanised accents filled the air. I saw Apes taking pot shots from high windows at anything that took their fancy, human or animal, but mainly human. The sound of breaking glass rang out across the city in place of church bells. Bodies began piling up on the streets. The air stank of fire and blood and the kind of cooked meat not even the hungriest Dog would touch. There was laughter too, but it wasn't right: there was horror in it, disgust, desperation, madness.

Everyone went a little crazy.

Through it all I kept walking, hoping against hope that one scene of terror wouldn't be replaced by another on the next block. Most times it was even worse. But I had to see: curiosity killed the Cat, although I hoped not literally. I kept thinking of what that mangy old Tom had said: 'Enjoy it.' Maybe being 'an insider' had softened my head, but I found that this kind of 'enjoyment' was the last thing on my mind. I felt numb.

And then, for a little while, I went crazy too.

I was five blocks from the office when four street Cats rounded a corner at the same moment I did, so we collided with each other. I backed up to let them pass but they just stared at me. Between two of them, something dark and bulky was being supported but I couldn't make out what.

'Well,' the tallest one said, looking me up and down. 'What have we here?' I didn't answer.

'He asked you a question,' the Cat next to him said.

PART 1: WHAT HAPPENED

'So he did,' I replied. 'I decided not to answer.' I tried to walk away but one of them stopped me. Whatever was propped between them didn't move.

'Well?' the tall one asked again. 'What are you doing out, *checkerboard?*'

I'd no idea what he was talking about. I opened my mouth to say so when the one next to him grabbed my face. 'No smart answers now, checkerboard.'

My back against the wall, I scanned each of them in turn. All had identical expressions: a sneer that showed violence was all they understood.

'I'm just going for a walk,' I tried to say with my squashed face. 'See what's happening.'

' "*See what's happening*",' the big one said, impersonating me. 'Well, what's happening right at this moment is—' I heard a Cat noise I knew all too well. Sure enough, a long, finely pointed claw gleamed under the streetlight. 'This.'

I was surprised when he turned away from me, swishing his claw into the bundle between the other two Cats. With a grunt, the bundle slumped heavily to the ground. The gang moved aside so I could see what it was. In the harsh light from a street lamp, I saw the trickle of red run along the concrete.

I felt my heart jump into my throat. I looked at the figure and the world froze. For a split second I thought it was Jimmy. One of them said something, but I don't know what.

'Hey, I'm talking to you.' A bloody claw jabbed me in the chest and that was it.

Before I knew what was happening, all my claws were out, my eyes had narrowed to slits, and I was hissing like a piece of frying meat. Instinctively, all four Cats backed off. All I could think was *that could've been Jimmy lying in front of me with his throat open, just so a few squalid alley Cats could get their jollies.* I took a swipe at the nearest one, the one who'd grabbed my face. He backed away as my claws flew towards him. Luckily for him all he lost was a lump of grubby fur. The two at the back were long gone, leaving just me and the tall one. When I raised my paw above my head he turned and ran, falling over the body before scrambling to his feet and fleeing down the next block.

For a few seconds the city was quiet again, and I looked down at the prone man. He looked nothing like Jimmy: his nose was too small and his smell was completely different under the blood. But it *could've* been Jimmy. And for a few seconds there I could happily have done to those Cats what they'd done to this man. For a split second I'd been as crazy as they'd been, and I didn't like it.

And then, perhaps in some strange way because of what had just happened, I got it into my head that Jimmy might still be alive. I went to the next block, hoping he'd be there. But he never was. All I saw were more wild animals turning the city upside down. Dispirited, I made my way back to the office, hoping it would still be intact.

I was relieved to find it was. Fourth floor, right above the third where I'd left it. All the windows were intact and in darkness. The street was empty too; anything in the other buildings must be lying low.

Stepping over the broken glass that had once been the door, I promised myself that if and when things calmed down, I'd have to get some new locks fitted.

I was about to take the stairs when I remembered the elevator. The last time I'd been in it, I'd been in a box. A box within a box. Pushing the button, the numbers on the panel went from four to one. Jimmy had been the last person to use it.

Inside the box I could smell him, mixed in with all his other odours; aftershave, sweat, those revolting cigars he used to smoke, hair oil. There were dozens of other smells in the box, none of them his. I noticed then that my sense of smell was only about half as keen as it had been: before, I'd

PART 1: WHAT HAPPENED

have smelled these things and more from outside the box. Clocking my endless reflections in the panels of glass, I got a good look at myself from the back. I judged that I was roughly the same height as he was. I said a few words out loud to myself, meaningless words just to hear the sound of my voice. I could definitely hear traces of Mr. J. Spriteman, Esq. in there.

The elevator opened and I made my way to the office. I knew instinctively that I walked like him too. As I passed each door I stood for a few seconds, listening and scenting the air. Nobody. All the doors were locked, except one. The one that I'd have to start thinking of as mine.

The clock in reception told me two things: that it was five o'clock in the morning, and that I could tell the time. Far away in the city, I heard a couple more muffled explosions. Then it went quiet. I was tired. I was bone-weary.

In the office, I looked down at the floor and laughed without humour. The basket with its tartan blanket next to the radiator looked warm and inviting, and way, way too small. Anyway, I knew from experience that the floor was freezing.

There was only one thing for it. Wheeling the chair over to the window I took one last look towards the city and shook my head. Figuring out how to lower the blind, I brought it down to the ledge and settled down in the chair.

I stood it for a few minutes, but in the end had to give in. Reaching into the basket, I grabbed the tartan blanket and lowered it over my body and closed my eyes against the cruel, cruel world.

2

WHEN I WOKE UP in the chair, I knew it hadn't been some crazy dream. I looked around the office and the corridor but nothing had changed. I seemed to have the place to myself, which suited me fine.

Releasing the blind, about four hours of bright sunshine rushed through the window. Below, the street was empty. I couldn't even hear much noise in the distance. It was The Morning After The Night Before.

I was thirstier than I'd ever been in my life. I bent down to the bowl of water beside the basket and poured the lot down my neck, despite its tepidness. Then I remembered the water cooler. I padded over to that with the water bowl when it occurred to me I could use a paper cup instead. I managed to knock back about a third of a cup before one of my claws punctured it. Next time I'd trim my claws. Or use a proper cup.

Back in the chair my eyes wandered around the room. Despite the best of efforts of Cynthia, Jimmy's secretary, and the building's cleaner, the office was a mess. Beneath the piles of stray papers, envelopes and manila files spilling yet more papers and envelopes, was the desk. The two black leather chairs on either side of it had seen better days, although the visitor's chair wasn't as badly worn as the one I was using. To the right of the desk next to my basket, bowl,

PART 1: WHAT HAPPENED

and litter tray, was a large, grey filing cabinet. To the left of that a sorry looking specimen drooped in the plant-pot, mainly because I didn't always use the litter tray.

I went over to the cabinet and opened a drawer. Scanning a file at random it became clear to me that instead of looking at a series of meaningless black ink dots on the page I could now read every word: then I remembered the previous evening, noticing shops signs and things like that. I'd been so het-up at the time I hadn't given it a second thought. It made me think about how many other things I'd taken for granted.

Behind my basket was my food bowl, half full of last night's dinner. I gave it a sniff, then stuck a chunk in my mouth and chewed for a few seconds before ejecting it back into the bowl. Evidently my tastes had changed too. In the small cupboard squeezed in next to the filing cabinet were two bottles of scotch, (along with the one always in the desk drawer) a tin-opener and four cans of *Chewy-Chunks*. In the space of a few hours they'd lost their appeal. Strange, as up until then I'd liked *Chewy-Chunks*. Rifling a few more drawers produced nothing any more appetising. My stomach growled as if in protest. I tried to ignore it, by going through to reception.

The contrast between Jimmy's room and Cynthia's was marked; the only signs of chaos here were the ones Jimmy had created on his way out the night before, the contents of a waste-paper basket all over the floor. Or maybe it'd been me; it all happened so fast. But the desk was nice and neat, and the few papers on it were in piles or in plastic trays. I started to think about Cynthia, and what might have happened to her. Some weekends she went out to visit her mother in the country, but she'd told Jimmy she had a date this weekend. Jimmy hadn't been interested, which had annoyed Cynthia. Maybe she'd try and get back here, but I doubted it.

THE TERROR AND THE TORTOISESHELL

My stomach growled again. I couldn't put it off any longer.

I had to go back out there, into the jungle.

✣

Passing Moe's Coffee Pot for the second time was much quieter than it had been the first. Sure, I saw a few Grizzlies raiding a grocer's and something with a long stripy tail flying between the streetlights using its tail to propel itself from light to light, but generally things had calmed down. In the far distance there was shouting and roaring but I didn't pay it much heed.

Heading towards me along the empty street was an enormous black Cat, perhaps a foot taller than me. As we got closer both of us slowed, unsure how to behave. He sniffed the air, nodded. I did the same. I said the first thing that came into my head.

'Who's the stripy guy?' I jerked a claw back over my shoulder.

'Lemur,' the black Cat said, licking a paw. I must've looked blank. 'Didn't you hear? They busted the Zoo apart. Animals took it over. It's full of people now, all caged up. Wild, huh?'

The black Cat was called JuJu. I asked him about some of the other things I'd seen the night before. He was much more worldly than I was.

'How come you're so knowledgeable?' I asked.

'I spent a lot of time outdoors. My "owners"—(he used the word sarcastically) well, I say *owners*... You let them *think* that... I was only there as something to talk down to when there was nobody else around—anyway, they went out last night. They didn't come back this morning.' He grinned.

As he was so knowledgeable I decided to go for the big one. 'Did you know that all this—' I couldn't think of the

PART 1: WHAT HAPPENED

right word. I swept my paws in the air to indicate everything, 'was going to happen?'

'Oh, *yeah*. Well, I knew *something* was on the way. Didn't you?'

I shook my head. 'I didn't get out much,' I told him.

'Ah. House-cat, huh?'

I looked around me. 'Not anymore.'

Saying goodbye we went our separate ways, and never saw each other again. I couldn't believe all this had been brewing and I hadn't had a clue. Jimmy had seemed his usual self, so had Cynthia. Sitting on the radiator looking out over the street every day I hadn't noticed anything untoward; Jimmy talked on the phone as usual, people came in off the street to complain about missing money or frisky husbands. Once in a while Jimmy would catch me looking at him and he'd say things to Cynthia like 'I swear that cat understands every word I say'. But I decided that was just a figure of speech.

When my stomach informed me that such thoughts could wait, I went back to hunting for food.

I took the opposite side of the street this time, poking my nose around open doors and through broken windows—a hairdresser's here, a clothes shop there—and realised that I'd no idea *what* I wanted to eat. In the past I'd been quite picky; now, I could have anything I desired. I must've walked three or four blocks before I caught the scent of fish.

The last thing I'd expected in the fishmongers was a queue. There must've been a dozen or so other Cats in there, Tabbies passing me with paws full of over-ripe mackerel, Ginger Toms loaded down with halibut. By the time I got to the front there wasn't going to be much in the way of pickings. I spotted a shelf along the back wall and slowly eased my way towards it. No one objected; I doubt anyone even noticed. Grabbing as many tins as I could carry I pushed back out through the door.

THE TERROR AND THE TORTOISESHELL

On the return journey I went a different route, hoping I'd see fewer bodies piled up in the street. Bad move; by the time I got back to the office I reckon I'd counted fifteen more corpses than on my way to the fishmongers, most of them in a coach that'd crashed into a garage wall. As I went past I closed the coach's door, as much to protect my nostrils as to preserve the bodies inside from further disturbance.

Later, I saw another group of animals hanging around outside another shop, creating a lot of noise. Popping up among the throng like he'd come up through the floor, an elderly mongrel started to speak through cupped paws. 'Listen,' he shouted, 'I don't care what you did in those other shops—you can sniff around here as long as you like, but the merchandise stays under wraps until I see some currency.' I wasn't sure I'd heard right. But then the group of assorted Dogs, Cats and others shuffled, hopped and skipped away. 'You're crazy, old mutt!' one of them shouted back. As I walked along the street clutching my free tins of salmon, I had to agree. But as it turned out, he had the right idea.

Back at the office, the salmon tasted wonderful. I threw the remaining tins of *Chewy-Chunks* into the trash.

3

ONE MORNING ABOUT A week later I was awoken once more to the sound of screaming. 'Not again' part of me thought. Another part of me hoped it was me doing the screaming and that in some strange way a reversal of what had happened the previous weekend was under way, and I'd be able to go back to my old self.

Looking down I saw nothing had changed: my oversized paws were still on the edge of Jimmy's desk the way they'd been when I dozed off. Getting up I drew the blind and looked out the window. I had to pick *that* very moment to draw the blind.

I was just in time to see two large Cats dangling a man and woman out of a window on the seventh floor of the office block across the street. The man and woman had just begun to plead for their lives when the Cats dropped them at the same time. I never believed that things could happen in slow motion, but when I saw the pair of them free-fall past the brick and glass to the street below with their mouths and eyes wide open, their faces turning crimson as the world shot past them, I saw my error. The man crashed down into the trash-cans below a fraction of a second before the woman. Screwing up my face I shuddered and turned away.

'That's another one you owe me,' a voice called out behind me. 'I told you he'd kiss the ground first.'

THE TERROR AND THE TORTOISESHELL

The whole scene upset me, but for different reasons it would have done a few days earlier. For a start they were the first Sappies I'd seen in three days. A part of me had hoped they were all dead or had escaped or something. It seemed there were still a few about after all.

It wasn't as if that'd been the first time I'd seen such a show. For a while such pastimes were the norm: throwing people out of windows to see who landed first, firing guns at their feet to watch them dance, or stringing them up from trees and swinging them about as all and sundry threw rotten fruit. Some of these things stayed in my head even when I closed my eyes. One day I passed a group of Cats arguing in the street. I hadn't heard the whole conversation but I could get the gist. One of them said 'Why? Because they had it coming. They've been doing it to us for years. *They deserve it!*' A part of me agreed, part of me didn't.

On my now daily trips out of the office I began to take note of the things going on around me, in the hope I'd start to see things settling down a bit. Walking through the city was still the novelty for me that it didn't seem to be for others—I was seeing *everything* for the first time, regardless of my form. It was still exciting and frightening. It was an education. I learned that the rapidly declining human population had become known as 'Humes', or more commonly 'Sappies'.

'It's from *Homo Sapiens*,' a Gorilla called Prometheus told me one afternoon. I'd been about to suggest that he and the Sappies weren't that far removed when I noticed the badge on the breast pocket of his suit: "Do NOT call me 'Guy' under any circumstances as it will cause offence." So I kept it shut.

Another reason seeing the two Sappies going out the window had bothered me was the fact that I'd started to notice signs of civilisation. Dogs and Cats walked along the streets without any apparent friction, as did every other species; it was only when anybody saw a Hume that things

PART 1: WHAT HAPPENED

changed. The old mutt I'd seen trying to flog his wares on the street wasn't the only one wanting something in return for his goods now; it seemed that everyone wanted 'currency'. When I wanted food I'd had to start taking things along with me to trade with. A few days more and I realised the office would start to look a bit sparse. Luckily I came across an old hardware shop that hadn't been looted yet, and as I was in possession of Jimmy's set of skeleton keys I managed to get in and out and take whatever I wanted whenever I pleased. I'd picked a good place—everybody was suddenly trying to repair the damage after days of rioting—there seemed to be an inexhaustible need for hammers and nails.

As the streets began to feel safer, my daily trips lengthened. One day I saw a Birman wearing a beautiful long coat that matched her dazzling blue eyes. Minutes later I spotted a Tabby kitten (it must've been a kitten as it was only three feet tall) coming out of a door leading into a mall. Inside, several well-dressed Cats and pooches sauntered past in slacks, shirts, ties, boots, you name it. Feeling decidedly under-dressed I looked around for a tailor's and eventually found one. Sticking my furry face through the entrance, something with an equally furry face composed of black and white showed its teeth at me.

'Can I help you?' it asked, its voice low and dusty.

'You could tell me what you are,' I said. 'I'm new to this game.'

'As are we all, sir. I'm a Badger, sir. Are you looking for anything in particular?'

I looked around at the racks full of cloth. 'Um, I'm not that sure...'

'Well. Come this way, please.' He beckoned me with the longest and sharpest claws I'd ever seen. I felt compelled to follow.

Passing the chest-high racks, I thought of the only clothes I'd previously been aware of.

THE TERROR AND THE TORTOISESHELL

'I think I'd like a suit,' I said.

The badger turned his snout to me, wrinkled it and said 'Sir, we sell a wide variety of suits to a wide variety of clients. In fact, only this morning I sold a beautiful morning suit to a fellow from the Zoo. I think he said he was an Ocelot. A relative, I believe.'

I decided I'd have to take his word for that. I looked around hoping that something would leap out at me and command me to put it on. And what do you know, something did.

'I'd like the pin-stripe in the corner there.' I remembered seeing a large man with a cane, white hair and moustache in the office one day wearing one. It turned out he was a good guy, but he looked fantastic.

'Certainly, Sir.' The Badger bowed slightly. 'An excellent choice.'

Paying the Badger with some of the money I'd found in the office's safe (they only accepted *proper* money, he told me, a practice that was becoming increasingly popular), I asked him how long he'd been in business. 'Since Monday,' he said, as though it was the dim and distant past.

I walked out of that shop and felt about six inches taller. Checking myself out in unbroken shop windows, I saw I looked good. Hell, I *felt* good. Seeing that my bare paws didn't go too well with the overall look, I decided to invest in a pair of shoes.

Each day more and more shops were opening. Opening, that is, in the real sense of the word. The unwritten rule was that whoever got into a property first (if it hadn't already been occupied by the previous owners' 'pets') took possession. Crude repairs were made to windows and doors, to which I made my own modest contribution, and of course, profit. You couldn't help but marvel how quickly it was all happening. Most animals seemed to take to it easily and, oddly, without question. Wondering why made me uneasy, so I stopped.

PART 1: WHAT HAPPENED

I was strutting back to the office in my swanky new suit when a thought struck me: I should go and see Jimmy's place. I never knew, he might be there. At the very least his apartment should still be. I vaguely remembered the way. When Jimmy bought me from the pet shop, that's where he'd taken me. After a couple of days of me scratching the curtains, he decided that as he spent most of his time at the office perhaps I should as well. The office's cleaners had objected at first, but a few well-placed purrs soon got them on side, or so I thought. It turned out later that Jimmy had sorted out a problem for someone in the building and was owed one.

I went back to the office first and dumped my supplies on the desk in reception and took a drink from the sink. Next door I looked out the window to get my bearings. It occurred to me as I looked that I'd been avoiding going to one or two places on my foraging trips—Jimmy's was one, the Zoo was another. I had a bad feeling about that place, brought on by the big Cat I'd spoken to.

After giving it a bit of thought, I came to a decision: Zoo first, Jimmy's second. But not today. I had to gear myself up a bit. The best way to do that, I reasoned, was by sleeping.

The next morning I had my already regular breakfast of milk and tuna, gave my paws a lick, wiped my face, and set out. I decided against the suit, so I found some old paint overalls in a cupboard and put them on. Not exactly stylish but they'd do. Sticking the keys in my pocket I left.

The Zoo was straight up through the other side of the business district, past the empty Cop Shop and half-a-mile from the recently re-opened fairground. Nice to see folks had their priorities right.

As if on cue, I thought I got a whiff of something incredibly sweet, and knew it was candy apples. How I knew it was candy apples I've no idea, as to the best of my knowledge I'd never smelled them before. As I got closer to the Zoo

THE TERROR AND THE TORTOISESHELL

something in my stomach tightened. But I knew I had to go and make sure, even if the prospect of what I might find there wasn't appealing. Catching a strong animal scent in the air, I reluctantly followed it.

Then I heard the music coming from behind a row of nearby apartment blocks: a sharp burst of brass bellowing out before being eaten by horrendous clashing cymbals. A cheer went up and then the lop-sided music started up again like some drunken attempt at *oompah* music (again, I've no idea how I knew what "*oompah*" music was). The closer I got, the more I could make out individual instruments being badly played, with wrong notes and even wrong time signatures. The effect was like a band trying to play while falling down a flight of stairs. Getting level with the apartment block beside the Zoo, I saw an animal face at almost every window—furry faces, bald faces, wrinkly, smooth, long, pug—all looking down over the high wall into the Zoo. The music began to rise to a terrible crescendo of noise before stopping abruptly.

Then I heard a blood-curdling scream and my fur froze. It was a Human scream, followed by an animal cheer. I tried in vain to put half-heard stories from my mind. A hole appeared in the wall partially covered by a big Cat and a turnstile. I went towards the turnstile, the Cat urgently beckoning me.

'Hurry up there, hurry! The *real* fun will kick off in approximately—' he looked down at a watch in his massive paw '—thirty seconds.'

I tried not to look too apprehensive. I was about to ask what it cost to get in when he waved me through the turnstile, a free ticket into some kind of newly-minted Hell.

The first shock to the senses was the odour. The second was what was causing the odour: Humans, dozens of them, naked, smeared brown, huddled into the former animal's cages and enclosures. Faces young and old, male and female

PART 1: WHAT HAPPENED

pressed against the bars and mesh of their prisons, so many per cage there was no room to move. A few feet away from every cage, animals of all stripes jeered and threw things between the bars as the mad brass band from the Pit played drunkenly on. A huge grey Elephant shot a jet of liquid into one of the cages. It wasn't clean water; at least, nobody got any cleaner. Grabbing a hold of myself, I moved swiftly along the nearest path.

To keep my eyes off what was in the cages I kept them on the crowds instead. To begin with all I could see were leering faces egging on the Zoo's new 'wardens'. But then I began to notice other expressions: shock, disgust; I was relieved to know it wasn't just me. Passing another cage full of people I saw that the gap between the bars was wide enough for some of them to escape. But what would they be escaping into? A few minutes later I found out, when a woman began squeezing through the bars, and a large Ape stepped forwards with a short pole in his leathery mitt and thrust it through the bars. There was a short buzzing sound followed by a sickening crackle as the pole made contact with the woman's flesh. I don't know if I imagined the smell but I walked away ashamed, my head bowed.

Seeing the Monkey like that brought back a conversation Jimmy had had just a few days before everything changed. He'd been telling someone about the amount of time he spent at the Zoo; he even had a season ticket.

'It helps me to think,' he'd told the voice at the other end of the phone, his feet up on the desk. 'You learn a lot about life down there.'

Heading for the Monkey house, I hoped I'd find a couple of things out myself, but doubted that I would. The first was about Jimmy. The second was something Jimmy had said in his phone call. Behind me there was a roar so loud it drowned out the music. I hurried on.

As the path zigzagged upwards the things in the cages decreased. Instead it was mostly empty wire enclosures with

THE TERROR AND THE TORTOISESHELL

busted doors. To my left, a big striped Cat with a chair in one paw and a whip in the other snarled at something small in the corner of a filth-filled cage. I tried not to notice. Then, something large and hairy and orange was loping towards me. Despite using its feet, it somehow gave the impression that it was walking with its shoulders, the way it swayed from side to side. In one of its long dangling fists something sloshed about inside a can. Its smell made my eyes water.

'Excuse me,' I asked it. 'I'm looking for something called a Capuchin.'

The orange goon stopped for a second. 'Capuchin,' it repeated, its voice guttural. 'Used to be over there.' He pointed out one of the enclosures I'd already looked at. 'Not there now. Gone. Left. All left.'

A goon of few words. He lumbered away to be met by a similar sized creature. 'You got the matches?' it asked. 'We're late.'

I didn't know what they were late for, but those words spurred me into action. I had a terrible premonition of what was about to happen and I knew there was nothing anybody could do to stop it. In a heightened state of panic I knew then that even if by some miracle Jimmy had been in the Zoo, he'd probably be dead or close to it.

Rushing past the grunting Apes towards the turnstile, I tried not to take in the things I'd seen on my way to the Monkey house. But it was no use, and new images impressed themselves upon me: people being pelted with waste and rotting fruit, being forced to jump as the whip cracked at their bare and bruised feet, having to roll over and beg for a small morsel of food.

Behind me the heavy tread of the Apes stopped, replaced by the sound of the can's contents being sloshed around, the humans in the cages screaming, pleading. I couldn't bear it. I tried to shut my ears to it but the noise got through anyway. Then one of the Apes began counting down with his big, dumb, emotionless voice.

PART 1: WHAT HAPPENED

I kept going, past the smells and the colours and the noise, making it through the turnstile just in time. I was passing the Cat when he tapped me on what was now my shoulder.

'Hey, you're going to miss the big one, pal! I know it's a little late, but better late than—'

His words were blocked out by a noise that must've sounded like a giant clearing its throat. The air rippled with heat, blurring the skyline as I instinctively looked back to the source. Red and yellow ropes of flame and black clouds of smoke rose and fell all around, the heat so intense it could cook your eyeballs.

Staggering away from the carnage, my breakfast hit the pavement at around a hundred miles an hour. Getting my breath back and trying to flatten my fur, I moved away from the crowds now clogging the streets on unsteady paws. All of a sudden Jimmy's apartment seemed like the most welcome place on earth.

✣

It took me a while to get my bearings again. It didn't seem to matter how far I got from that flaming freak-show, whichever street I went down I could still hear the screams. A part of me felt that I should've gone back and tried to help, but it would have been pointless. I think it was at that moment the idea of starting up the agency again came to me. Finding Jimmy's place put the cherry on it.

Eventually the screams decreased as I put more buildings between me and them. Instead, the streets became eerily quiet; the various shops and houses I passed all looked empty. A few looked like they'd never been anything but empty. Then, at the upstairs window of a large detached house, I saw a human face, its mouth opened wide, hands pressed to the sides of its head, like that famous painting, 'The Scream'. I tried to mouth back to the figure that they were safe from me, but I don't think it registered.

THE TERROR AND THE TORTOISESHELL

Looking at my watch I saw it was the same time as the last time I'd looked. Then I pulled up as I noticed the change in great patches of my fur along what had been my right paw and was now my right arm: huge chunks of fur, which had once been thick and luxurious, were now a brittle grey, singed at the ends. I hadn't been that far from the explosion after all. Brushing at the grey fur with my left paw, I was alarmed to see it break off in tiny little flurries of ash that fluttered away on the breeze. The fact that I'd just started wearing clothes had probably helped stop me being turned into a walking cigar. Before anything else occurred to me, I got moving. I turned into the next road along and looked at the street ahead.

And there it was.

At first I wasn't certain. On the surface I was just looking at another in a series of similar buildings, the like of which I'd been passing since I left the Zoo behind. But as I crossed the road I saw the leering faces below the windows and knew this was the right place.

The rather grandly-named Shefton Heights is twenty-two floors of sturdy brown stonework topped with a row of jagged turrets which, due to the regular patronage of the city's Pigeons, were now stained white. Just below each and every window a gargoyle jutted out, each floor having a different design. Perhaps the higher up you went the uglier the gargoyle, I don't know. Looking along the rows I didn't spot a single broken window. I managed to finish crossing the street just as something small and spiny on a bicycle tringed its bell at me before speeding off.

Stepping into the lobby, memories started to come back to me. The faded rose carpet was still there, as was the reception desk tucked in an alcove underneath the stairs. The man who'd sat there reading the paper had gone of course; Josh, they called him. Used to rub behind my ears. Nice guy. Over to the left of the desk was the elevator. As a

PART 1: WHAT HAPPENED

memory of Jimmy grumbling about living on the fourteenth floor came to me, I headed for its closed grey door.

In the close confines any odours of human life were rapidly fading; the smells were mostly from Cats and Dogs.

At the fifth floor the doors opened, and a fluffy orange-faced mutt stepped in beside me. 'Fifteen,' he said, as though to a flea.

'Push it yourself,' I told the mutt. He shrugged and pushed the button. I pressed fourteen again.

As the car ascended, my whiskers began to quiver. The mutt smelled of fancy soap or scent or something. I turned and caught him sniffing at me. Then he looked me up and down.

'What are you?' he said, as if addressing something with three heads.

'I was going to ask you the same question.'

'If you mean my breed,' it sniffed, 'I'm a Pomeranian.'

'If you mean mine,' I sniffed back, 'I'm a Tortoiseshell. Or "Calico", if that's too difficult to pronounce.'

'I'd heard they were all females,' it replied, looking me up and down again.

'Not this one,' I snarled.

'I believe this is your floor,' it said, pointing to the numbered board. Leaving the elevator, he continued to stare at me until the doors stopped him. I waved goodbye but for some reason he didn't reciprocate.

Going right from the elevator I took in the blood red carpet as if seeing it for the first time, ditto the cream doors and peeling green wallpaper. Every door I passed was closed. I decided this was a good sign. Turning a corner onto a long landing, I came to Room 1404.

I tried the handle and found it thankfully locked. Taking the keys from the overalls' pocket, my paw shook. Somehow, I knew which key to pick and tried it in the lock. I pushed and the door moved softly inwards over the carpet.

THE TERROR AND THE TORTOISESHELL

'Jimmy?' I peered into the darkened hall. Empty. I closed the door behind me slowly, went through to the living room.

The apartment was much smaller than I remembered it, but then again I had been much smaller the last time I'd been here. Scenting the air, I knew Jimmy hadn't been here for quite a while. Probably hadn't been back here at all. I'd expected that, but it still managed to be a disappointment.

I went through the formality of checking the rooms anyway. The living room and kitchen were all part of the same large space. In the lounge area a black leather sofa occupied the centre of the floor, with an armchair across the way and a small footstool in front. Jimmy would sleep in the armchair when he got in from a case, usually in the early hours of the morning, zedding away with his coat across his chest. To the right of the chair a small table struggled under the weight of the full ashtray balancing on the edge. On the floor beside it a few magazines and books overlapped one another, gathering dust. In lieu of carpet, a few rugs had been scattered randomly about.

In the kitchen the dregs of a hurried cup of coffee had congealed on the breakfast bar, the cup surrounded by a blizzard of crumbs and a mouldy crust. Opening the fridge, I found plenty of things inside which had once been solid. Wrinkling my nose, I closed the door.

Back in the living room, I stood by the window and looked out over the city. From up here things didn't look too bad; but then I caught a ball of fire over to the right. I shut it out of my mind.

Something fluttered just below me, making me jump. I looked down in time to see a Pigeon take off just below the window ledge, and for a few seconds I was a kitten again.

One hot afternoon, Jimmy had left the window open. A Pigeon had been sitting on the gargoyle, so I'd padded out onto the ledge to get a better look at it. I'd jumped right onto the gargoyle just as the bird had fluttered off, leaving me

PART 1: WHAT HAPPENED

suspended there for an unknown period of time, hundreds of feet up, looking down at the ants crossing the sidewalks, the smell of Pigeons in my nostrils. Eventually Jimmy saw me through the window and pulled me back inside, slamming the window shut behind me. 'That's one of your nine gone,' he'd said as he dropped me onto the sofa. Not long after that, I was being led through the streets in a small box on my way to the office.

For old times' sake, I planted myself back on the sofa. Another memory came to me: Jimmy sitting in the armchair, head in his hands, a small pile of photographs on his lap. I'd gone over and rubbed against him, but he never noticed. 'Adele,' he'd muttered into his hands. 'Oh Adele.' I never heard the name again, except when Cynthia mentioned her. Jimmy would clam up when she did. I never found out who she was.

In the distance there was a loud popping noise. Over at the window, I saw another fireball shoot into the sky. Seconds later a nearby building emptied ants onto the pavement that ran in all directions. It made me think of Jimmy running from the office like that, into that gang of big Cats.

Thinking of the Zoo and Jimmy reminded me of the Monkey I'd been looking for down there.

I'd thought nothing of it at the time, of course. It'd just been another one of Jimmy's endless telephone conversations which meant that I didn't get the attention I felt I deserved.

It had been a few days before the big change, Jimmy with his feet on the desk, his chair leaning back so it almost touched the window-ledge. He'd been talking to somebody called Bernie.

'Yeah, well I like the Zoo,' Jimmy had said. 'That's why I got a season ticket. You should try it.' There was a pause and then Jimmy laughed. Grinning, he shook his head before speaking into the mouthpiece again.

'Dumb creatures, nothing! Listen, you should've seen the little fella I saw this morning, over at the ape house.' A

THE TERROR AND THE TORTOISESHELL

pause, then 'Yeah, very funny. No, really. Over at the ape house there was this little capuchin monkey, you ever heard of 'em? Well, this little fella sees me walking over to him, cocks its head to one side and rushes along its branch near the mesh of the cage, over to the far side. So I follows it over. Stop laughing!' Jimmy shook his head again. 'Anyway, when I gets there, he starts chattering nineteen to the dozen, his eyes never left mine, his hands were gesturing, the look on his face; you wouldn't have laughed if you'd seen that look. It was trying to tell me something—quit laughing—and whatever it was it was *urgent*. I'm telling you Bernie, God made a big mistake when he dropped us down here. He should've left the world for the monkeys.'

Sitting there on the sofa I kept playing this little conversation over and over in my head. Had the Monkey been trying to tell him something? Was it possible that it *knew*, like some of the Alley Cats knew? Ultimately I don't suppose it mattered. It *had* happened and that was the long and the short of it.

I got up and had a look round the apartment some more. The living room was pretty sparse; Jimmy didn't seem to have gone in for personal possessions much. In fact the only stuff I found that interested me were the two bookcases full of crime fiction, both ancient and modern: pulp magazines and cheap paperbacks with faded covers, depicting lantern-jawed gumshoes in fedoras smoking cigarettes while distressed blondes lurked somewhere in the background, or of cars high-tailing it around corners, or a close-up of a smoking gun with a body slumped on the floor nearby. The gumshoe pictures were like little portraits of Jimmy. On the second shelf of the second bookcase an extremely well-thumbed paperback called *The Devil You Know* seemed to take pride of place; Jimmy's scent was all over it. This book looked like it had been read. A lot.

On the bottom shelf a book called *The Big City After Dark and Other Stories* caught my attention. Unlike the

PART 1: WHAT HAPPENED

others it had an almost zesty smell about it, like perfume or hand cream. Inside the front cover was the inscription: *It took me a while to track this down but I got there eventually! All my love, Adele.* It was in much better condition than the others, despite being much older.

After that, I noticed the zesty smell on maybe a dozen other books, although never as strong as on that first one. I began wondering if there were other signs of Adele in the apartment.

Next to the bathroom a small box room was fit to bursting with battered suitcases and old junk. Even if I could've got in, I doubted I'd have found anything in there. That left the bedroom.

Despite the closed curtains there was still enough light for me to see. Even compared with the lounge, this room was sparse: just a bed and a nightstand, with a closet on the right and a set of drawers to the left.

I sat down on the bed, next to the nightstand. Another yellowing book lay open on top next to a pair of reading glasses and an empty ashtray. Underneath, three drawers whispered 'Open me'.

I found what I was looking for straight away in the top drawer and put it on the bed next to me. The other two drawers were full of the kind of junk that second and third drawers were invented for.

Taking a deep breath I turned back to the oversized book on the bed. PHOTO ALBUM it said in gold leaf on the cover. Before I had a chance to change my mind, I flipped the book open. It didn't take me long to find her.

She was slightly smaller than Jimmy in her heels, perhaps five-nine or -ten, elegantly dressed with medium-length brown hair and dark skin. It looked like she was laughing at something Jimmy had said to her as the picture was being taken. The smile he was giving her back was a new one on me, not the usual lop-sided smirk. Instead, he was *beaming*.

THE TERROR AND THE TORTOISESHELL

Flipping through the rest of the pictures, Jimmy's expression or clothes rarely changed, but Adele's did; she appeared to have a wide variety of expressions and gestures, some wistful, some joyful; all graceful. Almost feline... and he ended up with me, I thought wryly. Some replacement.

The last picture in the album had Adele sitting on a park bench with her legs crossed, hands on her knees, staring right into the camera, both eyes and mouth smiling. On the next page however was a small square of folded paper in the empty photo pocket. Taking it out, I unfolded it and read an inky newspaper clipping about a woman called Adele Robbins who had died in a car accident on her way home from work. Her fiancée, it said, was devastated.

Closing the album, I let out the breath I didn't know I'd been holding and went to the kitchen. I found a packet of ground coffee in one of the cupboards and put the kettle on. Over the past month or so I'd developed quite a taste for it, which was more than I could say for liquor. When I'd tried some of the rot-gut Jimmy'd kept in his desk, it came up as quickly as it had gone down.

After finishing my coffee, I put the photograph album back in the drawer, took the cup into the kitchen, and left. Locking the door behind me, I was glad the corridor was empty. In fact the only other souls I saw before I left Shefton Heights were a rather sulky-looking Labrador and an old Husky having a muted conversation on the ground floor. Neither gave me a second glance. Walking back to the office, my pads felt like stone inside my new shoes.

Anyway, on that walk back to the office I made a decision, or at least kidded myself that I had. I couldn't help thinking that the decision had been made days earlier, but I'd been too stupid to realise. Whatever. By the time I arrived back at the office I knew what I should take with me and what I should leave behind. There wasn't that much to take.

The next day I moved into Jimmy's apartment.

PART 1: WHAT HAPPENED

It was an odd feeling, dropping these few odds and ends of mine into Apartment 1404, with Jimmy everywhere and nowhere. But I knew it was the right thing to do; I'd known it the second I'd put the key in the lock and stepped over the threshold. Despite the mixture of sadness and apprehension, the place felt like home.

4

As July became August, a bit more of the craziness went out of things. A big factor in this change was what had happened at the Zoo. It wasn't just Sappies that got crisped that day, and the deaths seemed to shake a lot of the madness out of a lot of animals. I think it was also starting to sink in that *whatever it was that had happened,* was now permanent. You had two choices—live with it, or go gaga. The quieter evenings, fewer explosions, and lack of broken glass on the sidewalks suggested that most had chosen to adapt; animals by and large were getting on with each other. There were no cartoon-style street scenes, with the Dog hitting the Cat who in turn hit the Mouse. It was only where Humes were concerned that things changed. You could still see the odd Sappy being chased along the street or dropped from the roof of a parking lot if you kept your eyes peeled. I daresay that some of them deserved it too, and worse. But all of them? No matter how hard I tried I couldn't get used to the sight of those obscene piles next to the kerbs, yet alone the smell that came from them. Occasionally you'd see garbage mutts dumping the corpses into the crushers at the back of the trucks. That's progress for you.

But generally things were improving, and it was pretty evident that Cats were at the top of the pile as far as 'society' went, with Dogs a poor second, and then Birds. Irrespective

PART I: WHAT HAPPENED

of breed, it was the creatures formerly known as 'domestic pets' that now had all the brains and power, effectively taking over where their owners or keepers had left off.

Not all 'pets' had been so lucky. Fish were no better off than they had been; when they came up for air now they could talk a fair bit, and most Cats only considered them food in the direst of circumstances. Fish also tend to have terribly short memories; they knew they were angry about something but kept forgetting what it was. The few that could keep an idea in their heads for longer than a couple of seconds demanded transfers to bigger tanks, but generally nothing changed.

Even the biggest enemies of the Sappies had to admit that they'd been responsible for some pretty cool things, and that a hell of a lot of those things were worth keeping to maintain the quality of life we now felt we deserved—transport, decent food, accommodation—all these things needed continuity to function. So we had to keep some semblance of order. Sure, things weren't quite the same—the majority of animals are rotten drivers for instance—but where possible things were kept pretty much as they had been, although without the stifling (and often baffling) rules that Sappies invented for everything; we'd more than enough to be getting along with, thank you very much.

But at the same time it became apparent that we weren't quite as different as we thought we were, as most animals appeared to have taken on the characteristics of the Sappies they'd been nearest to. For example, me and Jimmy: I dressed well, washed regularly and ate junk, just as Jimmy had. The more I used my new voice, the more I could hear Jimmy's caustic tones: slightly aloof (natural enough for a Cat anyway), but not uncaring either. Another example was Minsky, the Abyssinian who ran a deli and coffee house downtown, who'd taken to wearing long, black, flowing skirts and had a thing about feather boas, like the lady who'd run the deli before had. She also says she now has a quick temper, which she claims she never had before. In some ways it wasn't so much change as a perverse progression, which made it an everyday occurrence for a Cat to walk around the town in shoes and a fancy suit. It just *felt right*.

In my new home in Shefton Heights, I began to see who and what my new neighbours were. I had most of the fourteenth floor to myself, presumably because not all the apartments had had animals in them. But there were a few others, such as a great lolloping Dalmatian called Inky, a Tabby by the name of Tigger and a four foot high Parrot who appeared to be called Shove Off. At the back of the building, a bin began to fill up with redundant baskets and cages, which stunk to high heaven until the garbage mutts swung into action and took them away.

With all this integration of the species going on, other odd things started to happen. I'd heard the rumours—Cats dating Dogs and Dogs dating Birds (how that works I don't want to think)—but it was still a shock when I stepped out of the elevator one day and saw two creatures about five feet tall—one fat, bald and pink, the other green, bug-eyed and stinking—trotting and hopping through the lobby, grunting sweet nothings to one another. In amazement I watched as the Pig (only the second I'd seen) jabbed its trotter at the thirteenth floor elevator button, then moved aside so the Frog (first one I'd seen) could go in first.

I bumped into the Pig the next day. After a joke I didn't understand about bringing home the bacon, he informed me that Francine was expecting. And so it proved: the little "Frigs", as they came to be known, were soon a regular sight in Shefton Heights, running and hopping around the place; ugly but surprisingly cute little creatures that did nobody any harm. By and large, offspring from such unions was rare however; there was a rumour about a Frog and a Duck, but I'd no real desire to find out what a "Druck" would look like.

PART 1: WHAT HAPPENED

But as I've said, things were, by degrees, starting to settle down.

And then, one misty morning, it all went off again.

From a rather sleazy drinking den on the East Side called Slaggers, a few citizens of that rather rough area had heard gunfire. After a safe interval, they'd gone to investigate. Inside, the locals found a pride of Lions gunned down among the broken seats and shattered glass. A large note was pinned to the bar, informing the city that The Society for the Prevention of Cruelty to Humans was responsible and we could expect to hear from them again soon. The SPCH were thought to be a group of half-crazed Sappies that believed one day it would regain power by destabilising the city with a concentrated campaign of kidnappings, bombings, shootings, poisonings and 'anything else we think of. *There are more of us than you think'* the bottom of the note informed us. As they promised, there were indeed more shootings, along with the odd poisoning and explosion, and once more everyone started to worry. Then, a stupid rumour started: a Hume had been seen in the vicinity of the Zoo just prior to the explosion. Tensions rose. Something had to be done.

And that's how the Police Force got started.

5

THERE WERE STORIES GOING about that nearly a hundred animals had been taken out in various despicable ways by the SPCH in the space of a week. Everybody had their own ideas how to deal with them, usually with Cats on one side and Dogs on the other. The last thing any of us needed was a species war.

It took a rather ineffectual but well meaning speech, by the Reverend 'Snoopy' Smith held on the cathedral steps, to make the factions see sense. He put forward the idea that the reason something like the SPCH could rise up was because the city, despite its progress, was still essentially a lawless place. Perhaps, he said, if there was some kind of organisation who could deal with such things... this simple (and glaringly obvious) message was duly noted.

Step forward Sammy Bachman, proprietor of Bachman's Fruit & Veg Emporium. Later, when I saw the photograph of a black and white Mongrel, he looked suspiciously like the old boy I'd seen demanding currency for goods a few days after everything had changed. The story I heard was that, as he'd been the first to think up such a far-reaching idea as paying for goods again, this somehow meant that he had the necessary chops to run a Police Force. As I said, the old Sappy rules just don't apply anymore. Perhaps he was just the first to put himself forward, I don't know. Besides,

PART 1: WHAT HAPPENED

he looked harmless enough. I suppose the logic was that any Chief of Police was better than none at all, regardless of credentials.

Directly below Bachman and—according to some, the real power behind the Force—was a mangy old Tom called Scragg who had half an ear missing and claws that could shred glass—or so it was put around. Below Detective Scragg were various Cats and Dogs enticed by the recruitment posters: 'Can YOU *think of another job that can bring security to a whole city (and get you all the doughnuts you can eat)?'* Within days the Police Force was full.

But it all seemed to have the desired effect; the SPCH attacks trailed off considerably, but they didn't entirely stop. Amazingly, no suspects were apprehended, as the freshly inaugurated rag *Fuller News* took great pleasure in telling its fledgling readership.

The paper had re-emerged under the editorship of a gang of mutated Rats—who lived in the cellars below the building—after they'd figured out how to operate the printing press. So, to the delight of all, we were treated to the sporadic, barely literate, and mercifully short offerings of a gang of Rodents with grudges to bear. The first issue wasted no time in criticising the Police (apparently old Sammy had been a ratter in his younger days, which didn't help), citing the 'pineapple story' as a sign of their gross incompetence.

The 'pineapple story', which turned out to be apocryphal, ran something like this: a small team of officers were staking out a property believed to be the hiding place of the SPCH. Detective Scragg, desperate for results, took the decision that these terrorists should be taken either dead or alive, preferably the former.

'Okay, we're gonna smoke 'em out,' he told his squad after finding an open window at the rear of the property. He instructed one of his raw recruits to 'throw in a pineapple'.

Minutes passed, but the expected explosion failed to materialise. Scragg asked the officer to show him exactly

THE TERROR AND THE TORTOISESHELL

what he'd done. After he'd done so, an enraged Scragg was supposed to have yelled at him, and I quote the paper here, 'You @~≤;¥≠*! idiot, you were supposed to take it out of the can first.'

Scragg, to his credit, didn't respond to the slur in print, but a day later a hastily assembled *Fuller News* reported than a large tin of fruit salad had been hurled at one of their reporters, nearly causing him serious injury.

With the criticism of the city's finest gathering momentum, I began to wonder about starting up the agency again. It had been at the back of my mind for a while, and I doubted that I could be any worse than the 'official' law.

Just to make sure of my ground, I had a look around to see if anybody else had had the same idea. Apparently, no one had. I also made a few discreet enquiries with store owners, local residents, *etcetera* to see how they rated the police. The replies were far from positive: the number of animals that believed the 'pineapple story' was downright scary.

Another motivating factor was that I'd finally have something to do—I had all this time to kill, spending day after day reading Jimmy's crime novels, waiting to fall off the edge of the world.

So the decision was made, and in the second week of September, the Spriteman Detective Agency came into being for the second time.

※

Taking note of the Police recruitment campaign, I decided to advertise in *Fuller News*. I hoped the advert would be noticed by the Force and they'd contact me and beg for my special assistance in helping to apprehend the SPCH. I'd do just that, they'd think I was wonderful, and we'd all live happily ever after. It might even have worked out that way, had that fink of an Editor put the ad in his paper.

PART 1: WHAT HAPPENED

I went up to the offices personally and met the head Rodent, a large brown Rat who stank of booze. He stared at me over his desk with his sneaky little eyes.

'What you want me to do, huh?' he said, wiping crumbs from his chest and onto the piles of scrap paper surrounding him. 'You think I don't have better things to do than print private ads for Gumshoes? Go on, take a hike, buddy.' I was about to take a swipe at him when I clocked those long yellow choppers of his. I came away with the impression that he didn't like Cats very much, or Dogs, or indeed any other form of life. He was in the right profession.

So that avenue of publicity didn't go too well.

Next I decided to try leaflets. On a full-sized sheet of paper I wrote who I was, where I was, and what I was offering (I kept this deliberately vague, not being sure myself just what I *was* offering), Xeroxed the sheet several hundred times until I ran out of paper, then went over to the park at the other end of the city with my paws full of leaflets.

I found for a Cat I got on very well with Pigeons; they're friendly if rather messy Birds, and I like the way the sunlight plays off their feathers like oil in a pool of water. They never run when I approach them. Unlike Ducks. Perhaps I'd chased a Duck in a previous life and now they all knew about it.

'Hi Benji,' one of them said, looking up from the bag of corn they were all eating from. 'What you got there?'

'Wages,' I told them. 'If any of you are interested.'

They were. Telling them what I wanted and then what I had to offer, beaks turned in my direction immediately. One by one they waddled over to me, each pecking a wad of leaflets from my paws before soaring off into the sky. Within a few seconds the sky was raining adverts over the entire city. It was quite beautiful.

Leaving the park, I still had a stash of ads under what was now my armpit. On the edges of the park, small gangs of kitties clogged up the pathways like litter. I asked them

THE TERROR AND THE TORTOISESHELL

if they thought a can of tuna each for sticking a few leaflets through mailboxes and shop fronts was a good deal, with a bonus for the one who finished first. They seemed to think it was. By the time I made the long trek back to my office, three of them were already waiting for me. I suddenly had a bad feeling. Reluctantly, I handed over the cans.

Once I'd got rid of the kitties the Pigeons started to gather outside the window, precision-bombing pedestrians on the street below, demanding their payment. Scribbling down the address I'd told them about, one of them flew off while the others perched on the windowsill (not easy when you're twice the size of the ledge) or hovered around, doing their best to crap on any cars that zipped past on the street. A few minutes later the Pidge came back and told them he'd found Nut Heaven. Thanking me, they all flapped off. The window ledge looked like the side of a chalk cliff.

All I had to do now was wait. Cats are good at waiting; or rather, we're good at sleeping. Not as good as before, but still not bad. After a couple of hour's shut-eye I was startled awake by something I hadn't heard for a long, long time.

'Yeah, hang on a second!' I yelled at the empty office, looking for the phone. In the end I found it stuck under the desk where I'd been using it as a paw-rest. I pulled it up onto the desk.

'Yeah, Spriteman's Detective Agency?'

'Who?' a small whining voice said down the earpiece. 'I'm looking for Bendy.'

'*Bendy?*' I snapped. 'Who the hell's "Bendy"?'

'Bendy happens to be a friend of mine. Is he there?'

'Look pal, I think you've got the wrong number.'

He read the number back to me. He'd put an extra two in there somewhere.

'Oh,' the whiny voice said, and hung up.

It took me a while to realise why the call had bugged me so much. I looked at the leaflet I'd written and saw that I'd

PART 1: WHAT HAPPENED

put my address on it but neglected to put my phone number.

So a couple more lazy days passed and the situation wasn't improving. The SPCH carried out more attacks and managed to get away with them. Me, I snoozed a lot.

So.

I'd tried to put an ad in the paper, but that had come to nothing. I'd hired a gang of Pigeons to drop leaflets across the city. To their credit they did what I asked them. But a few days later I saw great piles of leaflets trampled into sidewalks or stuck in the branches of trees, or languishing in puddles. I'd also hired the kittens, but deep down I knew they'd probably dumped the leaflets the second I was out of sight and then turned up at the office for the pay.

And time continued to drag endlessly, tortuously on.

Then I had a great idea: why not redo the *Spriteman* sign in the window?

Which I did.

Back-to-front.

What a chump.

Outside, the explosions kept everyone jumpy.

♯

However, over the next couple of days, the explosions began to get further and further apart. Out on the streets the atmosphere gradually grew calmer but nobody knew why.

Then one morning I was in the town and saw various animals with their snouts and beaks stuck into newspapers. It'd been nearly a week since the last edition and I'd been beginning to wonder if the news office had been hit. Hope springs eternal, as they say. I bought a paper and was treated to the usual array of typos and God-awful writing.

SPCH FOYLD the headline read, GANG APRE—TAKEN IN. Finding a bench free of the stench of Pigeons, I sat down and began to read.

THE TERROR AND THE TORTOISESHELL

It looks today as if Sammy «The Pineapple» Bachman has today saved his own fur after the surpyse arrest of over a dozen members of the SPCH in a dorn raid on an abandunned house on the city's east side. According to Bachman «the city is now sayfe again as we now beleev we have apre—got all excep a few miner members of the unit calling itself The Soceity for the Prevenshion of Cruelty to Humans. Ordinary aminals can now sleeep safely in there beds.»

Details of the operation ar sketchy, according to Bachman, and will not be reveeled to the publick at larg, other than a large amount of explosifes were found at the scene.

However, we here at the *Fuller News* beleive the raisin for this alleg secricy is the fact that the matter was probly brought to a cnoclusion not by detective Scragg but by the ever modest Leuïtenant Dingus, infromed sauces tell us. «Dingus is a wizz, man, an absolute jeeny-us» one unnamed officer told us. «He got the job dun, not Scragg, who couldn't find his ass with a stick.»

Attempts had been made to scratch this last part out but not very good attempts.

However, the misterous Detective Dingus—who appears to not have any other name—was keping quite yesterday, his only comment was «I was only doing my job.» Perhaps it is about time that Dingus reseevd some kind of comadætshun for his stirling work.

After reading the article I had to admit I was relieved. But at the back of my mind was the thought that perhaps if my ad had been in that rag, maybe, just maybe, I could've played some part in it all.

PART 1: WHAT HAPPENED

But the overwhelming feeling I had after reading the piece and then the rest of the paper from start to finish—all seven pages of it—was this: never, never, *never* leave a Rat in charge of a printing press.

※

So with the SPCH out of the way, things again returned to 'normal'. The problem was, nobody knew what 'normal' was anymore. But as a kind of routine began to establish itself those Big Questions began to intrude: How? *Why?*

Of course nobody knew, and our options for finding out were limited. The radio stations had been dead since It all happened, so our main source of communication was gone. The telephone system worked but only locally, as I found out one day when I tried phoning some of the numbers Jimmy had kept in a book in Shefton Heights; numbers in other counties, states, even countries: every one was dead. You couldn't even get a dial tone. It was like we were the only place on Earth. Were animals all over the world trying to contact us and getting the same response? It was frustrating, to put it mildly. But suppose we *were* alone? Suppose we were 'It'?

Not that we lacked for anything. Now that most businesses and industries were operating at least some kind of service like the 'Old Days', it was unlikely we'd ever be in short supply of anything again.

Meanwhile, the city's population grew. On an average day I could see all manner of creatures hopping, crawling, swooping and sprinting along the streets as I took my morning stroll. I even spotted a winged Dog once, and a bright green and yellow Monkey. But they were one-offs. At least they were if we were the only ones left...

And then old Sammy Bachman, buoyed presumably by the abrupt halt to the SPCH's activities, had a bright idea:

what if a party of animals were sent out beyond the city limits to see what they could find?

The next issue of *Fuller News* suggested that nobody would be interested. Who knew—or would want to know—what kind of Hell awaited us beyond the boundaries of our fair city?

But, to the Rat's—and my—surprise, a lot of animals took up the opportunity. Perhaps it was because they were bored and fancied the adventure, or their new lives weren't all they'd hoped they would be. Whatever the reason, a lot of animals were soon leaving.

When after five days there'd been no contact from any of the explorers, Fuller printed an article which amounted to a great big 'We told you so'. But Bachman made a statement to the press the next day saying that he'd heard from the group's leader and everything was 'going to plan'. How (or even if) they were managing to keep in touch, nobody seemed to question. But it had the desired effect of keeping us all quiet for a while. Me, I wasn't convinced, but as I had no intention of finding out for myself, I wasn't really that concerned. Leave that kind of thing to the fools who thought of themselves as heroes. Needless to say, most of the explorers were of the canine persuasion.

I'd started to take walks along the riverbank, which was only five minutes from the office. I enjoyed the silence, the wonderful silence which gave me time to think. It was the only place I knew that wasn't full of other animals. Shefton Heights was quiet most of the time, but I liked the fresh air, and unless you went up on the roof there wasn't a lot of it on the fourteenth floor of an apartment block. So out I'd go, alone, just me and myself on the towpath.

I say 'alone', but occasionally I'd bump into another animal. I'd hear a voice in the distance sometimes, but more often than not I'd smell the onion first. Today it was the former.

PART 1: WHAT HAPPENED

'Come out of there you miserable sons of—' Flipper's gravelly voice carried along the path.

Flipper was the maddest old Tomcat I ever met. Without fail, every third or fourth day, regular as clockwork, I'd take my walk along the bank and there he'd be in his grey dungarees and checked shirt, sitting on a small striped deckchair with a green satchel at his side, a large fishing rod in his mitt which bent in the middle above the water until it looked like it might snap, and an onion on the end of the line bobbing about on the surface of the dirty water.

'You think I don't know you're there, huh? Well I do. By God, I do!' he mumbled to himself, the onion worrying the surface of the water.

Why Flipper was called Flipper I don't know. The first time I saw him he asked me if I enjoyed being able to talk and stand on two legs. I said that for the main part it was great. 'Been doing it for years,' he told me, grinning. 'The old man never batted an eyelid.'

Anyway, after seeing him a couple of times, the onion started to bother me; he'd even *peeled* it. It made my eyes sting.

'Come back here you—' I turned, thinking he was talking to me. Instead I saw him reeling the onion back in. It looked like it had been about to slide off the hook. Sitting back on his chair, he peeled another layer and threw it into the water.

'They get too soggy after a while,' he told me. 'No good to anyone then. Loses all the smell.'

Not from where I was standing. 'What's it for anyway?' I asked.

He looked me up and down, weighing me up, his strange eyes squinting into the sun. That onion was *humming*.

'They,' he hissed behind a mangy paw, looking down at the water, 'they *cry*, Fish you know. Don't ask me how I know, but I do. And this—' he pointed at the big white onion, 'helps them along. When they cry, you see, they have to come up for air or else they drown. Too much water see, even for them. And when they do—' he mimed casting out the rod, 'that's when I gets 'em.'

So there you have it: mad as a hatter. Harmless, but mad. A few more walks along the river convinced me that he never caught a damn thing. My guess was he lived on berries. Or invisible Fish.

Anyway, on this one particular day I heard him, then smelt the onion, and then eventually saw him. He wasn't sitting on the striped chair for once, instead he was having an argument with the water.

'You think so, do you? Well, I'll have you know—hello Benjamin,' he said without even turning round. 'I'll have you buggers know that I could catch any one of you any time I liked.'

To my surprise, another voice answered him. 'You wanna try now? I mean really try? *He's* got more chance than you have.'

It took me a while to trace the voice: a Fish with its scaly head slightly above water. Another head popped up to have its say.

'Flipper! That's a joke. You ain't ever caught one of us yet.'

'Why you cheeky little beggars! All it'd take would be one paw in the water and—'

'Just try it and I'll sink my teeth in it,' the first Fish said. All of a sudden there were at least a dozen Fish baiting the Fisher instead of the other way around. When they started in on me, I grabbed a pawful of stones and threw them in the water. Once the ugly heads sank and the ripples stopped, all became quiet again.

'Sorry Flipper.' I said, feeling a bit embarrassed.

'S'alright, Son. S'alright.' He patted me a bit too hard on the back.

I changed the subject. 'Not seen you this far up before.'

PART 1: WHAT HAPPENED

'No. Thought I'd give it a go. You never know. Could be Salmon along here somewhere.' Looking at the molasses-coloured water I doubted it. 'So,' he asked, casting his line once more, 'what's happening in the big bad world?'

Yanking a blade of grass from the bank I chewed on it and told him about the SPCH and the explorers.

'Aye, I suppose it had to happen.' He nodded sagely. 'They won't find anything you know. Nothing out there worth looking for. Best to stick to what you have. Especially now.' He brought the line out of the water again and took off another layer of onion. Suddenly my nose was twitching and my whiskers were quivering. Whatever I was smelling it wasn't onion.

Flipper saw my nose twitching. He started to sniff the air himself.

'Where's it coming from?' I asked him.

'Not sure. Not the water. Let us have a root around see.'

Leaving his tackle on the bank we walked further along the path. Despite the various other odours—cigarettes, rubbish, dog turd—it, whatever it was, was still the dominant smell. A *familiar* smell. Suddenly I knew what it was. But I couldn't see anything. Then Flipper started sweeping his paws through the long grass. He stopped, crouched over something. Turning, he beckoned me over. As I got closer, I saw the large brown cardboard box.

'Wouldn't believe it if I wasn't seeing it with my own eyes, Benjamin,' Flipper told me as I looked over his shoulder.

Inside the box, a litter of seven tiny kittens were trying to fasten themselves onto a large female who glanced up at us without any kind of fear as her babies clambered blindly over each other, emitting the odd squeak.

'They're Olds,' I said quietly.

Not all animals it seemed had changed the way most of us had. There were some that hadn't changed at all. They become known as Olds.

THE TERROR AND THE TORTOISESHELL

The longer I looked into that cardboard box the stranger I felt. Why had we changed but not them?

I was just about to ask the question when I realised its futility. Instead I tried making an 'Old' noise to communicate with them. It sounded plain wrong coming out of me, and the mother never even looked up from her litter. I realised that a part of me had become extinct. You feel funny, finding out stuff like that.

We continued to stare into the box for a while, neither of us speaking. There was nothing to say. It was Flipper who broke the silence.

'Listen,' he whispered, 'I'll keep an eye on 'em. I live just over that hill in the distance there. I'll see they come to no harm.' I nodded. 'Gives you a funny feelin' though, don't it?' I nodded again.

From that day on, every time I went for a walk down there I saw Flipper. He said he'd taken the kittens back home with him, but every time he came fishing he brought them with him. He also said that any Fish he caught would be theirs. I nodded, neutrally.

One day I took a carton of milk with me and a large bowl. While Flipper was 'fishing' I slipped the bowl into the long grass near the kittens and poured some milk into it. I didn't want to offend Flipper. He was doing his best in the only way he knew how.

Pouring the milk, I looked into the kitten's eyes, which had now opened, and they looked right back at me. It made me feel kind of sad. They didn't look any less complete than I was, or deprived in any way. Perhaps I envied them.

One day Flipper's voice behind me made me jump. 'Cats—we're never satisfied with our lot,' he said as if he'd been reading my mind. I agreed and went back to the office.

I hoped that when I got there the phone would be ringing. I was bored and confused at the same time; a strange combination. It's an odd feeling, not knowing who or what

PART 1: WHAT HAPPENED

you are; *why* you are, for that matter. But the phone wasn't ringing. It didn't ring for a long time. It was like we were all waiting for something to happen.

And then one day an elderly Tortoise called Horace picked up a book in a library and began to read.

6

As he told *Fuller News*, Horace hadn't been looking for any particular kind of Truth that day; only something decent to read.

It had been a normal enough day, he informed Fuller the Rat—when the latter turned up at the Municipal Library armed with a tape recorder and a hip flask full of scotch, in case, he said, the old guy felt the cold—'just another day in this new world of ours.'

Horace had lived in a box in one of the back rooms of the library for over fifty years. Nobody remembered any more how he came to be in the library, or who he'd belonged to, but visiting children were particularly taken by his slow-witted exploits, sometimes to the point of ignoring the books themselves. Whenever it looked like he was making a dash for the door someone would go after him, pick him up and dump him back down in his box. 'Plum got on my nerves,' he told the ratted rodent. 'Doubt they'd have enjoyed it either.'

And although the world had changed, Horace himself found that he hadn't changed that much, for which he was grateful. Granted, he was about five feet tall now (or 'long' as he put it) and moving about vertically, lugging his now redundant shell about as he shuffled around the library. 'Someone told me a while ago I should lose the shell,' he told Fuller. 'But I've had it this long, and I've grown rather attached to it, and vice versa.'

PART 1: WHAT HAPPENED

But by and by, Horace felt that he was the same old reptile he'd always been. In fact, according to Fuller's alcohol addled article, the Tortoise hadn't set foot outside the library since all the people vanished. 'You get set in your ways,' he'd said. 'Are you going to guzzle that whole flask yourself?' he'd then asked the Rat, who it appeared hadn't yet come to terms with the editing process.

But there was one great change he welcomed: finding in his dotage he now had the ability to read the books surrounding him. 'I felt like a kid in a candy shop! But that presented a problem in itself—where do you *start*? All those shelves, all those books... made my head spin.'

In the end he decided to shuffle along the rows until he got tired, and wherever he stopped he'd pick a book from the nearest shelf and read that.

The first time he'd run out of steam had been next to a shelf full of books on cars. 'I found I enjoyed reading more than I could possibly say,' he'd stated, to the point where it became a regular habit, taking up virtually all his waking hours.

About a week before the story broke, Horace decided to open up the library to the public for an hour or two each day. Apart from 'an infestation of ancient Scotties hogging the radiators', the place remained quiet. Each day Horace would go about his task of searching out new and interesting reading matter.

'After a while I began to wonder, like most of us I imagine, why it had all happened,' Horace said. 'So, I began to look out for certain kinds of books. Found a load, too.' But after 'Devouring Darwin' and various other authors the Rat couldn't spell, the Tortoise felt he was none the wiser. Giving it up for a bad job, he decided to try something new: he hadn't read any 'made up' stories.

'So I went over to the fiction part of the building. Took me quite a while, though—I say, you'll have a sore head in the morning, young man,' the paper told the city, Fuller evidently now finished with his flask.

'Well, my mind must've been wandering or something as I found that I'd hobbled three-quarters way along one row before I realised it *was* fiction, row K to M. I was feeling a bit sleepy, so I grabbed the nearest book off of the shelf at chest height and headed for the nearest seat for a little sleep. I can't have been sat down more than a few seconds when I drifted off. And then I had the dream.'

When I turned the page, it appeared that part of the text was missing as the article continued mid-paragraph.

'...but the thing was this man knew that this was all *true,* you see—at least that's how it seemed to me. But he'd presented it as fiction, presumably knowing what people's reactions would be... and he was just about to tell me something else when I woke up. I looked down at the book in my lap—a volume of stories by someone called Arthur Machen. I opened the book and started to read.'

'Interesting stuff, all of it; stories of little people, the occult and the like. But it was that last story in the book that really made me sit up and think.'

Apparently, from what I can gather from Fuller's garbled account of the old dude's ramblings, the story in question was about a time when animals sensed that people were losing their grip on civilisation during the First World War. As a result, a few animals began attacking people, and at some point somebody came to the conclusion that *'the animals were trying to take over the world'.*

'Then I remembered the dream I'd just had,' Horace went on. 'They were eerily similar. Was this man from my dream the same man who wrote these stories? I believed he was.

'But in the story, called *The Terror,* it didn't come to anything—the people figured it all out before anything really changed, and again took the upper hand. But look at us now: where have all the humans gone? So my initial reaction was "Oh my God, this has happened before".'

PART 1: WHAT HAPPENED

A brief interlude is necessary here, I think.

Once, in the Old Days, I remember looking up from my basket in the office to see Jimmy shaking his head over an article he was reading in the paper. He'd tutted a few times and then muttered something to himself which at the time hadn't made a lot of sense: 'I see the silly season's here again, Cynthia.' Now, the remark made perfect sense to me.

Yes, we were now in the middle of silly season, steamrollered by the Rat proclaiming that this decrepit reptile had stumbled on none other than the 'Animal Bible'. *It had happened before,* the type told us. Forget the fact that last time nothing had come of it, forget the fact that last time it was presented as fiction, forget the hundred and one other inconsistencies, because *perhaps* they hadn't been ready for 'The Terror' then. *But we certainly were ready for it now.*

So an elderly Tortoise had a strange dream; what of it? I had a dream once where a Sappy was gliding along the street upside down with the aid of a roller skate strapped to his head; it didn't mean that the guy had sore feet. It didn't *mean* anything. But the Rat hadn't finished yet.

No, because remember—*out of all the books that Horace could've grabbed off the shelves, and out of all the places in the library he could've stopped, he stopped at the exact spot where* THAT *very important book was and instinctively knew* (as Fuller argued, that we all would've known), *that 'The Terror' was far more than a mere tall tale.*

The fact that Horace had picked up maybe hundreds of other books in the intervening weeks was conveniently forgotten. It was obvious what Fuller was up to: he needed a story, and, with a bit of tweaking here and there, he'd got one. Tagged onto the end of the article as a kind of PS, was the following: 'We have also lerned that Mackin rote another storey *which is in the same bok,* also set in the first world war called "The Angel of Mons", which, apprntly, is also true; so what other secrts had this man Mackin to tell us?'

Finishing the piece, I caught myself laughing out loud and shaking my head. Oh yes, the silly season was here, all right. How in Hell could Fuller hope to get away with it?

It just shows you how wrong a Cat can be. Over the next couple of days, when I went out for my morning walk, I began to notice something extraordinary happening.

The article was being taken seriously.

Not by everyone, of course. I heard a fair few arguments on the streets between believers and non-believers. Me, I kept my trap shut; just discussing it at all was fanning the flames. It surprised me the number of Cats who thought there was something in it. You'd expect better of Cats. My theory is that these felines must've had religious—or gullible—owners. Jimmy, the natural born cynic, was an atheist through and through.

But then I took to wondering: *did* all these creatures really believe it? We were living in strange times, exciting times, frightening times; everything that we'd once known was extinct. Maybe most of us *needed* to believe something, needed the security of belief, regardless of how off-the-wall that belief was; perhaps it was better than believing nothing (personally I preferred nothing. It didn't let you down as much). But at least we now had a name for what had happened: The Terror. It certainly fitted.

Back at the river the kittens were all wide-eyed now, heedless of what was going on in the 'real' world. As usual, despite staying in his own little fenced-in universe, Flipper knew all about what was going on; the family of Pigeons who lived in the bridge further downstream kept him informed, he said.

'Guessed as much,' he told me one day, spitting into the river. 'The old boy used to read stories aloud to me. It's all there, in the printed word. If that's what they believe, let

PART 1: WHAT HAPPENED

them get on with it. Ain't none of our business. They ain't doing anybody any harm. Yet.' He spat in the river again. That one word kept rattling about in my skull on the walk back to the office.

♯

So, after all the false starts and twists and turns, things did finally settle down into some kind of pattern. Most of us had our days planned out, our beliefs in place. The world continued to spin, if a little shakily. It was still early days.

And then one day at the beginning of October, I was interrupted whilst watching a Gorilla on his window-cleaning round when a Longhair called Taki appeared in my office looking for a Tortoiseshell. But I already told you about that, and it'd be kind of painful to go over it again.

But despite that fiasco things did pick up, and a couple of weeks later the delightful Taki was working as my secretary. The in-tray was full of paper, the streets were full of animals.

And the Spriteman Detective Agency was in business once more.

THIS IS AN **ALA "Reading List"** EDITION & IS NOT FOR RETAIL SALE OR DISTRIBUTION

Part Two

—

Down to Business

7

'Sphynx.'
 'Different colours, with eyes usually matching the colour. Hairless. Suede-like skin. Prone to cold. Big ears. Give me another.'

Taki looked down at the book again, flipped a few pages and came up with Tonkinese. I told her it could be any of a number of colours, including brown and bluish-grey. It had a medium-short coat and markings like a Siamese. They were known for their hunting prowess. They were also late developers. She didn't contradict me, so I told her to throw me another.

Taki grinned from ear to ear, her blue eyes sparkling. 'Singapura.'

'Singapura?' I had to think about that. Then I had it—very rare, worth a fortune in the Old Days. 'How many of them am I likely to see in the city, huh?'

She purred at me. Maliciously. She wasn't going to let it pass.

'Okay, a Singapura has a short coat of a satiny texture with bronze markings. Its underside is usually lighter. It is also one of the smallest breeds in the world, weighing around six pounds. Or at least it did. Generally shy animals, but the females are excellent mothers.' I leaned back in my chair with my paws behind my ears, grinning.

THE TERROR AND THE TORTOISESHELL

'How did you get that?' she slanted her eyes at me.

It's strange how you can go from nothing happening to lots happening and back again so quickly. That's how it was with me. Suddenly, I had a business to run. It wasn't a glamorous business, or even a lucrative business, but it was a business and it was mine; and if animals wanted to pay me to look for missing Cats and Dogs, or to track down stolen goods or errant partners, then that was fine by me. The fact that the Cop Shop was about as much use as a bucket of steam was fine by me as well. Suddenly I had a pile of paperwork on my desk: step forward Taki. By the end of her first week all the paperwork was cleared and I'd sorted all my outstanding cases bar one: a young Mouse with a thing about fast cars kept getting pulled over by the Cops and whose mother wanted me to intervene. If I'd had other things to work on I'd have done them—chasing after a joy-riding Mouse wasn't my idea of fun. But it wasn't about the money, it was the hours.

Long gone were the forty winks that lasted eighteen hours a day; since The Terror I was lucky if I could manage eight hours a day, regardless of how tired I was. So anything that helped me fill the hours was welcome. Up to a point.

But at least the lull had given me the opportunity to brush up on a few things, such as boning up on the different varieties of beasts out there on the streets. I was hoping it would give me an edge over the cops.

'Hungarian Vizsla.'

'That's not a Cat, that's a mutt.'

'You didn't say it had to be a Cat,' Taki said.

I sat for a few seconds scratching my head. I wasn't so good on Dogs.

'Small, with long curly fur, usually cream. Its temperament is—'

'Wrong,' Taki took great delight in telling me. 'Completely wrong. Norwegian Elkhound.'

PART TWO: DOWN TO BUSINESS

I looked around the office for inspiration and came away with zilch. I blurted out the first things that came into my head. Taki's eyes widened, her tail swishing slowly over the edge of my desk. I stared back. She told me what I'd just described sounded more like a Hippo than a Dog. I asked her what was the difference. She'd just started telling me in no uncertain terms when the phone on her desk rang.

I swivelled my chair to look out the window. In the building across the street, two Great Danes were lugging an executive boardroom table from an office while a third stood and watched, presumably because he was wearing a suit. When the suit caught me watching I looked away to the street.

From the fourth floor I had a pretty good view, if you happened to like glass. Early November sunshine reflected off the countless panes, so it looked like every office had its own sun. Below a few cars buzzed by, windshields filled with large hairy faces, paws draped out of open windows, tongues and ears flapping in the cool breeze. In the distance something big and yellow looked like it could be a bus. All in all it looked pretty good from up here. Peaceful. But out there beyond the sun-filled windows somebody was far from peaceful.

Another of our ever-decreasing Sappy population had been found murdered, the sixth in under two months. But the strange thing was you never saw Sappies anymore. So where were they coming from?

I looked back to the furniture removal across the street. The Dane in the suit was rifling through a filing cabinet now. Great Danes, why couldn't she have asked me about Great Danes?

Suddenly my phone was wobbling on my desk the way it always did when it rang. I picked it up.

'Bootsy for you.' I told Taki to put it through.

'Yeah; Spriteman.'

THE TERROR AND THE TORTOISESHELL

'Hi Benji, how's tricks? Thought I'd give you a call.'

'Lucky me. What can I do for you, Bootsy?'

'I was just wondering if the city's finest PI knew there'd been another murder.' His tone suggested that I wasn't supposed to know.

'Yeah, I heard. Jungle telegraph,' or "Arnie", as I knew him. 'Why, what of it?'

'Oh.' He sounded disappointed. He didn't speak for a few seconds.

'Bootsy, you still awake down there? What's it to me?'

Again, silence. Then, 'Well, you know, we could pool our resources as it were, and—'

'But as you just pointed out, Bootsy, I'm a private, not a uniform.' He made an odd sound down the phone.

'But you do have some ideas, right? I mean to say, a Cat of your intellect must've given it some thought, right?'

'Yeah, I've given it some thought, sure.'

'Yeah? And, um... what conclusions did you draw, Benji?'

'What's this all about, Bootsy? Why the sudden interest in a few dead Sappies?'

'Because it's our orders! Look, Spriteman, just because you have no interest in a career—'

At last we were at the nub of it.

'You want me to help you out, is that it? What do I get in return, Bootsy?'

'—doesn't mean that the rest of us—hang on, what was that?'

'I said you want me to give you some help.'

'Well, I wouldn't have put it like that.' Over the line I could almost hear him back-peddling. 'But, well, as you say, yes.'

'Okay, let us say that I help you. What's in it for me?'

'There's the satisfaction of having helped a valued friend...'

I let that pass. 'Why the interest, really? Be honest. You must have more important crimes to be looking into.'

PART TWO: DOWN TO BUSINESS

'Because,' Bootsy lowered his voice to a harsh whisper, 'because Bachman thinks that if they can kill Sappies like that, then they'll get round to us when they run out.'

'Okay. Third time: what's in it for me?'

'Well, as you rightly pointed out, we do have a lot of other crimes to solve, more than enough to go round in fact, and some of that work could be given over to other organisations to look into...'

The previous week I'd have told him to take a hike, but this week...

'What the hell. Okay, Boots, I'll help you. Send over anything you think might be of interest. But I do have a *lot* of other work, you know.'

'Great! I'll see that you get the file A-S-A-P.' Hanging up I got the impression that Bootsy was holding back on something; he wasn't the generous kind. I decided to put it from my mind for the present.

I sat there for a few minutes drumming my claws against the desk, *rat-a-tat-tat, rat-a-tat-tat*, before reaching for the Cat book again. All told, I had a pretty informative hour.

I learned that Sappies thought Cats were complex creatures, leading strange double lives. Outside: predators, unsociable loners, unable to be trained like a mutt could be trained. Indoors: domestic and undemanding, affectionate when it suited us. An interesting theory, but the description seemed truer for Humes than Cats. At least it had been for the people Jimmy had dealt with. What else did I learn? That we have around thirty incredibly sharp teeth (I went to the mirror and checked), we have better night vision than Sappies, our eyes glowing in the dark; our hearing is much better than theirs; we have extraordinary co-ordination and balance, using our tails if positioned on a narrow ledge, and our whiskers are excellent for detecting atmospheric changes and air currents, which means we tend to bump into things less as long as our whiskers aren't damaged; we retain healthy appetites into old age and cannot be vegetarians (despite this the awfully-named *Nut Catlet* downtown does a roaring trade). I read a lot about Cat skeletons, Cat heart rates, Cat Weight, Cat reproduction, Cat life-span, Cat noises; tons of stuff. While I sat digesting all this information Taki dropped a small batch of stapled pages on my desk.

'Paper,' she said, going back to her office.

Flicking through it I was impressed: fourteen pages this time, and nearly all the headlines spelt correctly. Five pages were filled with Fuller's 'Editorial', telling us all what a wonderful job he was doing to *'enliten the city in these times of drkness... there are faucets at work in this city tht the police cannot control, and it is sup to every one of us to be vijilunt against such faucets.'* The Rat seemed to be talking about the killings. Either that or he was just having a dig at Bachman. Or both.

At lunchtime I sauntered down to Moe's, bringing back a couple of sandwiches for Taki and me. We talked about nothing much for a while until the phone rang. She handed it over to me. I said yes a couple of times, asked for directions, then hung up. Finishing my sandwich, I grabbed my hat from the stand and stuck it on my head, careful to make sure that my ears went through the holes cut in the sides.

'I'm going to see a Mouse about a Mouse,' I told Taki on my way out.

8

Ma Spayley was the fattest Mouse I'd ever seen in my life. On the telephone she had a tiny, high-pitched voice that sounded like it needed a balloon to tether it to the earth. The voice was at odds with the image in my head of a domineering matriarch in a pinafore and headscarf fussing around a group of squeaky rodents. Merrion Gardens was a fair distance, but at least it gave me a chance to walk off my lunch.

The case details had arrived one day while I'd been out doing something else. A Mrs. Spayley had called to see if I could do anything about one of her fourteen children who liked fast cars and was forever hot-wiring the ones that took his fancy. I was reminded of the joy-riding rodent I'd seen the night The Terror hit. It turned out it was the same Mouse.

Mrs. Spayley had told Taki that the law had picked him up so many times that they were getting pretty sick of him. She said they'd served her with some kind of notice to the effect that his sentence was suspended, but if he was charged again, then she, as his legal guardian, would face the consequences. It was a new one on me, and I wasn't sure it was strictly legal, but these days animals did what they liked; as long as some measure of law and order was being maintained, most animals didn't really care what it actually entailed. With thirteen other ankle-biters to keep watch on,

THE TERROR AND THE TORTOISESHELL

Mrs. Spayley was finding it difficult, and she'd told Taki she didn't know who else to turn to. I didn't think I could do much either, but Taki said she'd sounded so desperate... and then when I'd heard her myself I knew I couldn't turn her away. Perhaps I *could* think of something; there were no hard and fast rules saying I *couldn't* do anything. I was also more than a little curious to see how I reacted around all those Mice.

The house was on the far side of the park where I'd got rid of the leaflets. A wall ran around the outer edge of the park, so ancient it looked about as sturdy as a soufflé. After a while a half-destroyed metal gate broke up the brickwork, giving it a much-needed breather. Across the road were the rows of whitewashed bungalows that constituted Merrion Gardens.

Standing at the door of number seven I heard the squeaky voices of screaming Mice inside. I rang the bell anyway, half expecting that I'd have to knock to make myself heard.

'Yes?'

It was a good thing I hadn't knocked—the white object covering the doorframe wasn't a door, but a Mouse.

'Mrs. Spayley?' I said, trying to hide my surprise. 'Benji Spriteman. We talked on—'

'Oh Mr. Spriteman!' Her white bulk wobbled slightly. 'Oh, thank you for coming, Mr. Spriteman. Please, come in.'

As she backed into her kitchen something thudded against her. Turning to it she said 'Now Number Four, how many times have I told you? If you want to do that, do it outside.'

'Sorry, Ma,' a tiny voice said on the other side of Mrs. Spayley. 'Who was at the door?'

'Mr. Spriteman. He's come to have a word with Number One. Now, I want you and your brothers and sisters to go out and play while we talk. And if you see Number One tell him to come home.'

'Okay, Ma,' the unseen figure replied.

PART TWO: DOWN TO BUSINESS

Ma Spayley turned to face me. 'Would you come through please, Mr. Spriteman?' she shuffled awkwardly through the small door-frame and into the parlour, breathing heavily.

Before I had a chance to follow her I was besieged by a swarm of white and red, which nearly carried me out with them into the garden, maybe a dozen of them, three-foot high white Mice with red markings across their backs: '7', '9', '4', '6', and so on.

'Mr. Spriteman?'

'Just coming, Mrs. Spayley.' When it finally dawned on me, I smiled. To think that a few months earlier I might have chased them and tried to eat them. In the living room, Ma Spayley lifted a pudgy paw and indicated I should sit down.

'Would you like some coffee, Mr. Spriteman?'

'Yes, that would be nice. Seven sugars.'

'Ah.' She nodded. 'Cream? Silly thing to ask a Cat,' she chuckled to herself as she went back into the kitchen.

After a few seconds of clattering cups and saucers and steaming kettles, Ma Spayley appeared at the door.

'Nice place you have, Mrs. Spayley.'

I always said it, but this time I meant it. The room had a beautiful, thick, burgundy carpet which virtually begged me to take off my shoes. The walls were covered in large frame prints of cornfields and stately houses, although one frame contained a moving picture of me. The wallpaper matched the carpet, deep burgundy but broken up with gold stripes. On the mantelpiece, the various shiny knick-knacks looked on the pricey side. Despite being home to so many rodents, the room was extremely tidy.

'Why, thank you. The couple who had it before everything changed were successful people. They had a cage in the back room full of Mice for when their grandchildren came to play.' When she appeared with a large silver tray I took it from her and placed it on the coffee table.

'Thank you. Yes, there was enough room in the cage for a few of us. Until, that is, I had my litter—'

THE TERROR AND THE TORTOISESHELL

'How many did you have?'

'Fourteen healthy young 'uns,' she told me, handing me my coffee. 'Fourteen, and every one survived. Well, they couldn't decide what to do with us all and then it happened—The Terror, as they've taken to calling it—well, can you imagine what it must have been like for them, waking up to a broken cage and a house full of children-sized Mice?' She chuckled to herself again before flopping down on the sofa, breathing heavily.

'You have fourteen children, Mrs. Spayley? And it's Number One that's giving you the problems?'

'Yes, that's right,' she said, her whiskers sagging as her head dropped. 'Number One Mouse. You saw the numbers on their backs? Well, that's the only way I can keep track of them all, Mr. Spriteman. Sometimes I wish this "Terror" had never happened. It would've been easier, I think, the way things were. For us at least. Number One is the biggest, the "eldest". Strange, isn't it? You'd think they'd all be the same size. In case you were wondering, those red marks aren't permanent. It's only marker pen and it's already starting to grow out. When their fur's—'

'How many times has Number One been picked up by the police, Mrs. Spayley?'

'Seven times. I think it's difficult for him, being the eldest. He feels responsible in a way. We all muck in around the place, you know. But I think Number One thinks he should be kind of 'head of the household'. His father was mauled by a Cat, you see. Before The Terror, I mean,' she added quickly before going on. 'Anyway, from time to time he lets off a bit of steam with those cars and that's when the trouble starts.'

There was a long pause between us then, a long *comfortable* pause, as if we'd known each other for years. I liked Ma Spayley. It made it difficult.

'Mrs. Spayley, I have to be honest with you. I don't really know what I can do for your son.' For a moment she

PART TWO: DOWN TO BUSINESS

looked like she was about to start crying. 'But I'll have a word with him anyway, see if we can work something out.' She suddenly brightened.

'He should be here somewhere, but no doubt he's off gallivanting again.'

'No matter,' I told her, draining my cup. 'I'll find him.'

'We—' she paused, looked down at her dress. 'We haven't discussed a fee, Mr. Spriteman.'

'I haven't done anything yet,' I told her. 'If I manage to do any good we can discuss it then.'

Outside, the squeals of a dozen infant Mice filled the air. I gestured one of them over to me.

'No sign of Number One?' I asked.

'Hasn't come back,' the Mouse told me, puffing slightly, eager to get back to his play. 'Haven't seen him.'

'Where is he likely to be?'

'The graveyard. In the park.' The Mouse grabbed his tail and began swishing it through the air, round and round like a propeller. 'He's always there.' Before I got a chance to say anything else, the Mouse turned to reveal a big red number four on its back and galloped off into the garden, jumping every few paces. Making my way through the playing Mice I heard a female voice say 'Number Four, you can do that all you like. But you still can't *fly*.'

'I will one day,' Number Four replied confidently.

Approaching the park, I was surprised to see the wall still standing. Thankfully I didn't sneeze as I walked alongside it which meant it stayed up a little longer still. Passing through the gate, I was assailed by the overwhelming odour of Dogs.

Over to the right was some kind of huge wire cage, pictures of Budgerigars and other feather-heads stuck on the fence below. The cage was empty—a series of holes punched up through the wire ceiling told me why. Next to the empty prison, an incredibly disfigured tree wrapped its bald limbs around itself like a wooden straitjacket. Wedged between its two highest branches was a teddy bear with HELP ME! scrawled across its chest. The reek of canines was starting to make my eyes water.

The path headed up through more deformed branches, a couple of which were trying to tickle the muddy ground. To my left, something shot up a tree too quickly for me to see what it was.

Up ahead I saw something large and white sitting on the ground between a series of small stone monuments.

'You Number One Mouse?' I called up the hill. The figure turned and looked at me.

'Who are you?'

I decided to keep him waiting, not speaking again until I was within a few feet of him. When he stood up, I saw he was bigger than his brothers and sisters, but nowhere near the size of his mother. Unlike his brothers and sisters, he was wearing clothes.

'Name's Benji Spriteman. Your mother's worried about you.'

'Oh.'

'She wants me to have a word with you, see why you keep having all this trouble with the law.'

'Oh,' he said again before sitting back down.

'Mind if I join you?' I squatted down before he had a chance to reply, so I was looking at the stones. The largest was about eighteen inches high and inscribed with two words: MY MOUSE.

'Number Four said you'd be up here.'

'How long have these stones been here, do you think?' he asked.

I shrugged. 'Beats me. So, suspended sentence, eh?'

He lowered his head. 'If I do it again, they'll fine Ma', he told me, scratching at the dirt around the stones.

'Well I'm not the law, I'm a Private Investigator. A Dick, a Shamus, a Gumshoe. They're the polite terms for what I am.'

PART TWO: DOWN TO BUSINESS

'Yeah?' he was all ears now. 'You collar anybody interesting? You get any SPCH, anything like that?'

I shook my head then nodded at the stones. 'Why the interest in this place?'

'Dunno,' he said eventually. 'Just peaceful, I guess. Away from everything, you know?' I nodded.

I decided to take a chance. 'Why do you do it?' I asked him. 'You know, I think I saw you the first night, driving past my offices.'

'Where?' I told him. He said that'd been him. He crashed the car into a wall further on.

'You total a lot of cars, Number One?'

'A few.'

'Why?'

He screwed up his face, waved his paws in the air. 'I won't do it again! I told Ma but she wouldn't believe me.'

'Why won't you do it again?'

The Mouse stood up. 'I'll show you,' he said.

We tramped further up the hill and I saw more things clambering about in the branches above. The Mouse took no notice, so neither did I. We came to what looked like an enormous bush between two more dead trees. The Mouse began moving great mounds of grass and branches away from it, and something glinted from inside. It looked like a windshield.

'I found it dumped outside some empty houses,' Number One informed me. 'I waited a few days to see if anyone'd claim it but nobody did. So I reckon it's mine now.'

Sweeping away the last of the greenery, I found myself looking at a pretty decent little car. It wasn't old, it wasn't new. Neither was it the kind of car that anybody was likely to miss. The corners of my mouth rose as an idea came to me.

'Honestly, Mr. Spriteman, I didn't pinch it. It was just there.'

THE TERROR AND THE TORTOISESHELL

'Were the keys in the ignition?'
'Hell, no. I hot-wired it.'
I was impressed. 'You should find a garage for it.'
The Mouse smiled at me. 'You're all right, Mr. Spriteman.'
'And you're no villain. Who pulled you in?'
'It was all different ones. Er, there was Dammers, Toffee—he took me in twice—Paulin, Bootsy, Tober…'
I stopped him. 'This "Bootsy". Describe him to me.'
'Oh, *him*. Mr. Wise-guy. Persian, stuck up, not very bright.'
I recognised the description. I couldn't have put it better myself. 'Where did he pick you up?'
'Over on Fifty-First a few days ago. I don't think that was because of my driving, though. He didn't take me in. There were cops all over the place, and tape, too. I think it was a crime scene. He just shooed me away.' He looked round at me. 'I'm a good driver, Mr. Spriteman. Really.'
I looked at the car then I looked at the Mouse.
'Want to show me how good you are?'

♯

'Where are we going, Mr. Spriteman?'
As soon as the Mouse mentioned Bootsy, I knew I had to check it out. I now knew the real reason for his sudden need for co-operation: the murder scene—it had to be a murder scene—would still be relatively fresh, and he wanted a head start on the other officers.
'We're going wherever Officer Bootsy picked you up.'
Number One turned to face me. 'Have a hunch, huh?'
'Something like that,' I told him above the roar of the engine, then leaned across the dash and tapped the speedometer. 'The next time they pull you up I don't want to be sitting next to you.'
'Sorry.' He slowed down. All in all, he was a good driver. A very *agile* driver. Especially on two wheels.

PART TWO: DOWN TO BUSINESS

As we sped along I saw that I hardly knew any of the areas we were passing through, whereas the Mouse knew them in great detail. The further we went, the more exclusive the breeds became, the clothes more refined. When I saw a four-foot high Poodle wearing a fur coat I laughed so hard I thought I was going to have an accident. In a matter of seconds a jewellers, an exclusive clothes store, an antique shop, two bars and a fitness club disappeared behind us. High-class Poodles and Shih-tzu's pranced up and down the sidewalks adorned with sparkly trinkets and sunglasses; you could almost see the clouds of perfume they were all doused in. A Boxer limped along with the aid of a black cane embossed with gold. A pair of Siamese strolled along paw-in-paw, wearing identical morning suits.

'How long until we get to Fifty-First?' I asked, suddenly sick of the view.

'Couple of minutes.'

'When Bootsy stopped you, was there anyone around that looked official?'

'Could've been,' he said, honking the horn at a Spaniel on roller-skates in the middle of the road. 'I wasn't there long enough to find out. Here we are.'

Without appearing to slow down first, the car went from fifty to stop. When I'd got my breath back I opened the passenger door.

We were in a long, wide street full of large detached houses with big oak doors.

'Over here.'

The Mouse was standing before a rather austere, oblong-shaped building with a flat roof. Just inside the large parking lot was a wooden sign, the initials HFC writ large over some smaller, faded words just visible beneath—THE GOURMET CLUB. A name as austere as the building itself.

'An old restaurant,' I said. 'But what is it now? What's 'HFC'?'

THE TERROR AND THE TORTOISESHELL

The Mouse shrugged. 'No idea.'

'Wait here,' I told him as I stepped over the foot-high wall into the parking lot. 'Tell me if anyone shows up.'

I tried looking in the windows, but every pane was smoked black and all I got was my own reflection, good though it was. But I also got the distinct feeling that maybe somebody was staring at me a matter of inches away on the other side of the glass. I decided to put it down to imagination. The entrance door was padlocked, so I went round to the side of the building. As soon as I did my whiskers twitched. Two large cylindrical trash-cans stood a few feet apart before another heavily bolted door, presumably leading to what used to be the kitchen. Unlike the rest of the premises this area had been swept clean. My guess was that somebody had taken a hose to the stones, but the smell remained; the smell of claret, sausage-meat, violence: Sappies.

There was nothing else to see around the other side of the building, so I went back to the car and the Mouse. I asked him where most of the activity was the day he was pulled up. He told me it was next to those bins I'd been looking at. Driving back along the street we didn't pass a soul.

'Well, you were right about one thing,' I told the Mouse. 'You certainly can drive. Slow down a bit and I could give you a job.'

The Mouse turned and stared at me. After a couple of seconds I guided his face back to the road with my paw.

'You mean that?' His tail had started banging against the side of the gearshift.

'I can't promise you a lot of work, but—'

'Hell, I'm going to be working for a real, live Private Investigator! Wait till I tell Ma.'

'Well make sure that's all you tell. We haven't been here today, got that?'

He dropped me off near the office and told me he was going to find a garage. Once again I mentioned that my calls

PART TWO: DOWN TO BUSINESS

might not be that frequent, and about half-a-dozen other things running along the lines of 'don't get your hopes up'. He nodded, stupidly but charmingly, at everything I said before he zipped back across the city.

There was a new plaque up in the lobby: 'Ms Galbraith: Psychic Consultant'. A few weeks earlier I'd had the run of the entire building; now, various little operations had begun to invade: *Tigger Parsons' Home Security Services, Kitty Wellman, Piano Tutor, Spot's Luxury Tanning Studio*. I'd seen one or two faces around the place but had no idea if they were clients or were running the outfits.

As the elevator door slid open on the fourth I heard noises above, a cross between a foghorn and an opera singer followed by a few shouted questions to which there were no replies. I opened the door to Taki's office, better known as Reception.

'What's the racket upstairs?' I asked her.

'That is *Muzz* Galbraith, conducting a séance. She popped down to introduce herself just after you left,' she said without stopping her typing. 'She's nice.'

'*What* is she?'

'An elderly Pewter Longhair. A bit eccentric but very friendly.'

I pulled a face, about to move away.

'Oh, you had another visitor while you were out. A *very* important visitor. At least that's what he wanted me to think.' She held up a brown manila file stuffed with loose papers.

'Bootsy?' I said. 'He's keen.'

'He told me to tell you that you haven't had this file from him. He also told me to tell you that you *must* dispose of it when you've finished with it.'

'Did he now?' I took it from her and went through to my office, slapping it down on the desk. Taking my old water bowl from the bottom drawer, I filled it from the water cooler and drained it in seconds flat. For some reason the water tasted better out of the bowl than from those sterile plastic cups. Sticking my paws on the desk, I began taking sheets of paper from the file to inspect.

It was my first experience of police paperwork, and a profound relief to find that they were no better organised than I was. Hardly anything was typed and, when it was, the spelling was so poor I wondered if they'd asked Fuller to do it for them. Odd phrases were scrawled across other phrases, paw prints and coffee stains, and those little blue horizontal lines on the pages seemed to be there for decoration purposes only. The few photographs in the file were enough to put me off my food for several hours.

Having waded through it once, I went back in and waded through it again. After I'd finished I felt like I needed a long soak in hot water.

According to the file there'd been six murders so far, the latest at the mysterious 'HFC' had been sketched in at the end very briefly. All the victims were Sappies. Two things linked the crimes: all the killings had been carried out with expert precision involving very sharp instruments; secondly, each victim had been 'posed' to resemble an animal.

The body of the first victim had been found in mid-September on a dumpsite by two Birds leaving their old cage at the tip. When the cops arrived they found a Sappy probably in his mid-twenties, *rigor mortis* freezing him on all fours, tongue hanging out. On the ground close by were a pile of half-gnawed bones, a leash and a bowl of water. Taped to the Sappy's back was a sheet of paper, on it the words *Woof! Woof!* written in black crayon.

The other murders were just as brutal.

The body found on the seventh floor of Ronson Towers had been the third one. The officers opened the door on a dead man done up as a black Cat. Analysis later showed the black stuff was tar. The Man's hands—or paws, or what

PART TWO: DOWN TO BUSINESS

was left of them—were stuck in a ball of steel wool. The victim even had a tail; I don't need to describe where *it* was found. The word *Miaow!* was daubed across the wall with what was left of the tar.

The latest victim, the fourth male, had been found among the refuse outside an establishment known as 'The Beefsteak Rooms'; AKA: 'The Gourmet Club'; AKA: 'HFC'. This one had been made to look like a Parrot. *Pretty Pretty Polly!* was engraved into the man's 'feathers'. He even had a beak.

My mouth tasted vile, like something had died in it. I phoned through to Taki and asked her to put some coffee on.

'You all right, Benji?' she asked when she brought it in.

'I will be,' I told her, swallowing hot coffee. 'If you want a good nap in the next couple of weeks *do not* look in this file.'

'As bad as that?'

'As bad as that.'

I spent some time getting that taste out of my mouth and trying to clear my mind of the photographs. But I found I kept going back to it. Snatching at the phone I rang Police HQ.

'Detective Bootsy, please.'

'Who? Just one second.' I tried to deflect my musings by guessing the breed I'd just spoken to. A Dog, obviously. A small Dog, something like a Norfolk Terrier; happy dogs, good with children, oval shaped eyes, short powerful legs—

'Hello; Detective Bootsy.'

'It's me, the chump you dumped the file on. You could have warned me, Bootsy.'

There was a pause on the other end. I was sure I could hear him grinning. 'Not pleasant, is it? But that's police work for you. If you can't handle it you should've said—'

'Never mind. What does 'HFC' stand for?'

THE TERROR AND THE TORTOISESHELL

'Oh, that. You think it's important? It used to be The Beefsteak Rooms, 'cos it used to be a restaurant. That was its unofficial name.'

'Its official one being The Gourmet Club.'

'Right.'

'So?'

Bootsy paused again. I seemed to have confused him. 'So what?' He eventually replied.

'So what does it stand for?'

'Oh, *that*. Oh, we don't know.'

'You don't know.'

'No. We reckon it's still a restaurant, as that's what it was before.'

'You find anything in those bins?'

'Nope. Just the body nearby.'

'So why do you think it's still a restaurant?'

'What else could it be?'

'Have you checked out all the sawbones operating in the area, see if any of them has a grudge against Sappies?'

'Yep,' he told me, along with some other stuff. But I didn't hear the rest. Something had just come to me, something I doubted the police would've checked up on. When Bootsy took a rest to breathe, I hung up.

Rooting about under Jimmy's desk, I found the phone book I used to lie on top of in the Old Days. I got the number of the lab I'd made such a fool of myself in when looking for Ed Mahoney's tortoiseshell.

When I got through and told them who it was, I had to endure a few minutes playful teasing. Finally I got to ask a question.

'Are things still going walkies down there?'

They certainly were, I was told. I asked them to give me a list.

'You got a pen? There's quite a load.'

PART TWO: DOWN TO BUSINESS

Two minutes later, I had a pretty lengthy list of surgical apparatus that had grown legs. Thanking the Siamese, I hung up.

When Taki popped her head around the door to tell me she was going home I did the same. I decided I'd pay Arnie Murchess a call in the morning. If anybody had any ideas, it would be Arnie. For a fee, of course. Always for a fee.

9

I GOT UP THE NEXT morning to find that if that file had given me any nightmares, I didn't remember them. My glass of milk went down nicely too, now that I'd got that taste of death out of my mouth. Putting on my suit and hat, I locked the door behind me wondering who I'd bump into today.

Three mornings out of four I was guaranteed to run into at least one of my neighbours. Sometimes it was Inky the Dalmatian; others Tigger the Tabby, the elderly gent who I sometimes heard shouting at his deaf sister through the walls. More often than not it was one particular neighbour and our conversation was always the same. That morning I saw him coming out of the elevator.

'Morning,' I said.

'Shove off,' the red and yellow Parrot replied, waddling past me like a lame old man with his hands clasped behind his back. Maybe that *was* his name. Then again, perhaps he only knew the two words.

Leaving the gloomy, cavern-like lobby behind I stepped out onto the street. It was a warm morning for the start of November, and the streets were busy. Turning into the business district, I passed the two-ton Budgie with the cuttlefish stall, and the Ginger Tom with the shades and cane who pretended he was blind. Picking up a paper from the vendor, I rooted about in my pockets for change.

PART TWO: DOWN TO BUSINESS

'Anything worth reading today?' I asked the Saint Bernard.

'Only if you like a Rat with an ego,' he grunted.

As it was such a nice morning I decided to treat myself to a coffee at Moe's. She looked pleased to see me as always, but she looked pleased to see everyone. Next time round I decided I was coming back as a Snowshoe: tranquil and beautiful. We chewed the fat for a while; how her business was doing, how mine was doing, that sort of thing. I ordered eggs to wash my coffee down with.

'Looks like you enjoyed that, Benji,' Moe said when she took the plate away.

'Always do, Moe. You never know when things are going to change.'

'You expecting things to change, Benji?' she asked me, tilting her head to one side.

Suddenly I felt odd, the way I'd felt as I'd been looking over that damn file. 'You know, I don't know why I said that.'

※

Opening the door to the office, I felt the slight embarrassment I always felt when I saw Taki there before me, hard at work. She had the phone in one paw and a sheaf of mail in the other. I took the mail through to my office and went through it. Half of it went in the trash: junk mail, you can recognise the smell a mile away. Five minutes later the paper followed the mail into the can. The Saint Bernard had been right.

Picking up the phone I dialled Police HQ.

'Yep, Bootsy,' he said when they eventually found him.

'Do you have any new info for me?'

'I could ask you the same thing,' he said. I decided to shake things up a bit.

'That file was a mess, Bootsy. And incomplete.'

THE TERROR AND THE TORTOISESHELL

'What?'

'Come on, Bootsy! All those crime scenes and *no* suspects? You're holding out on me.'

'Now wait a minute, that file was bang up to date—'

'Phone me back when you feel you can tell me the whole story,' I said before hanging up. I reckoned he'd be back in touch sooner rather than later with some titbit of information he'd conveniently forgotten about.

Something green and ugly popped into my mind. On my way out, I told Taki not to be surprised if Officer Bootsy put in an appearance at some point. She said she could hardly wait.

Arnie's apartment block, the elegantly monikered Ronson Towers, was a modern building lacking the gargoyles and faded glory of Shefton Heights but still managed to look both bland and expensive in equal measure. Whoever the Murchesses had been, they'd had money.

In the lobby, I found that I could make my way to the lift without a flashlight; a nice change. A concierge sat behind an ornate desk reading the paper. For a second I wondered if it might be a Cop, but then I spotted he was reading without moving his lips. I slipped into the elevator and hit the button for seven. Nearly a month had passed since my last visit but I reckoned I'd still be able to sniff something.

I walked the entire length of the floor and was only two apartments away from the other elevator when I got the scent of blood. Looking up and down the corridor, it was clear. I knocked on the door, waited a few seconds and then knocked again, waited some more. As I waited, I took the skeleton keys from my pocket.

Opening the door, the smell hit me straight away. Through the short hallway and into the lounge, the smell got stronger. I shook my head at the sloppiness of the clean-up; anyone with half a decent nose could have caught the odour. You could still smell the tar the Sappy had been coated in. There

PART TWO: DOWN TO BUSINESS

were even dried brown stains on the wall. They hadn't even bothered to wipe off *'Miaow!'*. But despite all this, there wasn't anything here I didn't know already.

Locking the door behind me, I got the elevator up to the twelfth.

'Oh, it's you,' Arnie mumbled when he opened his door. As usual, he wasn't wearing any clothes. He told me once he didn't need them. I still harboured the suspicion that what he really meant was he couldn't be bothered paying for any.

'You want a beer or something? Oh, I forgot—you guys can't handle it, can you?'

'Which is exactly why you offered, Arnie.'

He shrugged. 'True.' Shuffling into the kitchen, he came back with a bottle and took a long swig from it as I sat down on his lumpy sofa. I felt like I was sitting on a bag full of porridge. Arnie stood in front of the window. The sunlight made his pale flesh look gangrenous. He stared down at me. '*Well?*'

'Well what?'

'I presume you're here because of the information I gave you.' He took another swig from his bottle. 'Did it pan out?'

'Yeah, Arnie. It panned out.'

He made a low grunting sound, nodded. 'And what about Mullen? You find him, eventually?' I told him I had.

He looked out the window. 'You like my apartment, Spriteman?'

I took a quick glance around at it. It was small and not particularly clean, but comfortable in its way. Before I had a chance to reply he spoke again. 'You see, I don't. It'd be nice to do the place up a bit. It needs a little—'

I cut off his leathery creak of a voice by rustling a few bills in the dusty air. Turning away from the window quicker than any Tortoise should be able to turn, he snatched the bills from me. 'That all? As you can see, I'm busy here.'

'Heard anything else about the murder on the seventh?'

THE TERROR AND THE TORTOISESHELL

'Nope.' He gulped the last of the beer. 'He was done up like a Cat is all I know. They're all done up like animals or something. The cops hung around for a couple of days.' Arnie belched, a noise like a crypt door slowly creaking open. 'Anything else?'

'Have you heard of a place called 'HFC?'

Arnie's eyes sparkled. 'Oh yeah, I hearda that.' He cackled, opened the window and spat.

'Care to tell me *what* it is, Arnie?'

'You mean you don't *know*?' He cackled some more.

When he eventually stopped laughing Arnie told me all about the HFC: what it was, what the initials stood for, the whole bit. When he'd finished I couldn't think of anything to say.

'Kinda makes you wonder where they get their meat, don't it?' Arnie laughed again. As I let myself out he was still laughing.

10

I FELT SICK, AS SICK as when I'd read Bootsy's file. In some ways this was worse. It meant that some of *us* were as bad as some of *them*. Arnie's info regarding the HFC explained the need somebody had for surgical equipment, also the thefts from the laboratory. It could also explain why these Sappies were being killed. But this theory went out the window when I remembered that the Sappies had been left intact. Also it didn't make a lot of sense to leave one of the corpses outside your own establishment. And, if this place was what Arnie said it was, surely they'd have their own silverware?

I had that taste in my mouth again. At Moe's I ordered a chocolate fudge sundae, extra chocolate. Before Moe had moved away I was working at it with the long spoon.

When I finished the sundae my face was all sticky. Turning to the mirrored wall, I gave my paws a lick and had a good clean, flattening down my fur and removing the stickiness of the sundae.

'Your secretary said I might find you here.'

Behind me in the mirror, Bootsy looked disgruntled. 'And now you have. Congratulations.' I carried on with my grooming. He glared at me in the mirror for a few seconds. I glared back, all innocent.

'The file!' he hissed at me, his teeth showing, '*what are your thoughts on the file?*'

THE TERROR AND THE TORTOISESHELL

'Nothing further springs to mind than it did earlier.' Flattening an ear with a paw, I watched it spring back up again. Flattened it again, watched it spring up again. 'And I can't tell you any more if you don't play straight with me. Why all the secrecy?'

Bootsy muttered under his breath as I licked my pads. Evidently he didn't know anything after all.

'You know what I think, Bootsy?' I said, turning from the mirror, 'I think you want me to do your spadework for you. But at the same time, you're making sure not to compromise yourself or your department. How am I doing?'

Bootsy didn't answer.

'I don't care either way, Bootsy. Just give me some of that extra work you promised and I'll play along.'

Bootsy stormed out, slamming tabletops. Something ticklish was rising in my throat. After a bit of hacking I launched the fur-ball into the can across the room.

'What was all that about?' Moe asked as she took the sundae glass away.

'Just keeping him on his toes,' I told her.

It was mid-afternoon when I got back to the office. I asked Taki if anything had come in while I'd been away. She was shaking her head when the phone rang. 'Hello, Spriteman's Detective Agency.' A few seconds later she repeated the greeting. After doing it a third time she hung up.

'It happens from time to time,' she said, answering my unspoken question.

I'd only intended to have a light nap, but when Taki woke me up she told me it was past five and she was going home. Saying our goodbyes I turned and looked out the window just as my belly rumbled. Despite the sundae I wondered if I should eat.

But then I remembered where I had to go later and decided an empty stomach might be the best policy. If that place was what Arnie said it was, I'd be doing well to keep my sundae down.

11

It was black as pitch when I left the office and there were a few others standing waiting for the bus. I could've called the Mouse but I wasn't sure what I'd be letting myself in for. Besides, the buses intrigued me—I'd heard they went anywhere you wanted them to, like oversized taxis.

After a half hour standing in the cold and wondering if this was such a good idea, a bus turned the corner into the business district, screeching to a halt about six inches from my shoes and sending various senior citizens inside flying towards the exit. As they got out, I heard a couple of them muttering about the youth of today and what the world was coming to.

'They're not happy unless they're moaning about something,' the driver, a grizzled-looking Bull Terrier in a faded peaked cap told me. 'Where to?'

When I told him his eyes widened. 'I heard it's dangerous up there.'

'Really? Actually, I'm going up to that new HFC place,' I told him once we'd got going. 'See what it's like.'

'You got an invite?' He asked over his shoulder.

'Do I need one?'

'That's what I heard. A high-class joint.'

Seconds later I heard disapproving voices behind me. I heard the words 'doesn't look the type'. I didn't know if they were talking about me or not.

THE TERROR AND THE TORTOISESHELL

The journey seemed to take forever, the bus stopping at and going through every tin-pot little street the city had to offer. We'd go through street after deserted street, then something hairy would fly out of a doorway and flag us down. After a while nobody seemed to be getting off, only getting on. A hundred different odours attacked my nostrils. I was crammed into a window seat by a Guinea Pig that needed a wash. Half the animals seemed to know each other and chatted across the length of the bus in loud voices. I looked back at the driver and thought he probably wasn't getting paid enough. Half-empty soda tins rolled up and down the aisle. The few lights inside the bus that still worked flickered on and off when we hit bumps in the road.

Seconds later, the bus ground to a halt. By now there wasn't enough room for anybody to be catapulted forward.

'Here we are: Human Food Club,' the driver cheerfully pointed out.

You could've heard a pin drop. Squeezing my way past the Guinea Pig, I thanked the driver above the whispers echoing around the bus. As it pulled away, I saw dozens of furry faces pressed against the grimy windows, mouths open, eyes wide, shaking their heads.

When the noise of the bus faded, I found the street was as dead as it had been the last time. The few streetlights that dotted the pavement were off and all the houses were in darkness. Across the street, I saw the sign in the parking lot. I had arrived at the Human Food Club.

♯

Opening the black door into a little alcove, I found myself in a queue with various overweight and over-indulged animals. At the head of the line, standing behind a wooden lectern, I saw a face from the past. Light-hearted banter danced along the line: *Yes, the special is superb tonight. Fresh as a daisy,*

PART TWO: DOWN TO BUSINESS

Sir. Getting to the head of the queue seemed to take as long as getting to the restaurant itself.

'Hello again,' I said to the big Cat behind the lectern when it was my turn.

'The Zoo, remember?' I reminded him. 'You let me in that day. For free.'

'Um, do you have an invite, *sir*?' he hissed. 'Because if not, I can easily get a member of—'

I leant over the lectern and grabbed the Cat's ear. 'I was reading in *Fuller News* that the police were still looking for animals connected with what happened over at the Zoo. Perhaps I'm on personal terms with the Editor.' I let go of him so he could dust down his velvet jacket and compose himself. Looking down at the book on the lectern, he ticked a page with a fountain pen. 'The bar's down there,' he mumbled. 'There's a forty-minute wait. Here's your ticket.' He didn't look up.

I sauntered over to the cloakroom and handed in my coat before going to the bar. I ordered an oil on the rocks, grabbed a handful of anchovies off the bar, and checked out the *clientèle*.

I didn't see any Pigs in there but that's what they reminded me of; flabby business types gesturing with pudgy trotters, all immaculately pressed suits and highly polished shoes.

At the far end of the bar were two doors, one leading to a poolroom, the other to the washrooms. In the poolroom two Bulldogs leaned over the pool table, talking business. On the walls were pictures of Sappies playing billiards in comical outfits. A nice touch. Behind me, the odd colourful name would crop up in conversation: Eddie the Quill, Boney Edwards, Fido the Fisherman, Reeky McStink. When one of the mutts went to the john, I turned to the remaining one and smiled at it.

'Evening.'

THE TERROR AND THE TORTOISESHELL

'Evening,' it replied with a voice like heavy velvet. 'Had a word with the waiter earlier,' he informed me, taking a swig of cognac from an oversized glass. 'Good menu tonight. *Damn* good.'

'Really?' I said, hoping I sounded interested. 'I've never been before.'

'Is that so?' the Dog gulped back another mouthful of brandy. 'Well, in that case my friend, you're in for a treat. The feet are to just *die* for.'

I wasn't sure I'd heard correctly. 'Feet?'

'Oh yes,' He nodded his jowls at me. 'Oh yes.'

There was a pause. I decided to fill it quick. 'Didn't I hear this place was once called The Gourmet Club?'

'Why yes,' the Dog took another swig from the bottomless glass. 'That was in the days when *they* ruled the roost. Its official name was The Gourmet Club, but it got the nickname The Beefsteak Rooms. Unofficially that's what it's still known as. Why, I'm not sure. I suppose because it sounds grand, eh?' His tongue wiped his face like a handkerchief before continuing. 'We're a marginalised group, of course. Apparently it was the same when the Humes ran it. The general riff-raff, then *and* now, don't really understand. So our palates are a little more refined, more *cultured* than theirs. So what? Huh. Plebs.' He swilled the red liquid around in the bottom of the bowl. 'It's rather odd, though: them being castigated for eating swans necks or whatever bits of the animal it was tickled their fancy. But *now*, since this Terror business, we have our own delicacies. I suppose some things never change, eh?' he snorted into his brandy bowl.

Suddenly I felt very warm. I was on my way back to the bar for another drink when my number was called out. Reluctantly, I followed the waiter into the dining room, its walls and ceiling decked out in caramel-coloured panels, the effect broken by the small yellow lamps on hooks which did

PART TWO: DOWN TO BUSINESS

little to relieve the gloom. Small round tables covered with burgundy tablecloths were slotted into every available space. Dark wooden chairs with red cushion seats nestled against the tablecloths. I felt like I was sitting down to eat in a well-upholstered cigar box.

'I'll just get a drinks list sir,' the waiter told me after easing me into a chair.

The second he left, I began eyeing up the diners gnawing away at unidentifiable lumps of meat, chatting politely to their equally well-groomed companions, the males all crooked bow-ties and cigarette holders, the females studded collars and frizzed up fur. A large aquarium tank full of water bubbled away against the back wall. The waiter was making his way back to my table when a Siamese laid a paw on him.

'Excuse me, Waiter, could you tell me the what the house red is this evening?'

'B Positive, Madam,' came the reply.

'A carafe of water for me,' I told the waiter when he asked. Something tried to crawl out of my throat but I forced it back.

'Your menu, Sir,' the waiter said. 'I'll come back in a few minutes.'

With a kind of dumbstruck awe I read the first page. Thinking my mind had played some hideous trick on me I read it again:

~Human Food Club~
~Menu~

~Kidney a la Maison~
Kidney succulently pan-fried and finished with a brandy sauce. Served with fried potatoes
~Roasted Liver w/ various seasonal vegetables~
(alcoholic's liver can be ordered on request)

THE TERROR AND THE TORTOISESHELL

~6 or 8 Braised Eyeballs~
Served with a light salad

~Deep-Fried Rump~
(choice of M/F) smothered with blue cheese sauce.

~Braised Feet Stuffed with Intestine Pâté~

~A selection of internal organs skewered with peppers and onions, served on a bed of fluffy white rice~

Looking up from the menu, I stared at the furry faces tucking into their meals; sharp teeth tearing, jowls working, 'wine' flowing, a cacophony of grunts, belches and flatulence. The air was so thick you could chew it. Napkins applied to greasy faces came away red and purple.

The waiter was hovering over me.

'Could— could you give me a couple more minutes?' I said after swallowing back more bile. With shaking paws I turned to page two of the menu, hoping that it was all some elaborate joke. *Tender lungs filled with a delicate mushroom sauce. Curried bowel in a variety of strengths. Sappy Thermadore.* Thankfully my dry retch was covered by the laughter from a nearby table, a Pug playing a rudimentary tune with a set of finger bones on the side of what looked like a specimen bottle.

The waiter was hovering over me again. I pointed down at the menu; something, anything to get rid of him.

'An excellent choice, sir,' he told me.

'Look!' a voice shouted out as he was walking away. 'Here it comes!'

Another waiter was coming out of the kitchen, wheeling a squeaky trolley containing a large domed serving dish. Two tables away from mine, he stopped. Bending slightly, the waiter lifted the lid of the domed dish, pulling it away with a flourish. An awed muttering went around the room.

PART TWO: DOWN TO BUSINESS

On the silver platter was a bright red shrivelled human head, lower jaw and chin covered with a tasteful selection of roasted vegetables. Stuffed into the mouth, a large red apple. Despite being eyeless, the head managed to convey an expression of great surprise. The diners applauded.

The large Mastiff who was sat next to this charming spectacle whispered something in the waiter's ear, who then tapped the side of a wine glass with a spoon.

'It seems we have a birthday girl in our midst,' the waiter announced. 'So if you'd like to raise your glasses and join me in a chorus of "Happy Birthday"...'

I took that as my cue to scat. As I left the dining room the last thing I saw was the Mastiff with a carving knife and fork poised above the head, waiting for the singing to stop. I was barging past the group of savages in the doorway looking to see what all the fuss was about when the waiter shouted 'Sir, your Thermadore!' I headed for the cloakroom.

Before disappearing behind the curtain to get my coat, the Dog on duty gave me a funny look. When it went behind the curtain I heard mumbled voices. A different Dog face peeped out from around the curtain for a quick look and then vanished. Seconds later, the first Dog appeared with my coat. As I headed for the door I turned to take one final look at the place and saw both Dogs standing in the corridor watching me. One grabbed the telephone on the wall next to him and began talking. His eyes never left mine.

Outside I tasted air so sweet it made my head spin. A couple of Chihuahuas passed me, chatting excitedly.

'...and the Thermadore! It just melts in your mouth!'

Suddenly, I was bent over and the contents of my stomach were decorating the concrete. Sappy Thermadore: that's why the aquarium was full of nothing but boiling water.

I should've hunted down a bus or a taxi, but that would've meant hanging around. Trying to get my bearings, I headed for what I hoped was the city. As if on cue a light

THE TERROR AND THE TORTOISESHELL

rain began to fall, the only sound on the otherwise empty street. I started to think about something marginally less sick, like the murders: why would they leave one body in the street when they could cook it in wine and garlic? Behind me, the gentle patter of the rain was broken by the steady *clop-clop* of footsteps. Two pairs, I was sure. Turning a corner, I came to a sudden stop and held my breath. The footsteps stopped a second later, leaving just the pattering of the rain.

The two goons from the cloakroom; had to be. When I'd been there with the Mouse I'd had the feeling of being watched through that darkened glass. Had they recognised me tonight? Did they think I was a Cop? I listened but heard nothing. Then I had an idea.

Removing my shoes, my pads felt cold on the pavement. On tiptoe, I crept forward. So far so good. Only I'd no idea where I was. The rain began to get heavy, thankfully masking the sound of my ragged breathing. Wherever I was, it was dark and the houses all looked empty, and the streets were virtually in darkness.

When I got to the intersection at the end of the street I had two choices. To the left, the road was flat and long and had nowhere to hide. To the right was an alley. Taking a chance I headed for the alley, stopping at its entrance. As I pulled up, I heard steps behind me again. I darted into the alley, keeping to the wall. At the end were four or five trash-cans. Along with rain and footsteps, I now heard sharp whispered voices.

Before I had a chance to react, there was a flash and a noise like a sneeze in reverse and something was whistling through the air a few feet from my right ear. There was a sharp *ping*! as one of the trash-cans went over with a clatter like a dinner gong wired up to a PA system, the lid spinning on the ground like a palsied plate. Another shot and another can took the bullet, the racket worse than a bomb going off in a monastery.

PART TWO: DOWN TO BUSINESS

My senses were all over the place; the hairs in my ears felt like they'd been fried, my eyes stung from the flash of the gun. The rain stuck to my clothes and turned them into wet paper.

'Go over and check, dummy,' I heard someone say.

Before I had a chance to think of the consequences, I was darting back out of the alley along the flat, open road. When I spotted a turning to the left I could've cried; how I'd missed it before I don't know. It led into another street full of dark houses. I secreted myself in the first alcove I came to, straining my ears for voices, but all I heard were violent scrabbling sounds among the trash-cans. When I chanced a peep around the alcove, all I saw was the alley wall.

The next few seconds felt like hours. Every drop of rain that blatted the sidewalk became a death knell. I took another look around the corner and my whiskers weren't shot off. There was no sign of them on the street. I had two options: to hide here shivering all night, or make a bolt for it.

I started moving, once again trying to get my bearings, half expecting them to be lying in wait for me somewhere up ahead. I figured town would be straight ahead, so that's where I went. Up at the end of the street, a car was parked against the curb. I ran for it as fast as I could, hitting the slabs when I reached it. I looked back and there was still an empty street behind me.

The rain was becoming torrential, falling slantways across the pavements in sheets. My whiskers were drooping so far I must've looked like I had a handlebar moustache. Flicking the water from them, I took off once more. The rain slanting across me gave the impression that I was getting nowhere. Ahead the sky seemed to solidify, darkening even further. Then I knew why: the darkness ahead was buildings, not sky. Several white lights in office blocks confirmed it. I still couldn't see anything behind me, and even if they were close by I was only one block away from the city. I knew I was getting closer to it when I heard the squeal of tires and suddenly a set of headlights turned the world yellow. That was why I hadn't heard them: they'd gone back for a car, probably figuring that if I was a Cop I'd be heading towards the station.

The car's hood loomed up closer and closer, raindrops disintegrating in its headlights. The car lurched up onto the pavement. I was only a few houses from the corner leading onto Main Street, but the car was on my tail, and it sounded so close I doubted that I'd make the corner in time.

To my right, the deep alcove of the last house beckoned me, identical to the one I'd hidden in earlier. Behind me the car was only a few feet away. I turned and saw two blurry figures in the front seats, their images continually swatted by windshield wipers. Because I'd turned back, I'd misjudged the alcove; I'd never be able to stop in time. In sheer frustration, I hurled both my shoes at the car's windshield as I splatted against the wall next to the alcove, sliding down it like a smear of mud in the rain, expecting to be swallowed up by the car.

There was a hideous screeching sound that went on forever, and it wasn't me. I saw the car veer off into the road, its brakes screaming. Then there was a crumpling noise followed by the chiming of broken glass.

The car was accordianed up against what remained of a series of bollards blocking off the street ahead. I looked up at the lighted windows of the offices, expecting to find myself the centre of attention, but there was nobody there. This part of the city was as quiet as the grave.

Without bothering to check the occupants of the car, I ran as fast I was still able through the city, looking back maybe every five seconds but nothing followed me. Absolutely nothing. I wondered if that was a good thing or a bad thing.

✣

PART TWO: DOWN TO BUSINESS

In the office washroom, I removed my clothes and tried to dry myself with paper towels, ending up like a *papier-mâché* doll in the process. Going through to the office I left the lights off, just in case. Dragging a coffee table through from reception back to the washroom, I piled my drowned clothes on top and positioned the table under the hand dryer, jamming the button of the dryer to ON. Then I went back into the office, flopping down into my leather chair. I picked up the phone and called Bootsy but he wasn't there, *quelle surprise*. I filled up my bowl with water and drank the whole lot in a continuous gulp. Parting the slats on the blinds, I looked out onto the street below, but it was empty. I spent a long, sleepless night in the office.

Draining the last of the milk in the fridge, I put the pot on for coffee. As I waited for it to brew, I remembered my clothes in the washroom. The whole room was like a sauna because I'd jammed the hand-dryer. Picking my clothes off the table I nearly burned myself. The clothes themselves were creased more than any clothes in the history of the world had ever been creased. I dressed in a suit that now resembled faded blue crepe paper. I had no shoes. I'd been shot at twice and nearly run over. I wasn't sure which of these offences was the worst. In the mirror, I saw a face nearly as crumpled as the suit. I realised I'd got off lightly.

Outside I heard the welcome clank of milk bottles in the street. I looked in time to see the cart driving away. Then an overweight Hamster wobbled past on a bike far too small for it, a sack full of papers across its back. It was still dark, only six-fifteen, but at least there were signs of life on the street.

Drinking my coffee, I realised that Taki wouldn't be in for nearly three hours. I decided to go home and try to get a few hours' shut-eye.

The streets were still swimming from last night's deluge. In the reflection of a shop window I looked like a badly

THE TERROR AND THE TORTOISESHELL

mauled kid's doll. Between the office and Shefton Heights I only passed two other animals—a snooty looking feline who looked like he hadn't been home for days and a Dog from the milk cart collecting empties. It was too early to exchange pleasantries.

In the apartment I removed my clothes and stuck them in the laundry basket. Flopping down on the bed I stayed there for two lovely hours.

I woke up ravenous. After polishing off some meat I found in the fridge for breakfast, I stood at the window looking down onto the city. It was approaching rush hour now, the roads and streets below filling with cars and animals. On the other side of the road from the Heights somebody was leaning against a wall. After getting a shower and digging out a clean suit and a pair of shoes from the wardrobe, I stood at the window knotting my tie when I saw the figure still leaning against the wall.

The phone ringing startled me. At the other end of the line Bootsy's whiney voice started chattering. I cut him off.

'You haven't got someone hanging around outside Shefton, have you?' He said he hadn't.

'There was a message when I got in this morning. I phoned your office. Taki gave me your number.'

'I'm glad she did. I had a bit of trouble last night.' I took the phone over to the window. The figure was still there.

'What kind of trouble?'

'Listen, can you come over here? I'd rather not discuss it on the phone.' It sounded paranoid but I had a reason for getting him here. He told me he'd be round in fifteen minutes. I sat by the window, watching and waiting.

※

It was about time for Bootsy to show when the figure moved away. I smiled. A few minutes later there was a knock at

PART TWO: DOWN TO BUSINESS

my door. Looking through the spy-hole I saw Bootsy and opened the door.

'I thought you weren't talking to me.'

'Bootsy,' I gestured him in. 'Spot anything unusual as you pulled up in your squad car?'

'How did you know I came in a squad car?' I told him about the figure hanging around outside. He said he never spotted anyone.

'So, what happened last night?'

I told him about my exciting evening at the Human Food Club and my eventful journey home. When I mentioned the car, he said someone had found a crashed car early this morning but there'd been no-one inside.

'You know, Boots, I wouldn't mind knowing why those two clowns went to such lengths to get me.'

He blinked a few times before replying.

'I don't know. All we know about that HFC place is that one of the bodies turned up around there. Beyond that—'

'Come on, Bootsy. You must've known what kind of a place that was. Why didn't you tell me?'

He shook his head. 'We'd heard rumours, but that was all. We didn't have a legitimate reason to bust the place, but I suppose we do now. Tell me those names you heard again.'

I told him. 'Can I use your phone?' he asked.

'Be my guest.'

I listened as he called Police HQ. He did very little talking and a lot of nodding. He could barely keep the excitement out of his voice when he did speak. I knew he still wasn't being honest with me.

Hanging up the phone he affected a weary sigh 'O-kay. It looks like there's going to be a raid on the place tonight, thanks in part to your information.' *Just like that?* I wondered, *because of some tip-off from an unreliable gumshoe?*

I decided to use Booty's lies to my advantage. 'That's good,' I said. 'What time will we be going?'

117

THE TERROR AND THE TORTOISESHELL

He picked it up straight away. '*We?*'

'If I helped set this thing in motion, then I think the least you can do is let me tag along. I may even learn something about real policing.' The raid may have nothing to do with the murders, but it felt important anyway.

'I'll see what I can do,' he said as he left.

12

WHEN I TURNED UP at the office, Taki took one look at me and asked what I'd been up to. I had thought I'd tidied myself up pretty well. I told her she'd make a good detective.

'Why's that?' she asked.

'Because you notice things.'

'Of course, you know what I'd be if I didn't notice things.'

'I've no idea,' I told her.

'I'd be male.' She lowered her head and clicked away at her typewriter.

I went through the mail, tossing about half as usual into the waste-basket. I dialled the number for the case that'd come through and asked for Dotty. I told her who I was and said that I could start looking for her missing kitten straight away. She told me that he'd just walked in the door not five minutes ago, but thanks anyway.

I sat for a while clicking my claws. Going through to Taki's office I took a carton of milk from the fridge.

'Going to see some kittens,' I told her.

The riverbank was blissfully quiet as always, just the oddly reassuring rumble of Flipper's voice nearby breaking the silence. From in between a tangle of weeds, two of the kittens batted each other playfully while another cleaned itself next to the water, its outstretched paw pointing to the heavens.

'Benjamin, are you well?' Flipper asked without looking up. 'How's life in the big bad world?'

In between gaps in Tales From the Riverbank, I told him. He ummed and aahed as usual, lost in his own little world. It was only when I told him about my heavy night that I had his full attention.

'Human flesh?' He threw his head back and laughed. 'Hah! Whole world's gone to pot! Human flesh... be cannibalism next, you mark my words.' He shook his head.

I said my goodbyes a few minutes later, leaving the milk in a discreet little corner.

I'd been back about an hour when Bootsy phoned.

'I've had a word with Scragg and he says it's okay for you to come. Also, *if* it goes well tonight then *maybe* we can put some work your way. Satisfied?'

'For now,' I told him. He mentioned a time. I told him that I usually had something to eat at a place near the station if he wanted to meet me beforehand. To my surprise, he agreed.

I was even more surprised when I saw him standing under Minsky's blue neon sign, looking uncomfortable.

'I didn't think you'd show,' I said as we walked in.

'I had an hour free and I was hungry.' It was an innocent enough thing to say but I didn't even believe that. I didn't trust Bootsy with the time of day.

Minsky's was divided up into two sections—the easy-going section and the formal section. The latter was all black tables, floors and counters, full of Cats in suits parked at small tables lit with candles. Bootsy started toward that section, but I pushed him left. He looked back at the restaurant side as though I'd snatched his favourite toy away from him. I told him, the things he was likely to see tonight he'd be better getting something cheap.

PART TWO: DOWN TO BUSINESS

I watched Bootsy's face as he took in the other half of Minsky's. He looked back at the restaurant side, then back to where we were standing.

'It's... different,' he said after prompting.

This side was the deli side, and things were much more informal. Brightly coloured rugs and canvasses hung on every available section of wall, and the seats were occupied by animals in loose-fitting clothing. The air was scented with dark-roasted coffee, imported cigarettes and sweet pastries.

'*What the hell is that?*' Bootsy hissed, pointing into a corner.

'You've never seen a Penguin before?'

'It's huge!' he said. 'It must be over seven feet tall. What's it doing here?'

'Watching over the place. He's the bouncer.' On the small stage the pianist, an elderly Pointer, played boogie-woogie. I ordered sandwiches and coffee which Bootsy said he'd put on his expense account. I said I'd let him.

'Where is she?' I asked the waitress who came with our order.

'Between sets,' she answered. 'She'll be back on in a minute.'

While I waited I tucked into the best tuna fish sandwiches the city had to offer.

I'd managed to get the lot wolfed down by the time the applause began.

Before Bootsy got a chance to ask, the curtains behind the Pointer opened and Minsky appeared, dressed as always in a floor-length black number, the feather boa around her neck trailing towards the floor, the wafts from her tail fanning it up again in slow, languorous movements. Turning to the Pointer she clicked her claws, a noise like the flicking of a switch. As the pianist began the intro to 'Summertime' various creatures clapped and whistled.

THE TERROR AND THE TORTOISESHELL

She gave her usual note-perfect rendition, her voice filling my head like a beautiful warm breeze. She played three, maybe four songs after that and I'm not ashamed to say I don't remember what they were. The songs didn't matter so much as the voice. She could've been singing the menu from the Human Food Club and the audience wouldn't have applauded any less.

Somewhere on the restaurant side a plate broke, and the spell was broken. Looking down at Bootsy's plate, it was still full of sandwiches. I looked down at his cup. It was still full of coffee.

'Like the show, Bootsy?' I said, nudging him in the side.

'Hmm? Oh yeah. Wow. *Yeah*.'

I pointed to his plate, but he said he wasn't hungry. He wanted to go backstage instead. I lied and said we didn't have time. Hell, I wished I'd never met him there.

Getting to Bootsy's car took longer than it should. He kept pulling up, asking stupid questions about Minsky. Jealously, I snapped the answers back at him. While he was in this state I tried to get some info on the murders out of him, but I'd have got more sense out of a waxwork.

'What time does the raid start?' I asked as he opened up the car.

'About ten minutes ago,' he said, looking at his watch.

'Are you okay to drive?' I asked.

'What's that supposed to mean?'

'Nothing. Let's get going.' He floored the accelerator, and the car jostled its way into the traffic.

We pulled up behind a not very subtle line of cop cars parked along the street.

'They won't know what's hit 'em, will they?' Bootsy didn't respond.

When I asked him, he put a few names to faces: the big, dumb-looking Officer standing by the curb nursing a blackjack was called Officer Toffee. Further along was

PART TWO: DOWN TO BUSINESS

Scragg, who did indeed have half an ear missing. I noticed that Bootsy didn't go over and introduce me to his colleagues. In truth he looked slightly uncomfortable.

'Where's Dingus?' I asked him. 'Or Bachman?'

'Bachman doesn't leave his office,' he told me. 'As for Dingus, I heard someone say it was his anniversary. Been together since before The Terror, apparently.' I thought about asking what kind of anniversary but changed my mind.

'Can I have your attention please?' a voice called out. Everything fell silent.

Scragg began a run-down of what was about to happen. 'There are concealed marksmen in the alley,' he shouted loud enough for anyone inside the HFC to hear. 'The patrons of this establishment will be given a few minutes to disperse naturally. If they fail to materialise, the place will be shot full of holes, after which we go in there and pick up the pieces; literally if we have to. Any questions? No? Good.' Several nervous-looking officers put their paws back down.

'Bootsy,' I whispered, 'tell me this is a joke, won't you?'

'It's a different world now,' he said out of the corner of his mouth. 'The old "rules" don't exist anymore. We just do what we can.' My mouth opened and closed but nothing came out.

I looked around and spotted several of the 'concealed' marksmen in the alley. Others crouched outside the parking lot, guns resting on top of the low wall.

'*This is the Police and you are surrounded,*' Scragg shouted through his bullhorn. '*You have five minutes to clear the building starting* NOW.'

The five minutes was getting close to fifteen, and there was no sign that anyone was going to come out. I saw Scragg speak to another officer and nod his head furiously. He held up a gnarled paw, three of its claws extended. I watched them retreat back into his paw. *Three. Two. One.*

What happened next was a strange amalgam of farce, bloodbath and organised bun-fight. All at once, the air was

THE TERROR AND THE TORTOISESHELL

singing with gunfire, all of it one way. The Human Food Club was ripped apart; its window and doors were breaking and splintering, erupting with acne-like pockmarks. Then, as suddenly as it started, it stopped. When it did I found I had an alarm clock ringing in each ear. And then the silence.

Complete, total, absolute, silence.

All eyes turned back to Scragg, crouching behind a squad car. Standing, he waved to the marksmen and the rest of the officers. 'Okay, let's get in there,' he told them.

As this was happening, I could see a large brown paw begin to feed a green hose out through one of the broken windows. The hose was bulging, as if something was working its way along it. Then without warning the air turned red as a large gout of thick liquid shot from the hose and out across the parking lot, over the heads of the marksmen and straight into the scarred face of Detective Scragg, the force of the jet knocking him backwards several feet before flooring him completely. Near hysterical laughter from inside the Human Food Club covered the sound of dozens of jaws hitting the ground.

Scragg, eventually getting himself off the ground, began wiping the blood off his face. *'Blub! Blub!'* he shouted. The marksmen opened fire again, filling an already well-peppered building with even more holes. Scragg was now sitting down on the sidewalk and Detective Toffee appeared to have taken charge. He was yelling frantically, but nobody heard a thing over the gunfire. Eventually, the firing stopped and the silence returned. There was no laughter from inside the Human Food Club now.

That was when the 'food' started flying through the broken windows: legs, heads, guts, gizzards and sundry other inedible edibles were hurtling through the air, splattering an already blood-soaked street with a series of soft squishes. When I saw a leg still clad in a half a pair of pants and a running shoe on its end turning somersaults in the air, I nearly laughed despite myself.

PART TWO: DOWN TO BUSINESS

'I don't think you'll find your killer in there,' I shouted over at Bootsy. 'That meat's nowhere near fresh.'

A head rolling past on the street drew my attention back to the restaurant. Dozens of officers were charging into it now, through the broken door and window frames. Interestingly, Bootsy stayed with me.

I was still looking across at him when the gunfire started again. Officers were pouring towards the side of the restaurant and round the back. Then after a while it went quiet again.

Scragg, now with most of the gore wiped off his face, tried to look in control as he squelched towards the restaurant.

All the remaining officers went inside, or at least up to the door for a quick look. Only one stayed behind.

⚔

An hour later we were in Bootsy's car heading for Police HQ. All they'd found were the long-dead corpses of eighteen Sappies, or 'Twenty-two if you added up all the bits' as one officer put it.

'I mean, after all that! One waiter! One lousy waiter!' The waiter was the only living thing left in the place after all the staff of the HFC had somehow managed to escape over a wall at the back of the restaurant; several sets of tire tracks were found in the woods that bordered the restaurant.

'They must've had a tip-off,' Bootsy muttered to himself.

'But if you only learned what the HFC was from me yesterday...' I said innocently. He didn't reply.

While Bootsy had wandered about like a headless fowl, I'd made myself inconspicuous and stood next to Scragg's car.

'Of course it's not fresh!' the waiter had told the detective. 'It's all been dead for months! The whole thing's just one big con!'

THE TERROR AND THE TORTOISESHELL

Shortly afterwards, the waiter—who'd only been working there for the past week—was bundled off to the station.

'Listen Bootsy, a deal is a deal is a deal,' I told him as we sped along. 'It's not my problem you loused it up.'

'Just get off my case, will you?' he hissed.

The station was a riot of activity. Bootsy, fuming, flounced off to the bathroom and left me standing at the reception desk. An Alsatian eyed me up.

'You on the raid?' he asked.

I nodded, showed him my badge.

'A private?' the Dog said. He ran his tongue across yellow teeth. 'I didn't know we were involving outsiders. No offence.'

'I was with Officer Bootsy,' I told him.

The Dog's eyes widened. '*Who?*'

'Bootsy. The guy who just went to the john.'

'Officer? He's no Officer.'

'Pardon me?'

'He kept hanging around here when we reopened and nobody had the heart to send him away. They tolerate him is all; let him wear the uniform and stuff. He has no authority round here. None whatsoever.'

'Can I ask'—I said slowly, carefully,—'how long this raid has been planned?'

The desk sergeant looked around him. 'Well,' he leaned forward, 'strictly speaking, we knew there was something going on there weeks ago, but the murder meant everything was brought forward.' I wondered if the Alsatian could see the steam bubbling up in my head as my blood began to boil.

When Bootsy came out of the bathroom, he took one look at my face and walked away.

'Hey!' I charged after him, grabbing him, spinning him against the nearest wall. 'You set me up, Bootsy,' I spat.

'Benji, don't be ridiculous!'

PART TWO: DOWN TO BUSINESS

'Okay, how about this: you're no more an Officer than I am. You're just a Cat that hangs around here pretending to be a Cop. You were getting nowhere, so you drag me into things to do some work for you which you'd get the credit for. You had no intention of passing me any extra cases because you didn't have any to pass.'

He didn't say anything. The whole station had stopped what it was doing to watch us.

Bootsy surprised me by smiling, an evil vindictive little smirk.

Bad move. I swung my paw at him so quickly it surprised us both. A swatch of fur from the side of his head fell onto the carpet, as did Bootsy a split second later, his eyes wide with fear as he slumped against the wall, holding his cheek.

'Don't ever come near me again,' I told him.

Stomping along the cold, dark streets I kicked at anything unlucky enough to get in my way. The office was nearer than the apartment so I went there. By the time I'd cooled down it wasn't worth going home.

13

I AWOKE TO FIND SOMETHING steaming inches from my face. Swinging my legs off the desk, I took the coffee Taki had brought in.

'Another hard night?' She asked.

I told her. She screwed up her face and went back to reception.

I left the office after finishing my coffee, and made for the nearest news-stand. I saw one copy of *Fuller News*, a new edition. My heart sank.

Parking myself on the nearest bench, I steeled myself to look at the paper. "SICK RESTRANT RAIDED, PIKTURES IN SID!" the headline screamed. Fuller must've been up all night. Reluctantly, I read the paper.

The front page was entirely filled by the headline, so I turned to page two. Under a slightly smaller headline—'*Heds will role*'—was a drawing of a human head with a knife and fork on either side. '*And we dont mean his!*' was written underneath, an arrow pointing up to the illustration for the hard of understanding.

> Chef of Police Samy «The Pineapple» Bachman was said to be seething list night after a ræyd on the Human Fod Club resulted in all the suspects escaping with there lifes after the oparation ended in farce.

PART TWO: DOWN TO BUSINESS

> In the end there were no causalities, despite the fact our old fiend Detective Scragg ended up covered in sevral gallons of HUMAN blood fired through a hose from a window. An unnamed sauce said «The only ones who came out of te affair with any dignity incact were the corpses and body parts themseles!»

Six pages later, the only other article was a small mention of a group calling themselves The Machenites, a pseudo-religious group who were taking the works of Arthur Machen as gospel. I couldn't bring myself to read any more. Tossing the paper into a nearby trash-can, I went back to the office and asked if Bootsy had called. He hadn't. I had nothing better to do so I went back and finished my nap.

When I opened my eyes, the office was in darkness. So was the pane of frosted glass leading to Reception. My watch told me Taki had left hours ago.

On her desk, a large sheet of paper was filled with writing: *Benji—no messages but* LOTS *of calls—of the silent variety. I didn't know you had a secret admirer...* Neither did I, Taki, neither did I. Minsky suddenly popped into my head and I found my heart and stomach both clamouring for attention. Leaving the office I hoped I could satisfy one or the other, preferably both.

When I got there, Minsky's was surprisingly empty. Then I remembered: it was the night she gave her tonsils a rest. I took a seat and waited for somebody to take my order. That somebody turned out to be the lady herself.

'It was a good show last night, Minsky,' I told her as she shimmied over. 'The best.'

'Glad you liked it,' she smiled.

'What's this?' I pointed to the pad in her paw. 'You on waitress duty tonight? Now, if you took me up on my offer I could spare you such hardship.' About once a week I made some stupid comment to her, suggesting we leave this crazy

THE TERROR AND THE TORTOISESHELL

world behind and do nothing but raise kittens somewhere quiet. My declarations of love were usually met with a polite smile, but that didn't stop me.

'And where does the lovely Taki fit into all this?' She said, her tail gently swishing the air behind her.

'I told you, Taki's made it quite clear she's there to work. But seriously, what about it? Your looks, my brains, your beautiful singing voice. Be quite a combination.'

'You're forgetting one thing, Spriteman. You're a Tortoiseshell, remember?'

'So? What's that got to do with anything?'

When I didn't return her knowing look she seemed surprised. She looked at me in a way that suggested I should ready myself for a shock.

'Well, a Tortoiseshell... a *male* Tortoiseshell...?'

'Yeah,' I said, 'I'm glad you noticed. A male Tortoiseshell what?'

She sat down beside me. 'Oh, Benji. You mean you don't know?' I gave her a blank look.

'Benji, can you ever remember seeing any other *male* Tortoiseshells?'

I thought about it. Now she mentioned it I *couldn't* remember seeing any other male Tortoiseshells. And hadn't that snooty Pomeranian in the elevator said something along those lines?

'So, I'm unique,' I told her. 'Even better.'

'That's not it,' she said. 'I'm not doing this very well, am I?'

'Doing what? Just tell me.'

She took a deep breath and pointed to the Penguin in the corner. 'Benji, a male Tortoiseshell has about as much chance of fathering kittens as he has.'

I just looked at her and looked at her, not knowing what to say. Later on, I consulted my Cat book and found that it was true. Somehow I'd missed it before. Either that or I'd

PART TWO: DOWN TO BUSINESS

read it and blotted it out, I don't know. Perhaps I'd always known, deep down. I'd never *really* considered a family before, but to find out the decision wasn't even mine to make was a bit of a shock. In a strange way, it made sense that I'd ended up with a guy like Jimmy, I suppose; both loners, two of a kind.

Minsky was saying something.

'What did you say? I was a little preoccupied there.'

'I said I don't like leaving you like this but I have to go. Someone's picking me up here later on.'

'Do I know him?' I said, not expecting a reply.

'Well, yes you do.'

'Hang on,' I said. 'Not Bootsy. Tell me it isn't Bootsy.'

'It *is* Bootsy. He called me and asked me out. He seemed okay to me.'

I left the restaurant in a cloud. Things couldn't get any worse. My work had dried up. Then, the Cat I love tells me I'm never going to hear the pitter-patter of tiny Spritemans. And on top of that she tells me she's going out on a date with the guy who's just made me a complete laughing stock.

Things could not, absolutely *could not*, get any worse.

Hah.

I entered the lobby at Shefton Heights and two Cats, a Dog, and a large Budgie I vaguely knew stopped talking. They watched me get in the elevator. As soon as the door closed, I heard their voices again. I was too weary to care.

The elevator opened and I got out. Tigger, Shove Off, Inky and a few others were congregated outside my door. I tried to walk through them, but Tigger's paw blocked the way. Then I saw my door, half hanging from its hinges.

'It's not pretty, Benji,' Inky the Dalmatian told me. 'They've ransacked the place.'

Before I could change my mind, I pushed through the busted doorframe and into the apartment to inspect the damage.

14

Inky hadn't lied—the place was a mess. They'd done everything except use the place as a toilet. The sofa and chairs had been upended, the coffee table was lying on its side like a dead heifer, the rugs were scrunched up on the floor like used tissues. The only thing in the lounge that wasn't broken was the bookcase, although apart from a handful of books, the contents had been strewn across the floor. I could feel my fur rising beneath my suit in anger.

'Okay,' I said to the animals in the room. 'Tell me what happened.'

Tigger said he'd just got in and was coming along the corridor when he noticed my door was slightly open. Knowing I'd probably be at work he thought it odd, so went and knocked on Inky's door. Together they'd taken a look.

'What time was this?'

'Half hour ago,' Tigger told me. 'An hour at the most.'

An hour at the most. But I hadn't been home last night after all the fuss of the HFC raid. It could've happened then.

'Do you want me to call the police, Benji,' Inky was saying, 'or... deal with it yourself?'

I thought about it. 'No, let's get them involved, shall we? But tell them not to send Officer Bootsy.' I laughed at that. Inky gave me a funny look, then phoned the station.

While I waited for the police to show I knocked on a few doors, but all I got was a nervous-looking grey Whippet on

PART TWO: DOWN TO BUSINESS

the floor below who said he'd seen a strange figure hanging around outside the building a few times. I asked him if it looked like a pile of rags shuffling along. He said that it did. It sounded like the figure I'd seen down there. Then I recalled Taki's remark about the silent phone calls…

I went back to my apartment. Tigger tried to keep me chatting to take my mind off things. He talked while I sat among the wreckage, looking at the books still on the bookcase, one half-propped up, looking like it was about to topple at any second. I stared at it, willing it to fall. When it became obvious my willpower wasn't enough, I marched over to the bookcase and swept the remaining books onto the floor. 'Can't have them making the place look tidy, can we?' I told Tigger. Like Inky had earlier, he gave me a look that suggested I wasn't myself at present.

'What's that smell?'

I turned to see who the unfamiliar voice belonged to. Shove Off the Parrot was standing in my front room, feathers bristling. After getting past the shock of hearing the Parrot's widened vocabulary, I took a sniff myself. I marvelled that I hadn't noticed it as soon as I came in.

'Jeez, it stinks like the Monkey house,' Shove Off said.

Whatever it smelled like, it was a strange combination of scents, as if it came from a whole bunch of animals. The thought sent a shiver through me. It was unlike anything I'd smelt before.

'The name's Captain, by the way,' Shove Off said, introducing himself. 'Not very original, but that's Sappies for you. So what do *you* think that smell is, Benji?'

I felt at a loss. 'I don't know.'

'It's strange, whatever it is. There's a bit of everything in it,' Tigger said. We were all thinking along the same lines, it seemed.

They all cleared out the moment the city's finest arrived. I didn't recognise the officers, but for Bulldogs they turned

THE TERROR AND THE TORTOISESHELL

out to be pretty smart. I told them of my movements over the past few days: the HFC raid and being followed afterwards, the mysterious calls we'd been getting at the office. One of the Dogs asked if anything had been taken. I had a quick look about the place but nothing appeared to have gone.

'Looks to me like it was the thugs from the HFC, finishing the job off. They probably spotted you at the raid and the management decided to shake you up a little.' I had to agree.

'You wouldn't think two Dogs could smell so bad,' I replied, sniffing.

'You know, it's a pity that Dingus is working on—'

'What he means is that Dingus has got the best nose on the force,' the other Dog interrupted.

I thought of something. 'This Human Food Club. Who is it running the joint?'

'Reeky McStink? Yeah, McStink.'

'I heard that name at the restaurant. Who is this guy anyway?'

'He's what the Sappies called a mobster,' the first Dog said. 'Claws in all sorts of pies. Hides behind a lot of associates.' I interrupted and threw in a few other names I'd heard. The first Dog nodded.

'So you're telling me I've got a gangster on my tail?' My fur stiffened.

'I'd take this as a friendly warning,' the second Dog said, indicating the mess. 'If they'd meant business, they'd have sent Eddie the Quill to see you and we wouldn't be having this discussion. You'd have more holes in you than a sieve.'

'How comforting. You guys really know how to cheer a Cat up.'

'All part of the service. See you around.'

Shutting the door behind them I went back to the lounge, wondering what I'd gotten myself into, wondering where I should start cleaning up first. All that wondering wore me out, so I went to bed.

PART TWO: DOWN TO BUSINESS

I hadn't checked the bedroom. Inside, I found it as I'd left it. I was just beginning to think about the kind of a mobster who would wreck an apartment but leave the bedroom untouched when I fell asleep.

⁂

I hadn't been asleep long when I awoke. It was still dark outside, the city was dozing. I spent the best part of an hour tidying the place up, had a wash and a coffee. While I'd been occupied the city had turned ash grey, the air heavy with spots of rain. I picked up the phone, dialled Ma Spayley.

She answered on the eighth ring. 'Hello?'

'Hello, Mrs. Spayley. Didn't get you out of bed, did I?'

She laughed. 'I've got fourteen children, Mr. Spriteman, I've been up since before five.' In the background several helium-pitched voices clamoured for attention. I told her what I wanted and she said she'd pass the message on. Thanking her, I hung up and went to the office.

Before Taki had a chance to ask me why I looked so dishevelled, I told her. She sat in stunned silence when I'd finished. I asked if there'd been any more of *those* calls. She shook her head.

'Hooray.' While I waited for my coffee to cool I tried to think it through. I buzzed Taki on the intercom.

'These calls from the mute, when did they start?'

She thought about it. 'Roughly the end of October.'

'And you think they're all from the same caller?'

'Well, I don't know. There's never any noise in the background, and they always hang up after I've said "hello" a few times.' Thanking her, I hung up.

I'd gone to see Ma Spayley about the Mouse on the first of November. It was now the sixth. The raid on the HFC had taken place the night before last, which meant the calls weren't down to the two clowns who tried to off me when I left the restaurant, even if they had trashed the apartment. So who were the calls from and what, if anything, were they about?

I was drumming a fairly nifty tattoo on the desk when I heard squealing tires on the street. I looked out and saw the Mouse's car parked on the sidewalk. I reached for the intercom again.

'The Mouse is on his way up. Tell him to come right in.'

A few seconds later, I heard Taki tell him to go through. The Mouse said please and thanked her about half a dozen times before there was a noise like somebody bumping into a desk. I wondered if I'd learned anything since taking over the agency. It was time to find out. As his silhouette hovered before the glass panel of my door, I called for him to come in.

'Hello, Mr. Spriteman,' the Mouse looked flushed. I covered my smile with a paw. 'You wanted to see me?'

'Sit down,' I told him. 'You never found a Cat attractive before, Number One?'

'How did you—'

'You look flushed. Water cooler's over there. Get me one while you're at it.' There was hope for me yet.

'I called you over because I wanted to ask you something and didn't want to discuss it within earshot of your mother,' I said when he sat down. 'I didn't want her thinking I was involving her son in anything dangerous.'

The Mouse stopped drinking his water. 'Why? Are you?' He looked like he hoped I was.

'Do the names Reeky McStink or Eddie the Quill mean anything to you?'

His ears pricked up. 'Yeah, he's a gangster. Eddie the Quill's his number two.'

'How did you know about them?'

'When I took cars I'd hear their names get mentioned from time to time. Some animals take their cars "to order".

PART TWO: DOWN TO BUSINESS

That's where I heard their names. Is that it?' He looked disappointed.

'That's it, that's all I wanted to know. You want me to put in a good word with my secretary?' I asked.

Bright pink skin showed through white fur. 'No! Um, I mean, no.'

'Okay,' I chuckled. Tearing a sheet of paper off a pad, I wrote down an address. 'You and your brothers and sisters like nuts, Number One?' He nodded.

'Here's the address of a place called Nut Heaven.' I handed him the slip of paper. 'Tell the Pigeons I sent you and that it's okay.' Hearing the outer door slam shut, I called Taki.

'I think you've got an admirer there,' I told her.

'Really? Hadn't noticed.' She continued clicking away at the typewriter.

The phone rang. 'Your favourite cop,' Taki informed me.

'Okay,' I sighed. 'Put him through.'

'Benji, I just heard about your pad. I'm sorry.'

'Really. What can I do for you, Bootsy?'

'Nothing!' He tried to sound offended. 'Honest! I just heard down at the station that you'd been turned over.'

'Did they tell you *why* I'd been turned over?' He fell silent. 'No? Well, I'll tell you. Out of the goodness of my heart, I got involved with a so-called law-enforcement officer who it turns out has about as much influence as a cookie barrel. Alleged Officer Bootsy says that such a collaboration could be beneficial to both of us. But guess what? One of us gets done over, in more ways than one. You figure it out.' He didn't reply immediately, but I knew what was coming. I could almost hear the cogs going round in his brain.

'Is this about Minsky? Because if it is, then I'm afraid them's the breaks.'

'I don't like being made a fool of,' I told him. 'You had no intention of passing me any work.'

THE TERROR AND THE TORTOISESHELL

'This *is* about Minsky, isn't it?' I could imagine the big Cheshire Cat grin at the other end of the phone.

'Go to hell,' I told him, slamming the receiver down.

Almost straight away the phone rang again.

'Hello? Hell-o? *Hello?'* Taki muttered something I didn't catch as she put the phone down.

I stuck my thoughts for an hour before I'd had enough. I told Taki to go home. There was nothing happening around here. What a way to run a business. What a business it was in the first place.

Jimmy had done it out of necessity. Me, I had a choice. I wondered how the hell he'd managed it.

The fourteenth floor was thankfully empty as I didn't particularly relish conversation. Flopping down on my bed I hadn't expected to fall asleep, but I did.

15

THE LONGEST SLEEP I'D had since The Terror ended when I heard the telephone ringing in the living room. I opened my eyes and was shocked to see the clock telling me it was five to three in the morning. I stumbled from the bed to the living room.

I picked up the receiver. 'Do you know what the hell time it—'

'At the old disused grain warehouse on Dennings Lane you'll find a door pried off its hinges. Meet me there in one half hour.' There was a click in my ear and the line went dead.

I looked at the piece of plastic in my paw like it was melting. Eventually, I replaced the receiver.

It had all happened so quickly, but I was sure the voice was Bootsy's. But he'd sounded different, wrong; frightened. *Really* frightened. And I was sure he'd said *'meet me there in one half hour'*. That wasn't how Bootsy talked. Reasoning it through, I came up with three possible answers:

One: he'd heard about my nuisance calls and decided to join in because I'd humiliated him at the station.

Two: he was in some kind of trouble. But why contact *me*?

Three: he was eager to make amends for his earlier failings and wanted me to have first look at some new evidence he'd uncovered. Unlikely.

THE TERROR AND THE TORTOISESHELL

One was a possible, but I was sure it was two. I was also sure I had to go and see. Already dressed, I left the apartment.

Dennings Lane was a shabby little nook lined with cobbled stones and long-abandoned shops and houses. I'd been there before following up leads and it wasn't a nice area. Despite its desolation, you got the feeling that every step you took was being watched, perhaps from behind the netted curtains billowing through some of the broken windows. I was tempted to ring the Mouse but decided against it, not knowing what I was getting myself into. I had to do it on foot, which meant running some of the way. Never the most punctual of creatures, I felt that I had to be this time.

I was just turning into Dennings Lane when I looked down at my watch, seeing that I had a couple of minutes to spare. Suddenly, the hands on my watch were obliterated as I was blinded by a set of car lights shooting along the Lane. When the tadpoles stopped swimming before my eyes, I took in the Lane. The moonlight managed to make it look even worse than it did in daylight, half the terrace row fire-damaged, the other half looking ready to disintegrate. At the far end was the grain warehouse. I could see two doors, one padlocked, the other slightly ajar. Walking along the left-hand pavement, I half expected long spectral claws to reach for me through the broken windows and drag me inside.

Then I was standing outside the old grain warehouse: a long, pockmarked, yellow-stone building blocking off one end of the street. The door that was ajar looked like it had been open for a long time. There was just enough room for me to get through. In my pocket I had a heavy flashlight with a powerful beam. For the time being I kept the flashlight off, hoping my eyes would adjust to the darkness. My fur was so stiff I imagined it was puncturing my clothing.

I stood in the darkness for a few seconds, but I couldn't sense anyone. In the Old Days I'd have known straight

PART TWO: DOWN TO BUSINESS

away. The floor was covered in dust and rubbish. I shuffled forward. Looking up, I saw that the floor above had fallen through. I felt like I was shuffling my way into a giant cave.

Then, my whiskers began to twitch. From nowhere, a sour odour had filled the air, and I knew then I'd walked into something very, very bad. Slowly I turned in a circle but I was still pretty sure I was alone. My paws, against orders from my brain, decided to take me forward. My breath was quickening.

Then I saw it, perhaps twenty feet away, a dark, indistinct bulk on the floor. A crate? But I hadn't seen any others; the place was empty apart from the trash. I was moving again, within fifteen feet of it now, ten, eight—

And then I stopped, and saw that it wasn't a crate at all.

I had to switch the flashlight on to make sure. Again my actions overruled my emotions and flicked the switch. White light lit up a scene like a frozen sculpture hemmed in by the darkness surrounding it.

I saw the thing in stages. First I saw a small rectangular black object, with a sheet of paper beneath it. Above it, a paw was reaching out to it.

The shaking torch in my paw jerked the beam up so another part of the puzzle came into view: a body stuck inside a large jerry-built mousetrap; only this one was imprisoning a Cat. When the flashlight's shaky beam shone into Bootsy's dead eyes, it lit them like opals.

I realised then that the rectangular black box was a tape recorder. On the sheet of paper under it would be the words I'd heard Bootsy recite on the telephone. They'd made him read the note into the tape, then put him in the trap. His body was stiff as a board. The sharp click I'd heard at the end of the message was the killer stopping the tape. By the time they'd phoned the message through, Bootsy had been long gone.

The car I'd seen leaving Dennings Lane.

THE TERROR AND THE TORTOISESHELL

How long I stared at that hideous tableaux, I don't know. I was rooted to the spot. Even when I heard the sirens on the street outside and the door burst open, I still couldn't move. It was only as the two officers were dragging me back through that rusted door that I came to my senses, and by then it was too late.

16

AFTER WHAT FELT LIKE a decade in the cells, the two officers dragged me out along a corridor and into an interview room, where I was dumped like a sack of garbage into a plastic chair.

The journey to the station was a bit of a blur; I vaguely remembered one of my claws getting stuck in an officer's jacket as they hauled me towards the squad car, and then almost being blinded by the vast array of headlights in Dennings Lane. There must've been twice as many officers there than there'd been for the HFC raid—and all for little old me. Talk about using a bulldozer to bury a Sparrow.

The door to the interview room opened and a ragged-looking old Tom Cat with half-an-ear missing came in and glowered at me.

'Good evening, Detective Scragg. I hope your officer's ineptitude didn't get you out of bed.'

'Enough of the wisecracks, Spriteman. You're in serious trouble.' As he focused his heavy gaze on me, my attention was continually drawn to the missing chunk of ear.

'The last time you were in this station, half my officers saw you attacking Bootsy. Yesterday, a colleague of Bootsy's was sitting right next to him when he was on the telephone—to you. The colleague distinctly heard a loud voice at the other end of the phone telling Bootsy to "Go to Hell". Now,' Scragg leaned across the desk, engulfing me with his stale

THE TERROR AND THE TORTOISESHELL

coffee breath, 'perhaps you'd be so good as to tell me what you were doing in Dennings Lane in the early hours of the morning?'

'I'd have told you an hour ago,' I said, looking at the officers, 'given the chance.'

'Well, never mind. Now's your chance.'

I told him about the call I'd received and he held up a scarred paw.

'Whoa, hang on there. Given your recent encounters with Bootsy, why bother going at all?'

'Because he sounded terrified.'

'So why didn't he call us first?' Scragg asked. I didn't have an answer.

'Okay, let's put that to one side. Have you got anyone who can corroborate this story?'

'No, I was alone. I left my office early and went to bed. So, do you think Bootsy's killer is the same guy killing all those Sappies?' I carried on before he had a chance to stop me. 'You see, the reason me and Bootsy fell out was—' I told him the tale.

'So that's where the file went,' he muttered into the silence that followed.

'The file's still at my office if you want to check. Bootsy told me to destroy it, but I haven't got round to it yet.'

'That damned fool,' Scragg was pawing at the table angrily.

'Can I go now?' I asked.

'In a while. Can I tell you something, Spriteman? I believe you. I don't like you, but I believe you. Shall I tell you why I believe you? I believe you because we received a very strange telephone call ourselves at three thirty-three. A distorted voice, but you can understand it if you listen closely. Would you like to hear it?'

Scragg looked over at one of the officers who went outside and came back with a tape recorder.

PART TWO: DOWN TO BUSINESS

'We've only started recording incoming calls in the past week,' Scragg said as he rewound the tape. 'This is what the tape picked up.' He clicked PLAY.

'Hello, Police—*Never mind the formalities. If you want to find your "Sappy Killer", I suggest you go to the grain warehouse on Dennings Lane and see what you can trap.*' The line went dead.

'Well?' Scragg said.

'"See what you can trap"?' I said. 'I've been set up, obviously.'

'Obviously. But I want to know why.'

'Wish I could tell you.' I asked if he knew about my nuisance calls and the break-in and he nodded.

'You've no idea at all? Absolutely none?'

'Absolutely none.' I told him about all the cases I'd handled recently. It didn't take long, and none of them warranted such heavy-handed revenge.

'Okay Spriteman, you're free to go. But, as they used to say, don't leave town.' I laughed.

Outside, the sun was shining. My belly began to rumble. I had to see Minsky. Somebody was going to a lot of trouble to set me up and I wanted answers. And if I asked nicely, maybe I'd get something to eat.

When I got there the place was closed. I rapped on the door for a while before a small and tired voice spoke through the mailbox.

'Who is it?'

'Minsky, it's Benji. I need to talk to you about last night.'

Reluctantly she opened the door, pointing me to a seat in the formal part of the place. She said the police weren't long gone and she was tired. With a sigh, she asked me what I wanted.

'Did the police tell you that I was arrested for Bootsy's murder?'

THE TERROR AND THE TORTOISESHELL

She looked at me like I'd slapped her. '*You?*' I was pleased to hear the disbelief in her voice. I told her what happened, only leaving out a description of Bootsy at the grain mill.

'Somebody set you up.' I nodded.

'I know you'll have been through this with Scragg, but I need you to go through it with me too.' Looking me directly in the eye, she took a breath and started talking.

'He came in while I was doing my second set. We'd arranged to have a drink here, then maybe go for a meal when the club shut. I came off stage and he wasn't there. I asked one of the bar staff, Polly, what had happened to him. She said there'd been a call for him and he'd left soon after.'

'Did Polly take the call?'

Minsky nodded. 'Yes. But it was so noisy she couldn't make out the voice. It was definitely male though, and the line was bad so the voice sounded funny, kind of raspy.'

'What time was that?'

'I finished my set just after eleven. He came in about a quarter of an hour before that, so some time between.'

There was an awkward silence. My appetite had vanished. I was wondering how best to get out without seeming rude when Minsky spoke, a sly smile on her face.

'You ever had a drink, Spriteman?'

'I tried some of Jimmy's scotch once,' I shook my head. 'Never again.'

'You shouldn't drink *that* stuff,' she said, rising from her chair and heading for the bar. 'We can't handle the hard stuff. But *this* stuff,' she took a tall yellow bottle from a high shelf. 'Care to try an eggnog, Spriteman?'

'What's in it?' She told me. 'Sounds sweet.'

'It certainly is,' she put the bottle down on the table along with two glasses, 'and best of all, not too strong.' Tilting the bottle over my glass, something resembling set custard coated the sides. I took a sniff.

'Mmm. Not bad. Who shall we drink to?'

PART TWO: DOWN TO BUSINESS

She tutted and looked at me as if I'd asked a silly question.
'We didn't exactly get on, Minsky. He conned me.'
'Do it for me.'
'Okay.' Clinking our glasses I took a mouthful of yellow gloop which slid down my throat in one sugary velvet movement. Immediately, I took another.
'He wasn't the right one for you, Minsky,' I told her, setting my glass back on the table.
'I never said he was. In truth, he was a bit full of himself.'
'Not very bright either,' I added helpfully. She gave me a dirty look.
'Sorry.'
'To Bootsy.' We clinked glasses again.
We sat drinking eggnog and chewing the cud until the bottle was empty. Great company, great booze; at one point I told her I was going to put eggnog in my morning milk. I also asked her if there really was alcohol in it, as it seemed to have no potency to it at all.
Then I stood up to leave, and there was a definite swagger in my walk that hadn't been there when I came in.
Saying our goodbyes, I stepped out into the fresh air and wallop—*that* was when it hit me—my head felt as light as a balloon and as heavy as a cannonball at the same time; it was like I was on all fours again. Flagging down a Yellow Cab, I asked the cabby what it was like driving around in an eggnog bottle all day. He asked me where to.
I can't remember what I told him but we pulled up across the street from Moe's. On the street I got a waft of exhaust fumes that made me gag. I decided the best thing I could do would be to have a stroll to clear my head.
I wanted somewhere quiet, so there was only one place. As I left the concrete behind for grass and earth, some of the buoyancy I'd felt at Minsky's also left me.
Swaying under the bridge that led to the riverbank, I tried to cheer myself up by looking at the Pigeons nesting in the

THE TERROR AND THE TORTOISESHELL

bridge supports. Their cooing always gave me the giggles. One of them called down for me to watch where I was going. Taking the command literally, I looked down to find I was only six inches from the water's edge.

'Thank you!' I called up to the Pidge. 'Thank you for saving my miserable little life!' The Pigeon plumped itself up to the size of a cushion, which brought on another fit of laughing.

The weeds and grass along the towpath had grown quite a bit since my last visit. Either that, or I wasn't walking in a straight line. 'All that rain,' I decided.

Suddenly an ugly grey head poked out of the water.

'If you're looking for the crazy he's not here,' it said.

I could go see Flipper! What a wonderful idea!

'Has he gone home? Tell me, where is home?'

'Just keeping walking,' the Fish told me.

'If I can,' I told it. 'If I can.'

After tramping through the undergrowth for about ten minutes, I wondered if the Fish just wanted rid of me. I encountered nothing but foul-smelling greenery. I was starting to get a headache and my throat was dry. Then I spotted a small bridge up on the left leading to some kind of farmhouse. What at first glance looked like a series of growths at the back, turned out to be corrugated tin sheds clinging to the brickwork. Neither the sheds nor the farmhouse looked like they were occupied.

Crossing the bridge carefully, a paw on each rail, I must've looked like I was crossing a high wire. I clopped down the wooden steps. Putting paw to grass once more, I heard a *Miaow*.

'Flipper?' I called out. There was no reply. At the second attempt, I managed to get through the gate leading into the unkempt garden, at the far end of which the river bubbled merrily away. Before knocking on the door, I caught a waft of stale air from inside. When I knocked, the door opened slightly.

PART TWO: DOWN TO BUSINESS

'Come in,' a muffled voice said.

I was in a kitchen where the floor was smeared with something resembling mud, and a pile of dirty dishes bloomed out of the sink, threatening to spill over the lip of the sink onto the floor.

'Ah, dishes. I hate doing them. Benjamin, are you well?' Flipper was standing in the doorway, eyeing me up. Leaning forward, he began sniffing the air.

'By God, have you been *drinking*?'

I was about to answer when he carried on. 'Well, thank heavens for that. I thought I was the only one. Tea?' He went over to an old silver kettle with a fist-sized dent in its side and filled it with water. 'You won't have tasted tea like mine! Go through, go through.' He waved a paw into the room he'd just come from.

Immediately, I was attacked by dust motes. The room was in such a poor state it made the kitchen look reasonable.

'My place looks better and *it's* been turned over.'

'What's that?' Flipper called from the kitchen.

'I was just asking what's so special about your tea.'

'Oh, that. Special ingredient. Wait and see. Well, take a seat.'

I plonked myself down on the first pile of books that looked like it wouldn't topple over.

I say 'books' because that's all the room contained; if there was any furniture, it was hidden under paper and bindings. The walls weren't painted, there was no carpet; just books, piled higgledy-piggledy from floor to ceiling. A few piles were only a foot or so high, so I presumed that they must be the 'chairs'.

'It's like a library in here,' I said for something to say.

'Aye, that was the old man.' He called from the kitchen. 'There's all kinds of stuff if you've the time to look. Here, get that down you.' Flipper shoved a cup filled to the brim with brown liquid at me. A strong tangy odour emanated from it. I took a quick sip and screwed up my face.

THE TERROR AND THE TORTOISESHELL

'What the hell is it?' I said between splutters.

'That,' Flipper said as he sat on a pile of books opposite me, 'is the old man's tea. He always put a drop of whisky in it.'

'A *drop?*' The second mouthful wasn't as bad as the first one. The next one wasn't as bad as that. By the time I'd finished half the mug I found myself enjoying it, even if it was curdling the eggnog in my stomach.

'Good, eh?' Flipper said, tasting his.

'—Yup.' I coughed another mouthful down.

'You don't strike me as a drinker, lad.'

'I'm not,' I told him.

Before I knew what I was doing, the alcohol was performing one of its tricks. Me, usually such a reserved creature, started blurting out everything that'd happened over the past few days, and probably a few things that I'd mentioned the last time I'd seen him. He got my life story. He got The Works. When I told him about the murders he shook his head and gave me a look that said he was glad he was away from the big, bad city. As I talked, he made more tea. The room began to spin whenever my head dropped.

The last thing I saw before my eyes closed was one of the Old Cats come flouncing into the room. Seeing me, it stopped, took a sniff, and jumped onto Flipper's lap, where he sat stroking it. The Old Cat gave me a look that suggested it didn't know what on earth it was looking at. I was starting to wonder the same thing myself when everything went black.

17

I opened my eyes and everything was still black. As my eyes adjusted, I could see I was in a room filled with rows of proper seats, not books. I was sat in one of the seats on the back row. A thin beam of white light passed my left ear, the beam full of small motes of dust. Fascinated, I followed the beam as it struck the far wall of the room.

In front of me, row upon row of furry heads were watching the small, blank, white screen that had materialised. Apart from the gentle hum of the projector behind me, the room was completely silent.

I watched the blank screen for a while and began to grow impatient. But I seemed to be the only one: none of the other heads appeared agitated. I was just about to look away when the screen began to shrink from top to bottom, so that I had to bow my head slightly to see the nothing everyone else was so avidly watching. My neck was beginning to ache from having to press my head so far down into it, when I saw that all the heads in front of me were now only inches from the ceiling. It wasn't the *screen* that was shrinking, it was the ceiling ahead of me that was lowering over *their* furry heads. The ceiling continued to descend at a painfully slow rate, giving everyone the chance to escape, but either they didn't realise what was happening or they chose to stay, because the heads continued to watch the white screen; and now the

THE TERROR AND THE TORTOISESHELL

ceiling was only an inch or so above the heads, all of which appeared to be the same size.

As I continued to fold myself into my seat, I saw that the screen now had something flickering across it.

Seeing what was on that screen became the most important thing in the world. I crushed myself even further into my seat until I found a position in which I could see it.

Instinctively I knew that what I was witnessing was very important: a field full of domestic animals milling around, evidently waiting for something, tongues lolling, tails wagging. Some sat, some stood. And then it happened: the animals on the screen started to grow before our eyes. Dogs, Cats and other creatures were stretching upwards and outwards, colliding with each other as they grew. Some of them were now five or six times the size they'd been seconds earlier. And there were other changes: some animals went from four legs to two, their backs began straightening out, rising with the speed of a second hand on a clock; faces began to shrink or grow so that they were roughly proportionate to their new bodies; limbs thickened, heads became rounder, more and more human.

Frightened, I began squirming in my seat. The realisation that I was able to squirm at all meant that something had changed. This knowledge made my panic even worse; I lurched toward the lip of my chair, seemingly in slow motion, it took so long. Looking over the edge of the seat I could barely see the floor, which was now a canyon hundreds of feet below, and the black chair I was clinging to was a slippery cliff I was flailing about on the edge of. Then my paws were cart-wheeling madly in the air in front of me as I fell off the chair, down into the canyon.

Despite the great distance, I wasn't in the air long enough to let out a scream. When I hit the floor I felt no pain; I landed on my paws. Looking back up to the chair, the descent should've taken minutes, not a split second.

PART TWO: DOWN TO BUSINESS

Slowly I began to crawl forward, my body to the ground. A crazy idea came to me that I should try to walk on two legs, but the idea was *ridiculous*. I carried on, crawling across the wide expanse of floor. Above, a white beam of light like a melting star burned the way ahead for me. As I slithered towards the light, I heard deep murmuring voices far above me but carried on, even though the voices might be important. Suddenly there was a blinding flash of light in the darkness and I raised my paws to my eyes to shield myself from the glare.

When I opened my eyes, my paws were covering my face. Lowering them, I jumped as Flipper's face came into view. On the pile of books next to him was a small table lamp.

'Wake you up, did I?' he said as he moved away. 'And not before time, if I'm not mistaken. Sounded like you were having a nightmare.'

'Of the worst kind,' I told him as my heart hammered.

'I thought it best to let you sleep off the booze, you not being used to it. How's your head?'

'You don't want to know. What time is it?'

Flipper looked blankly at me. I checked my watch. At first I thought my watch must be drunk too.

'It's nearly midnight?' I said, stunned.

'Did I not do the right thing, Benji?'

'It doesn't matter,' I told him. 'I had nothing special planned anyway.'

Getting up to leave, I tried to ignore the fact my paws were wobbling around without my say-so. I said goodbye to Flipper and stepped into the night. The river gurgled like an evil black potion, capable of sucking the fur and flesh off your bones. Climbing the bridge steps cautiously, my stomach and head cursed me with every shaky step.

On the far side, one of the kittens was watching me. 'After you,' I told it. With lightning speed, it flew past me.

THE TERROR AND THE TORTOISESHELL

I stopped halfway across the bridge to give my stomach a rest. I leaned on the rail and looked out at the covering of trees in front of me. Despite being only fifteen minutes from the city, I was in a different world.

Before my eyes began to droop, I forced myself down the steps. Back on solid ground, I suddenly found I had a strong desire to do something I hadn't done since The Terror. Perhaps it was a yearning for the past, or more likely, something to do with that damned nightmare I'd just had.

I looked around for a suitable place. When I found one, I took off my shoes and pants, then squatted. As I conspicuously went about my business, I looked up at the starry sky. For a brief moment I felt like I was doing the most natural thing in the world. Putting my pants and shoes back on quickly, I began to bury the dirty deed.

I stopped when I saw a large pair of luminous eyes staring at me from a pile of weeds. Another kitten, looking at me like it couldn't believe what it was seeing, or, as was most likely, just seen me do. Patting the dirt off my paws, I started the walk back to civilisation. Behind me, the kitten was still staring. Had it been capable of speech, I dread to think what it might have said.

18

Because I felt so awful and it was nearer, I figured the office would be the best place to stay that night. I took the stairs because I thought the elevator might make me sick. Inside, the moon poured light through my open office door and onto a note on Taki's desk. Taking it through to my office, I looked at it by moonlight and dropped it on the desk. In the cupboard I found my old blanket and wrapped it around myself, curling up in my chair, shivering. If this was what alcohol did to you, you could keep it.

I awoke when my whiskers began to twitch. Coffee. On cue, Taki walked in with two mugs and placed one in front of me.

'You look *awful*.' She sat down at the other side of the desk 'And not for the first time lately.' She began to sniff. 'Have you been *drinking?*' Suddenly I felt like a guilty kitten with its head in the fridge.

'Yes, ma'am, I have.' I took a long slug on the coffee. 'Tell me about yesterday.'

'You read the note? *Nine* calls yesterday. Same as all the others.'

I nodded. 'Have you ever heard of Reeky McStink?' The name seemed to have lodged in the back of my brain. She nodded.

THE TERROR AND THE TORTOISESHELL

'Eddie the Quill?' She nodded again. 'A girlfriend of mine told me about them. Says they're best avoided.' Again I wondered if I was the only one in town who *hadn't* heard of them.

I looked down into my mug. It was like looking down into a cupful of river water. I pushed it away.

'You're not involved with Reeky McStink, are you?' Taki sounded anxious.

'His goons trashed my apartment, I don't know.'

'And you think these calls might be—'

'Some of them might. I don't know that either. Some detective, huh? If it is them, why single *me* out? I'm no threat. It doesn't make sense. According to the two cops who showed up at my apartment, if they'd really meant business I'd be history by now.'

'Perhaps they are just crank calls after all.' She sounded as convinced as I was.

When Taki went to do some work, I spent the rest of the morning nursing my sore head. There were no calls, crank or otherwise.

Around two, I kidded myself into thinking that I should maybe try put something in my stomach. I couldn't face Minsky's, and Moe would want to talk. I remembered Quaffers and headed over there, trying to blot the roar of traffic from my ears.

I was pleased to see the place was nearly empty. A waiter appeared from nowhere and I asked me where I wanted to sit.

'Right next to the ugly guy in the corner there,' I told him. The waiter bowed slightly and went over to check it was okay. He came back and said to go straight over.

'Hi, Arnie,' I said as I sat down. He looked up for a second from the greenery on his plate and then ate some more.

'Heard about your involvement in the raid,' Arnie said, his mouth full of lettuce. 'Sounded fun.'

PART TWO: DOWN TO BUSINESS

'Why didn't you tell me Reeky McStink ran the place, Arnie?'

'I assumed you'd know already. He runs a lot of things in this city. Wields a lot of power.'

'Is he the kind of guy to go round smashing up animals' apartments?'

'Only if he couldn't find you.' He stopped eating and thought about it. 'Even then, it's doubtful. You'd have to be pretty important to him. And if you were *that* important, he'd have found you by now.' He stabbed at something red on his plate and shoved it into his wrinkly face. When the waiter came over, I ordered steak.

'What about funny phone calls? The silent treatment.'

'Nah. Not his style either.'

'Is that good, Arnie?' I indicated his plate.

'Very. I would offer you some but—' he left it hanging.

'It certainly does look good. Good enough to pay for.'

Arnie eyed me up whilst taking another couple of mouthfuls. 'Reeky's a very important creature, Spriteman. He has bigger fish than you to fry.'

'Such as?'

'Well,' he took a long swallow of water, enjoying his moment of power. 'Whoever's killing all those Sappies for a start. It might be beneficial to him if he was to apprehend the villain. He has friends in high places, or so I've heard.'

'A reward?' I'd never thought of this.

'Perhaps, perhaps. But,' Arnie waved his fork in front of me, 'who knows what form a reward could take?'

The waiter came over with my steak. I suddenly found I was ravenous.

'Would McStink kill Bootsy, do you think?'

'The cop done up in the mousetrap? Uh-huh. No holes. If the body wasn't full of holes it had nothing to do with McStink. If it had've been, he'd have used Eddie. "Kills with quills"—hah!' Arnie came as close to a smile as a Tortoise can. He forked the last piece on his plate and plopped it into his mouth.

'Well,' Arnie rose, his dry, green flesh creaking like parchment, 'that's me finished. See you around, Spriteman.' He went over to a waiter and pointed back at me before leaving the restaurant.

The waiter came over, discreetly placing a saucer and the bill on the table. As soon as he went to another table, I inspected the damage. It was turning into an expensive lunch.

As I chewed over the rest of my meal, I began to wonder about Bootsy's murder. Why kill a harmless sort like him? He hadn't the brains to be onto something big... unless it was by accident. It also looked like—or was meant to look like—the Sappy murderer and Bootsy's killer were one and the same. If Bootsy *had* stumbled onto something then perhaps I was in the firing line too because I'd dealt with him, and that's why they'd gone to the trouble of setting me up, temporarily at least, for Bootsy's murder. Perhaps I was being warned to back off. But who from? And what were the calls in aid of, which started *before* my involvement with Bootsy and the raid?

My head was swimming with it all, and my headache came back with a vengeance. The piece of meat in my mouth turned to elastic. I spat it onto the plate. I wasn't hungry any more.

I'd barely set a paw in the office when Taki told me we'd just had another call.

'It could be nothing, Benji,' she said.

The rest of the day dragged. When Taki eventually popped her head round the door to wish me goodnight, I was already waiting in my hat and coat. I walked down to the entrance with her and asked if she wanted to go for a coffee. She said she was visiting friends later on and had to

PART TWO: DOWN TO BUSINESS

get home to get ready. Patting me on the shoulder, she made her way towards the bus stop.

I felt weary as I walked home that night, looking at the faces passing me by, wondering if one of them kept calling my office and not speaking, or if they'd trashed my apartment, or killed Bootsy and set me up. The sky was far too low and the air felt like jelly which I kept bouncing off. I seemed to be picking up every noise and detail around me with painful clarity. I felt like I was red raw, new to the world and its awfulness.

Eventually, Shefton Heights loomed up ahead like a mountain covered with carved gargoyles and Pigeon droppings. Crossing the street, I made my way over to the eternally gloomy lobby.

In the elevator I pressed the button for the fourteenth floor, slumped back against the wall, and let out a great gust of coffee fumes as I closed my eyes.

The doors were almost shut when they began to open again. Something resembling the tip of an umbrella was forcing them apart to reveal what looked like a huge bulk of clothes standing in the lobby. With one swift movement the figure squashed itself into the elevator beside me, pointing the umbrella in my face while sticking something sharp into my ribs.

'Not a word,' a muffled voice said beneath all the clothes. The umbrella, held by a shapeless mitten, moved away from my face to the panel of buttons, and the tip pressed the button for the fourteenth floor. Slowly, we began to go rise.

19

IT HAD NO FACE.
It was the only thing I could think about as the elevator took us up to the fourteenth floor. Its entire head was bound up with cloth and material, scarves criss-crossing the whole area; where the eyes should've been, a pair of cheap sunglasses: the figure I'd seen hanging around outside the building. I felt like I was entombed with a Poor Man's Mummy or Invisible Man. The confusion of smells that surrounded the figure didn't make me feel any better; there were so many scents it made my eyes water. They were the same ones I'd encountered in my apartment after it was ransacked.

Whatever was being stuck into my gut never moved. I prayed that another tenant would press for the elevator, which might buy me some time to create a distraction as the doors opened, but it never happened. Each time the number on the panel went up another floor, my heart sank a little lower. They were taking a risk, whoever they were. Then again, they were crazy enough to—I began to sweat, my fur sticking down against my clothes. Finally, the doors opened and the figure nudged me out onto the empty landing.

'Move,' it said.

The entire floor was deathly silent—I couldn't even hear the Frigs downstairs making their usual racket. I shuffled towards my apartment with the metal in my back.

PART TWO: DOWN TO BUSINESS

At my door, an arm leaned over my shoulder and pushed the still busted door inwards. Whatever was in my back pushed me into the apartment.

When we were both inside, the figure closed the door and leaned back against it. Despite the coverings and the shades, I could feel its eyes on me. When I realised the low rumbling noise coming through the layers of clothing was muffled laughter, I began to shake. Eventually the laughter stopped, and the pile of clothes in front of me spoke with its awful muffled voice.

'Hello, Benji,' the voice said. 'It's been a long time.'

I was too shocked to answer when one of the mittens begin unwinding the scarves from around the head and neck. For a brief second, I was terrified there'd be nothing underneath. When the glasses came off, I saw a pair of mad eyes; mad but smiling eyes. As more of the scarves were unravelled, hair, eyebrows, pale white skin and a set of pink ears appeared. Then the mittened hand rose to the face and pulled something from its mouth; I watched as two wads of cotton fell to the floor like gigantic snowflakes. When they hit the ground I looked back up at the face, and spoke.

'Jimmy,' I said.

THIS IS AN **ALA "Reading List"** EDITION & IS NOT FOR RETAIL SALE OR DISTRIBUTION

Part Three

–

The Country of the Blind

20

'A CAT BRINGING ME COFFEE—I must be going up in the world.'

We'd stared at each other for probably only a few seconds, but it felt like a lifetime. Happiness, shock, relief: all these conflicting emotions and more went through me as we stood in his—my—apartment.

The main emotion, without doubt, was shock. The Jimmy I'd known—the well-fed, well-groomed man about town, a half-decent crack away from a wry smile—had gone. This Jimmy was a stick-thin, bedraggled animal with a permanent grin and glassy eyes. And the *smell*.

'You broke into my apartment,' was all I could manage to say.

'You know, I haven't had coffee for over four months,' he said, as if he hadn't heard me. 'I like it black. Two sugars.' As his grin got even wider, I was sure I saw something crawling in his beard.

Stunned, I went through and made coffee. As I stood waiting for the kettle to boil, a hundred questions ganged up on me: How? Where? *Why?*

I put his coffee down and sat opposite him on a chair I dragged from the bathroom. I couldn't think of a single thing to say. Instead I watched him drink coffee.

'Yeah, I broke in all right,' he said, finishing off the still boiling coffee. 'Didn't take anything though. Left the

THE TERROR AND THE TORTOISESHELL

bedroom and the john untouched too, I hope you noticed. Didn't that strike you as odd? Any cookies?'

I sat there like a dummy, trying to take in what he was saying. 'Uh. Sure, I'll get you some.'

In the kitchen I tried to compose myself, took a few deep breaths. I grabbed the cookie jar and went back through. The second the jar was on the table, Jimmy's dirt-encrusted nails were prying the lid off. He shoved four biscuits into his mouth in one go, the crumbs falling into his empty coffee cup.

'Didn't that strike you as odd, Benji?' he said through a mouthful of cookies.

My brain seemed to be lagging behind. He opened his mouth to speak again when I answered him. 'It might've, if I'd thought for one minute you were still alive. That smell—' I waved in his general direction. 'What is it? I thought it was a gang.'

He nodded furiously. 'That's what you all were supposed to think. There's this chemical plant down near the canal. Interesting place. I knew I had to disguise my scent so I broke in and doused myself with as many different things as I could. I've also been going through trash-cans. I find any interesting odours in them, I smear them on myself. Found some pork fat in a can near here the other day.' He grinned again. I counted at least four teeth missing.

'Chemical plant?' My ears sprang up. 'Did you take anything else?'

'Just a long knife I keep strapped to my leg.' He tapped his shin. 'Protection. I didn't fancy ending up as another dead Sappy done-up like an animal.'

'You know about the killings?'

'Oh, sure. *I know a lot of things, Benji.*' I imagine the look he gave me was supposed to convey warmth, but instead it unnerved me. I asked if he wanted more coffee. He nodded, long greasy strands of hair falling in front of his eyes.

PART THREE: THE COUNTRY OF THE BLIND

'Yes, Sir, I know things. That's why I came here, to the apartment. Didn't you notice the clue I left?'

I frowned. 'What clue?'

Jimmy shook his head and laughed. 'It was a *bit* oblique I suppose,' he said as I went to make more coffee. 'The books on the shelf? The one at the front was called *The Devil You Know*. Ah well.' I told him I'd been so angry at the time that I'd swept the books off the shelf without even looking at them.

'Doesn't matter,' he told me when I came back with the coffee. Sticking the cup under his nose, he inhaled like it was a magic potion.

'But I was sure you were dead!' I was almost shouting at him. 'I saw those Lions chase you up that alley! I heard screams. *Human* screams.'

'You heard human screams all right, but they weren't mine.' He was sipping at the coffee now instead of gulping it. 'You make good coffee. What are you like as a cook?'

'I'll make you anything you like, if you tell me where you've been.'

He grinned again, but it wasn't as unnerving as before. 'It's a deal,' he said.

21

'WHEN I BROKE IN I never went near the fridge either, you notice that?' Jimmy said between mouthfuls. 'I was so tempted I can't tell you. But,' he gulped, 'if I'd started I wouldn't have stopped, know what I mean?'

I nodded as Jimmy scooped another handful off the plate, the pattern re-emerging like a series of sped-up slides. When the last of the meal disappeared, he ran a dirty finger along the china to get at the crumbs he'd missed.

'So the scream I heard wasn't you,' I said, trying to get his mind back.

'Hmm,' he swigged more coffee. 'No. Some guy I'd never seen before. I was stood against one wall, he was stood against another. The entrance to another alley was between us. This guy must've weighed three hundred pounds. The Lions took one look at me and one look at him. An easy decision: I would've been half the meal and would've struggled twice as hard. So they jumped him. They could probably have got me too, if they'd wanted.'

'Enjoy the meal?' I asked.

'Me or the Lions?' he sniggered. 'Sorry. It's just—' He gave up, shrugged.

'It must've been Hell.'

He let out a deep breath. 'Hell would be a good word for it, yes.'

PART THREE: THE COUNTRY OF THE BLIND

In a quiet, dispassionate voice he began to describe what he'd been through.

'When the Lions took that guy, I actually *stood* there for a few seconds watching them *dismantling* the poor sap. Somewhere close by, a window smashed and it brought me round. I ended up about two blocks away, in such a panic I could barely see. But I kept going. Then I tripped over something on the sidewalk: an Old Dog.' He threw back his head and laughed. 'Do you know that Dog actually *bit* me? The only animal that got hold of me and we were kind of on the same side!

'The bite cleared my eyes, if nothing else. I got up and ran. Everywhere I ran smelled like a slaughterhouse. I was heading out of the city, hoping I could get out to the freeway or something—maybe I'd see a carload of humans and get a ride—but then it occurred to me: who the hell would stop? Besides, if this *thing* was happening here, it must be happening everywhere else too. So I kept running.

'I eventually ran out of breath near some kind of disused office complex on a run-down estate. I'd never seen it before. The bottom floor windows were all smashed, but not recently—it looked like nobody except kids had been there for months. I was debating whether to go inside when I heard animals yelling close by, so the decision was made for me. I smashed the remaining shards of glass from one of the windows and climbed in.

'The room I was in had a locked door. I aimed a few kicks at it and hoped that I didn't raise anybody in the process. In the corridor, I headed for the first flight of stairs I could find. The higher I went, the less vandalised each floor was. The top floor—the ninth—was virtually untouched. I looked out of a window onto the estate below. I couldn't make out any yelling up there. I was just starting to feel a bit easier, when I heard breaking glass way below me.

'I ran along the corridor looking for an open door or one I could easily force; but they were all those heavy fire resistant doors. I had a penknife in my pocket that I used to peel apples. I worked at the lock of one of the doors. Eventually it gave.

'I slipped into the dark room and stuck my back to the door while I tried to catch my breath. The racket below was still going on. My eyes were adjusting to the darkness of the room. When a cloud moved away from the moon I had a good view of the layout.

'Apart from a rusting filing cabinet, it was empty. I decided not to take any chances with the noise, so started on the cabinet. It took me about ten minutes to jam it up against the door.

'About five minutes later, I heard shouting below. I inched my way over to the window and looked out. On the ground, a group of about twenty animals were beating-up a handful of humans. My legs started to shake and I flopped to the floor, realising how lucky I was.'

When Jimmy stopped talking, he was out of breath. Letting my own breath out, I went into the kitchen to get the bottle of brandy stuck at the back of one of the cupboards. I set the bottle and a glass in front of him. Filling the tumbler to the brim, he gulped down half before continuing.

'I was holed up in that office for roughly four days. At some point my watch had got smashed, so I wasn't sure of the time. Apart from a group of Dogs sniffing around outside one time, I saw no one. I was starving. I started seeing things—things worse than Dogs on two legs. I had to get out.

'I waited until it was dark. Before I left, I checked for any unlocked rooms in the building, looking for anything that might prove useful. I didn't find anything.

'That night was the worst: I was so hungry I had the shakes. I ended-up fishing a half-eaten banana from a trash-can and ate that, peel and all. Every night for about a week I ventured out, breaking into stores to get food,

PART THREE: THE COUNTRY OF THE BLIND

blankets, matches; anything I could carry which might be of use. Every night bar one I saw Humans getting killed. I think somebody up there likes me.' He smiled.

'You never got attacked?' I asked as he took more brandy.

'A couple of near misses, that was all. One night, a Bird grabbed the back of my shirt and tried to pull me into the sky. Somehow, I managed to fight it off. I've still got the scratches to prove it. I began wondering: was I the only one left? How come I'd escaped? Why me? You feel guilty, Benji.' Wincing, he emptied the glass, refilled it.

'How long did you stay in the building?'

'Until it burned down.'

'When was that?'

'About a week ago. Would you believe me if I said it was a relief? I was stagnating in there. Things outside had quietened down a bit: all that fuss about the SPCH and the Zoo was over, so the streets were a bit easier to pound at night.'

'You know about the SPCH and the Zoo?'

The 'SPCH, the Zoo, the murders. I'd find copies of that rag the Rat is putting out. I'd never been disturbed in that building, but I was beginning to feel anxious there. If somebody was seeking out Sappies... Anyway, one night while I was out on the prowl, I saw smoke pouring out over the trees at the edge of the estate. As I got a little closer, I saw a gang of Street Cats throwing lighted rags through the broken windows. The building going up had forced my hand: I had to move now. So I found another place to hole up that night.'

'You could've looked me up earlier,' I said.

'I considered it, but I'd never been that far into the city. And there was always the possibility you'd have turned against me.' I was starting to protest when he held up a hand. 'No, think about it. If you'd been seen with me earlier, maybe still even now, it wouldn't just be me for the chop. You'd be seen as a traitor.'

THE TERROR AND THE TORTOISESHELL

'So what's changed?' I asked.

'A lot has changed,' he said emphatically. 'And I promise you by the time this bottle is finished you'll know how much.' I gestured for him to continue.

'I decided that my best bet was to see if I could find any of my old colleagues. A lot of them had been Cops, so should have had better survival instincts than most. I went as close as I dared to their old houses. Most were full of animals, and the other houses had been abandoned. I found nobody. Again, I wondered if I was the last man standing.

'After that, I decided to try old friends.' He smiled. *'That* didn't take long. Nothing doing. But I kept finding these papers which hinted at things.'

'Dark faucets,' I said.

'Yeah. I also kept my ears open and heard there'd been this other murder. I heard a name one day too that rang a bell. I didn't know why but I decided to try and remember it.

'Anyway, I digress. Food was getting scarce and the only way to get more was to venture further afield. I couldn't do that as I was. I managed to steal a few sets of clothes from washing lines and wore the lot so nobody could see my face. My main concern about going further afield was that the further I went into the city, the denser the population would be. I didn't know if most animals' main sense was still smell, so I thought it best to take no chances, despite the clothing. I remembered this laboratory place down by the canal that manufactured scents. Rumour had it in the Old Days it had been involved in animal testing. One evening I managed to get in and stock up on "perfume"—various scents of different animals. I wasn't exactly sure what most of it was, but it did the trick. That night I managed to walk through the city (at two in the morning, admittedly) without being molested.

'On my walk about, I found several papers. I took them back to my hideaway. That name I'd heard was still bothering

PART THREE: THE COUNTRY OF THE BLIND

me. I looked through the papers to see if I could find it in any of them. Amazingly, I did.'

He started taking ragged pieces of paper from his pockets, dumping them on the table, rifling through them.

'There's been all those editions of *Fuller News?*' I said. 'I don't recognise half of them.'

When he'd found the one he wanted, he smoothed it out and handed it to me.

> ...the man found in the grage may bee the fifth victim, but stil the police are baffled.
>
> Here at *Fuller News* we can provi Police wth a clue. Thanks to a brillant peace of detection by one of are jœnralists, we have discoloured that the second victim, a moman called Veronica Kissler, actually worked at these very officers before The Terror struck, adding a smewhat po!gnant touch to for us regarding the murders themselves. They may only be Sappies, but wha is being done is an outage—and the police is sems, can do nothing to stop it.

'It's certainly up to Fuller's usual standards,' I said. 'What of it?'

'Adele—you know who Adele is, don't you?' I nodded.

'She was a journalist. She worked in those offices. That's where I knew the name from. *I'd met her.* But Adele introduced her as Ronnie, not Veronica, that's what threw me.'

'So?'

'When I was looking through the rest of the papers another name jumped out at me: another female victim, who was found with a purse containing her name and address. She was a journalist friend of Adele's too, only Fuller didn't pick that one up. Incidentally,' he said, dipping his hand back into his pocket, 'I lied when I said I didn't take anything when I was here.' He showed me what looked like a staff photo. Both of the murdered women were on it. So was Adele.

'So what are you saying, Jimmy? That the killer is targeting journalists?'

Jimmy was shaking his head. 'Not only journalists. I was onto something, Benji. It started as a hunch, but—you have hunches, don't you?'

'Sure I do,' I said, trying to humour him. 'What was yours?'

'Mine,' he said, leaning forward, 'was that Adele's death hadn't been an accident at all.'

22

'Hey, don't look at me like that!' This time when he smiled it was a good smile, despite the lack of teeth, a sane smile. 'I'll explain it to you. But first—' he slopped more grog into his glass.

'When Adele died I'd suspected foul play. I'd no proof, and there was nothing to suggest why anybody would want to harm her, or what they could possibly gain by it. But for a few weeks I couldn't get it out of my head. I even looked into it. The only thing that stood out was that a few days before she died, she'd been working on some big story. What it was she wouldn't say; she said it might jinx it. Whatever it was, the evidence went up with her in her car when it caught fire. I was suspicious because the car had only been in for a service a few days earlier. Also there was no evidence to show that any other cars were involved in the accident. Somehow it just caught fire on its own.

'I got nowhere with it. It was eating me up, but I couldn't prove anything. So I had to let it go, tried to get on with my life. Even bought a Cat.' He smiled. Not sure how to react, I smiled back.

'But, after all *this* happened—' he swung his arms wide, 'and I saw those names in the paper... Benji, what are the chances that two of those six people happened to work at the same offices? *And what are the chances that Adele*

THE TERROR AND THE TORTOISESHELL

knew them both as work colleagues? She died in suspicious circumstances herself, remember. And then something else hit me: what if the two journos *and* Adele—and maybe even the other victims, who knows—*were* all killed because of the same thing?'

By this stage I was beginning to feel really sorry for Jimmy. Heaven knows what he'd been through, and whatever it was it had seriously derailed his mind. He wanted answers. Any answers, it didn't matter what they were. To his credit, he still had enough about him to see what I was thinking.

'I know how it sounds, Benji, I've thought the same thing myself. But the idea *won't let go*. And if we're going to be blunt about it, I don't really have that much else to live for these days, do I? I'm practically obsolete, one of a virtually extinct breed. But I still believe that I'm onto something here.'

'Okay, Jimmy, let's just say for one second that you are right: Adele's death was no accident, and that all these others are part of the same thing. But Adele's death was *pre*-Terror; all the others came after. What is it that could still be relevant to both eras? Who would it matter to anymore?'

He was nodding like his head would come off. 'I know, it sounds ridiculous! So I did a bit more digging. In fact, down at the Cop Shop I'm sure somebody must be working on a series of unsolved burglaries as we speak...'

I realised the danger he was putting himself in.

'You're that sure about it?'

He nodded some more. 'A few months before Adele died, the two of us went around to Ronnie Kissler's for a meal. It took me a while to remember where she lived, but I found it eventually. Unfortunately, the house was full of the yappy little Dogs who'd taken it over. I managed to get them out of there by running a hose from the empty house next door through the Dogs' mailbox. I shoved a note through with

PART THREE: THE COUNTRY OF THE BLIND

the hose implicating a family of Alsatians in the next street. I'd no idea if there were a family of Alsatians in the next street, but the Dogs went to look anyway.' I wondered if I'd misjudged him. Maybe he wasn't mad after all.

'I knew I wouldn't have long. I found her study on the second floor. My luck was holding out, because it didn't look like anybody had been in there since The Terror. I rifled through desk drawers by the light of a street lamp. In one of them I found a check-list. At the top of it were the words "Adele's Job".'

'What else did you find?'

'That was it.'

'Oh.' I was back to wondering about his sanity again.

'The trail's gone cold. I'd been debating whether to contact you for a while. I decided now was as safe as it was ever going to get. So I wrecked this place and made a few silent calls, hoping you'd guess it was me. One day, when I was feeling especially reckless, I even hung around outside the building hoping you'd see me.'

'A *few* calls?' I said. 'There were dozens of them.'

He looked me square in the eyes. 'I called three times, Benji, that was all. Then I got the newspaper and saw all this about Bootsy, and you being a suspect. Obviously you were being set up.'

'It's in the paper?' I hadn't seen one for days with everything else going on.

'I think we've more in common than you realise,' he said.

I decided not to rise to that. 'So your trail's gone cold.'

'Yup. Done all I can do. But I was thinking about it. There's probably files in Fuller's, but me trying to get them would be suicide. So what I was wondering—'

'*You want me to break into Fuller's for you?*'

'Look at it another way: I want to be your client.' He smiled. 'At the moment I can't pay you, but I'm sure that at some point—'

THE TERROR AND THE TORTOISESHELL

'Hang on, hang on. Let me think about this.' I began pacing the room, trying to gather my thoughts. 'You're saying that whoever's killing these Sappies also killed Adele?'
'Yes.'
'So it's a Sappy who survived The Terror.'
'That's my belief, yes.'
'It could be you,' I told him.
He smirked. 'I suppose it could. But I had an alibi when Adele was killed. Also I didn't have the equipment to kill all those people.' I thought about the thefts from the lab—the same one he'd been to. Still I didn't think it was him.
'But you can't prove that,' I said. 'So... who killed Bootsy?'
'I'd say it's the same person.'
'Why set me up for it?'
'Because you're linked to me. Maybe you'd know the details of the case because I did; inherited them the way you have other things. I knew three of the victims, you knew Bootsy, you *know* me. Maybe because of your involvement with the police. Maybe you're onto something and don't know it. Same applies with Bootsy.'
'I was also shot at recently and followed home.'
'That doesn't surprise me. I said we had a lot in common.'
'So do you think this person knows you're alive?'
'Who knows? It's a possibility.'
My head was spinning. When we finished, it was still dark outside. Jimmy said he was going for a shower. I told him he could have the bed. I mentioned the police file I had. I also told him it wasn't up to much.
I crashed out on the couch before Jimmy had got out of the shower.

23

I AWOKE THE NEXT MORNING to find a strange looking man in the kitchen making coffee.
'Want one?'
'Please. Lots of cream.'
The man put the cup on the table and sat down. His hair was about a quarter the length it'd been the night before, and it looked like it'd been cut with a knife and fork. It probably had. The beard was gone too (I never threw any of Jimmy's shaving stuff out), under which his putty-coloured skin managed to somehow cling tightly to his face and sag at the same time. He looked better, but still looked dreadful.

'Quite a transformation,' I told him. Finishing my coffee, I got ready to leave. 'What are you going to do today?' I asked him. He said relax. I said I hoped he wouldn't go wandering off—it was a big bad world out there, you know. He was still laughing as I closed the door behind me.

Walking to the office, I realised the weight of the responsibility that was upon me. I wanted to tell somebody—anybody—but knew that I couldn't. I doubted there was a law for harbouring Sappies but I was sure one could be quickly put in place.

I was half-way across the road to the office when something pungent hit my nostrils. Further along the street,

THE TERROR AND THE TORTOISESHELL

a scruffy mutt in an overcoat was chewing on a cigar, a column of blue smoke obscuring its face.

In the elevator, I noticed the cigar smoke clinging to my suit. I wondered what could link a possible pre-Terror killing with a series of post-Terror ones. To Jimmy, I don't suppose it mattered; he wanted justice for Adele, that's what his life had boiled down to. Did I want justice for Bootsy? I wasn't that noble.

Sitting at my desk, I pondered the best way to get into Fuller's offices, and the best way to explain what I was doing there when I got caught. Next door, Taki suddenly started coughing. I caught the odour of rank cigar smoke, heard an unfamiliar voice. Then the intercom buzzed.

'Lieutenant Dingus here to see you,' Taki said, still coughing.

My surprise at finally getting to meet the famous Lieutenant Dingus had barely time to register when a cloud of smoke wafted through the opening door.

'Mr. Spriteman?' A gravelly voice said behind the smoke. 'Lieutenant Dingus, sir. May I sit down?'

When the smoke cleared it was hard to believe that this under-sized, squinty-eyed Basset Hound in a dirty brown raincoat could possibly be the same Dog I'd heard so much about.

'Sir?' He gestured towards the chair with his cigar, an earnest look on his face. 'May I sit down?'

'What? Certainly.' Dingus plumped down into the chair opposite me and began rubbing his barrel-chest with a wrinkled white paw. 'You'll have to excuse me, sir. I have a bit of stomach trouble this morning.'

The Lieutenant made a suitably comic display of reaching inside his dirty Trench Coat with his other paw and pulling out two small white tablets. 'Antacids,' he told me. 'They don't always work.' Somehow, he managed to chew the tablets and keep the cigar in place at the same time.

PART THREE: THE COUNTRY OF THE BLIND

'You ever get that, Mr. Spriteman? It just came on suddenly, about an hour ago. My wife, she says it's because of these cigars, but I tell her—'

'What can I do for you, Lieutenant?'

'Well, Sir,' he leaned across the table, 'it's about Bootsy.' He put the now dead cigar into the ashtray in front of him. 'You see, the more I try to figure it out, the less sense it makes. You ever have cases like that, Sir? The problem I have is that I have to check up on all leads. I'm sure you can appreciate that, Sir. I believe that you and Officer Bootsy had a falling out just prior to his death, and—'

'That makes me a suspect.' Immediately he held up his paws towards me.

'Oh no no no no.' He was shaking his head so hard that his oversized ears were smacking the sides of his face. 'But I get the impression you knew him pretty well. As you can understand, Sir, we don't have that much information about him. He wasn't an official Police Officer as such.'

'He bluffed his way in.'

'If you like, Sir, yes.'

'Did you really know about the HFC place weeks ago?' I asked.

'Pardon me? Oh yes, sir. Yes, I did. Do you mind if I smoke? Thank you.' He produced another fat cigar from somewhere inside the raincoat. 'We knew there was something not right about the place.' The room began to fill with smoke again. 'You could almost smell it.' I remembered a passage from my Dog book: Basset Hounds, famous for their sense of smell. *The best nose on the force.*

'I understand you were at the raid, Sir?'

'I was with Bootsy.'

'Yes, I heard that. I was out with Mrs. Dingus. We've been together since before The Terror. Is there anything you could tell me about Bootsy?'

THE TERROR AND THE TORTOISESHELL

I told him what I knew, which didn't take long. A small notebook appeared and notes were taken. Every so often he'd nod and mutter. 'Right, I see... uh-huh...'

'Can you think of any reason why anybody would want to implicate you, Mr. Spriteman?'

'Benji. No, I'm trying to find that out myself. It's got me stumped at the moment, though.'

'I understand, Sir—Benji. I'm just trying to build up a picture and—can I be honest with you, Benji?' He leaned across the desk again, rubbing the top of his head with the paw containing the cigar. 'I've been meaning to come over and speak to you for a while; before all this happened with Bootsy, I mean. You see,' he leaned even further across so his nose was almost touching mine, 'the guys down at the station, Benji, they're nice enough, but there's not many good cops among them. But you, you come from a detective background, so to speak, the same as I do—my owner, he was a Lieutenant too, you see—so I figured you'd have more of a clue than the guys down there.'

I was touched. 'Thank you, Lieutenant.'

'Oh, just Dingus, please.' He narrowed his good eye, until it was the same size as the one with the squint. 'Could I keep in touch with you?'

'Sure,' I said uneasily. 'I'd like that.'

Standing, we shook paws. 'Well goodbye, Mr. Spriteman—Benji. Hope to see you around.'

'Yes, goodbye, Lieutenant. And good luck.'

'Just Dingus. So long.'

As the door was closing behind him, I noticed that my fur was stiff. For some reason I couldn't fathom, he'd rattled me.

I was just sitting down again when the door opened and Dingus stuck his head back round the corner. 'Oh, just one more thing sir,' he said, scratching one of his ears. 'I almost forgot. Could you possibly drop by the station this

PART THREE: THE COUNTRY OF THE BLIND

afternoon? There's a couple of things I'd like you to see. Well, goodbye, Sir.'

Before I had a chance to reply, the door had closed and the Lieutenant was saying goodbye to Taki. Hearing the outer door close, I went through to her office.

'Interesting fellow,' she said. 'Friendly with it.'

'Yes,' I said. 'I wonder why.'

24

'Are you sure it's okay to go in?'
'Sure, Lieutenant. It's not pretty though.'
'Is Clancy in there too?'
'No sir. He's taken a late lunch. Be back in about an hour.'
'Right-o.'

After Dingus left, I tried to figure out what had just happened between us. If I'd had any work to get on with I'd have done that, but I didn't so I couldn't. I looked over the file Bootsy had given me again and remembered to take it back home for Jimmy.

I decided to have an early lunch. From a call box outside Moe's, I got through to Dingus's office and was told anytime this afternoon was fine. After lunch, I walked to the station to find Dingus waiting for me in an old, grey jalopy nearly as ragged-looking as he was.

'My guess is this isn't a police car,' I said.

He frowned. 'How did you know that? Get in. I've got something to show you.'

After a ten-minute bump-and-grind across town in Dingus's bone-shaker, we pulled up outside the coroner's office. The tenth floor smelled of disinfectant; cold white walls pressed you in. While Dingus was clearing things with an assistant, something lumpy under a sheet was wheeled

PART THREE: THE COUNTRY OF THE BLIND

past by a Great Dane so tall he almost knocked his head on the ceiling. I also caught a whiff of something unpleasant.

A warm paw touched my arm.

'Huh?'

'Ready, Benji?' Dingus squinted up at me.

'No, but lead on.'

Dingus opened the door into the morgue, a surprisingly large room filled with metal drawers. Against the far wall, two of them lolled open next to each other, like tongues sticking out from huge metal mouths. Their contents were thankfully obscured by the dissecting table ahead of us.

'Do I really have to be here?' I asked, wishing I hadn't had such a heavy lunch.

'Oh, yes,' he gave me that earnest look again. 'I value your opinion.' He shambled over to the nearest of the drawers. I followed. Reluctantly. He stopped between the two open drawers and turned to face me.

'Do you see the resemblance, Benji?'

'Hmm?' My gaze was firmly on Dingus's rain coat.

'The bodies, Benji.'

'Oh.' Taking a deep breath, I looked down and saw Bootsy, his dead eyes staring past me up to the ceiling. I flinched, looked away.

'Have you ever heard of Eddie the Quill, Benji?' Dingus said, pointing at the other body.

'Yes, I've heard of—' This time, I didn't see the face first.

The body next to Bootsy looked like an old Beagle, or it would've done had it not been for the holes peppering its torso.

'What the hell hap—'

'Eddie the Quill works for Reeky McStink,' Dingus told me. 'He's a Porcupine. He's also Reeky's personal assassin. Here's one of his business cards.' He took a card from his jacket and passed it to me:

THE TERROR AND THE TORTOISESHELL

*Shish-Kebab Your Enemies With
Eddie The Quill—Pest Exterminator
"Kills With Quills"
(If that don't get 'em, the lice will!)
Reasonable Rates*

'Catchy,' I said.

'You ever seen a Porcupine, Benji? You know how they kill their prey? They run *backwards* into their victims! Have you ever heard anything like that?'

'No,' I said, struggling to keep my dinner down. 'Out of interest, Dingus, what kind of goon is Reeky McStink?'

'Oh, he's a Skunk. Apparently, you smell him before you see him. You do know how Skunks—' I nodded. 'I've never smelled one, but I'm told it's pretty awful.'

'Can I ask, Lieutenant, why you brought me here to see this?' I pointed to the half-mutt, half-sieve in the drawer. 'Bootsy I can kind of understand.'

'Because he was killed in such a distinctive fashion we wondered if he was one of the Sappy killer's victims too, assuming that Bootsy's also one of them. If he *is* a Sappy victim, then Reeky and Eddie become chief suspects. You see, the holes are where Eddie must've—'

'I'd figured that out, Lieutenant, thank you,' I told him. 'But why am *I* here?'

'Well, Porcupines and Cats are both nocturnal creatures, and I wondered if you'd ever spotted—'

'You think I know Eddie the Quill? I told you I've never seen him before. Besides, I keep office hours these days.'

'Admittedly, it was a long shot.' Dingus raised both paws in the air then let them fall. 'So what do you think, Benji? Could it be Reeky?'

'I've no idea, Lieutenant.' Something stunk in here besides the corpses.

PART THREE: THE COUNTRY OF THE BLIND

'Well, like I say, I just wanted another pair of ears to hear how it all sounded.' *Awful*, I managed to avoid blurting out.

We left not a moment too soon. On the way out, an Irish Terrier in a white smock barged past us, muttering to itself.

'Excuse me a second,' Dingus said, following it back through the double doors.

I stood in the corridor alone, glad of the breather. From behind the door, I heard a raised voice which wasn't Dingus, followed by a quieter voice which was. Seconds later, Dingus appeared.

'Sorry about that, Benji.'

'Who was that?' I enquired.

'He's the city's coroner. Very good at his job, but highly strung.'

Despite my appeals for fresh air, Dingus insisted he give me a lift back to the office. On the way, he talked about the case, asking what I thought of his ideas. I said yes, there probably was a link between the bodies in the morgue and the Sappy killings. But somehow I doubted that he believed it any more than I did. And why get me over there to look at the Beagle?

On the fourth floor, I heard a crash of piano keys above me. Evidently Kitty Wellman's class wasn't going so well. Two doors short of my office, something bright on the left caught my eye. Turning, I found myself looking straight into a room full of overweight Cats in leotards, stretching, bending and jumping.

'What the hell is that two doors down?' I asked Taki.

'Mrs. Plumley's aerobics class. She's just moved in. She popped by to say hello.' Taki began giggling and raised a paw to her mouth.

'What's so funny?'

'I was just imagining you in a leotard.' She started giggling some more.

THE TERROR AND THE TORTOISESHELL

I slumped down in my chair and pulled my shoes off. Opening a drawer, I pulled out a half-eaten danish and the latest edition of *Fuller News*. FIDO THE FIHERMAN'S LAST CTCH! the headline yelled. The name rang bells. Where from? Then I had it: that night at the HFC.

> One of the Cities's leading villans, Fido The Fsherman has bin found full of holes—but not the kidn you'd get from a gun! He is believed to have ben the latest «gagland style» dispatch of Eddie The Quill, the lice-ridden Porkupine who is beleeved to be an asosiate of the equally shadowy Reeky M$_c$Stink.
> However, it was beleeved by sauces close to us that Fido ALSO worked for M°Stink. Was this a patting of the waves that Fido Didn't see coming?! Did he real out his hœk once too often? Was he—

I shoved the paper away, not able to stomach any more of the drunken Rat's lousy wordplay.

My stomach sank. Dingus had wanted me to see him. I was just starting to think why, when on cue the intercom buzzer sounded.

'If it's Dingus put him through,' I told Taki.

'I just thought you should know that we've found another dead human.' My heart leapt to my mouth. Jimmy had promised to stay in, but—

'Benji, you still there?'

'Yes, I'm still here.'

'Well, you remember what I said earlier, about having another set of ears? I was wondering if you'd come along with me to the crime scene.'

What if it was Jimmy? 'Er, okay, Lieutenant. Certainly.'

'That's great, Benji. I'll be there in fifteen minutes.' He hung up.

PART THREE: THE COUNTRY OF THE BLIND

No, it wasn't Jimmy. It couldn't be Jimmy.

I'd just started to dial my own number, when I remembered we'd agreed he wouldn't answer the phone. It seemed to take a lot longer than fifteen minutes for Dingus to show.

Slamming the door shut, discordant piano chords crashed down upon me like a portent of doom.

25

'Apparently a couple of Street Dogs found it behind some bins in an alley,' Dingus told me above the racket of his car's engine. 'Sounds familiar, huh?'

'Where are we going?'

'Near the fairground. You ever been to the fairground, Benji? I love it. I took Mrs. Dingus there once. You know we've been together since before The Terror?'

'So I heard.'

'Really? Well this part of town, I've never been there before. It's about a half-mile *past* the fairground. They told me at Headquarters to bring a gun with me. Me, I don't usually carry guns.'

I turned to him. 'A rough area?'

'Apparently so. There's a rumour that Reeky's been spotted out this way.'

'Now I wish I'd brought my gun.'

'Oh, *that*,' he waved a paw. 'I don't think Reeky's after you, Benji.'

'You know about that?' I asked.

'I know about that.' He nodded. Eventually, he put his eyes back to the road.

'What else do you know about me, Dingus?' I asked.

PART THREE: THE COUNTRY OF THE BLIND

'I've heard you're a good detective,' he said. 'Well, that's why you're here, obviously.'

When he finally gave the road his full attention, it gave me time to entertain all kinds of strange thoughts. I started to get paranoid. I had to keep reminding myself I was innocent.

The fairground came and went, replaced by block after block of concrete and weeds and mangy looking beasts standing on street corners kicking dirt into the gutters. Ahead, an officer waved us into a space between two cars: one a squad car, the other a torch job. Local toughs hung around taunting the half dozen officers at the scene, a thin piece of yellow "Crime Scene" tape all that was separating them. When I got out of the car, one of the officers moved aside, and I caught a glimpse of an alley with something nasty on the ground. My nerves began to sing.

The something nasty turned out to be a man made to look like a Porcupine or Hedgehog. Its back, arms and rump were covered in long sticks, hair stuck up to match. Whoever was responsible had even gone to the trouble of blacking up the guy's nose. When I was certain it wasn't Jimmy, a huge gust of air shot out of me. As I looked away, I caught Dingus squinting at me, one paw over his mouth.

'They must hate Reeky and Eddie pretty bad to go to this trouble,' I said once I'd regained my composure a little.

'Certainly looks like a frame up,' Dingus replied. 'But, if we rule the two of them out then we can rule Fido out too... which means we're back where we started, and that—'

He was cut short when the Irish Terrier I'd seen at the morgue burst his way through the crowd towards us.

'Get these animals outta here!' he yelled, gesturing to the officers. 'If you want fun go to the midway.'

Dingus stepped forward. 'Benji, this is Doctor Clancy the coroner I was te—'

'Hey, what's going on here, Dingus?' Clancy shouted. 'This isn't a public show. Get all these goons out of here, will ya?'

THE TERROR AND THE TORTOISESHELL

'Ah, sure. Clancy, this is Benji Spriteman, the city's finest private detective—'

'How do you do, Mr. Spriteman,' he said quietly.

Before I got a chance to reply, he was off at Dingus again. 'What do you mean, have I got the results for the Fido murder yet? I had to cut short my lunch to attend a meeting with Ashton about his measly budget cuts and you ask me about Fido! Let me tell you something, Lieutenant,' the medical examiner waved a paw in Dingus's face. *Irish Terriers have a tendency to be extremely volatile with other Dogs*, I remembered. 'Do you have any idea of the time it takes to perform a proper autopsy?'

'Well, I only—' Dingus replied.

'Yeah, you only. That's your trouble Dingus. You know what—'

I watched this one-way argument with great interest, the coroner gesticulating and working himself into a froth like he was three seconds from a coronary, while the Lieutenant stood before him with an unlit cigar in his mouth, nodding occasionally. You could've sold tickets.

Eventually, Clancy stormed off, muttering *'In the morning...!'* under his breath, leaving me and Dingus with the corpse. He shuffled around for a few seconds before turning his back on it. Lighting his cigar he shook his head.

'He's very good at his job,' Dingus assured me, 'but boy, is he hot-headed. Where were we?'

'You were saying something about being back where you started.'

He nodded. 'You know, this case, it's got me stumped. I think I'm getting somewhere, and then—' he slapped his head. 'Boy, oh boy. We can't do a lot here now, it's getting dark. Can I give you a lift, Benji?'

I asked him to drop me at Shefton. In the car, he asked me what I thought of it all.

'I think whoever's responsible, they like playing games.'

PART THREE: THE COUNTRY OF THE BLIND

'I'd agree with that.'

'Also, if that one was anything to go by, the killer is doing his work somewhere else—there was hardly any blood in that alley. Which means they must have transport. Did you mean what you said back there, about me being the finest private detective in the city?'

He lifted a paw from the wheel, gestured. 'Sure.'

'You do know I'm the only private detective in the city?'

Dingus laughed at that. 'I'm sure you'd still be the best even if there were others.'

Like a good chauffeur, he dropped me at the door. Waving him goodbye, I thought how strange it was, liking someone so much but also being suspicious of them at the same time.

On the fourteenth floor, I started to whistle the little tune Jimmy and I had decided upon as a signal for when I got back. If the door opened and Jimmy didn't hear the tune, it meant one of two things: either it wasn't a social call or I'd forgotten to whistle.

I found Jimmy sprawled across the couch reading one of his beloved dime paperbacks, a pot of coffee and a plate of cookies by his side. For a split-second he looked like the Jimmy I used to know, making me feel like an intruder.

'Good day at the office?' he asked.

'Another murder,' I told him, keeping the anxiety I'd suffered on his behalf to myself. 'At the morgue I saw Bootsy and a possible suspect called Fido the Fisherman.'

'What did the human look like?'

'Besides a Porcupine? It was hard to say. Whoever he was, they'd really gone to town on him.'

'So what do you think now, Benji?'

'I—'

We both froze when we heard the knock at the door. I was about to mouth at Jimmy to vanish, but he was one step ahead of me. As the bedroom door closed, I went to answer the knock.

THE TERROR AND THE TORTOISESHELL

'Sorry to bother you at home like this, Benji.' As usual Dingus looked suitably apologetic, rubbing his face with a paw. 'I forgot to say; Clancy's report on Fido and the Human will be ready in the morning. I thought you should know.'

I was there when Clancy said it, I thought. 'Thanks for letting me know.' I felt very uneasy. Again.

'You know, this case is really bothering me,' he continued. 'There's something that just doesn't ring true, and—oh, I'm sorry, Benji. You're tired.'

The yawn was a put-on, but it was the best I could manage in the circumstances. "Fraid so, Lieutenant. Need my beauty sleep.'

'Yes. I understand. Well, goodbye, Benji.'

'Bye.' I watched him shuffle into the elevator before I went back inside. I let out a sigh of immense relief, something else I always seemed to do when Dingus was around.

'Who was it?' Jimmy asked as I came back into the living room.

'That was Lieutenant Dingus. He's in charge of the case. How did he know my number?' I wondered. Jimmy's expression puzzled me. 'Why, what's wrong?'

'*Dingus?*' Jimmy looked like he couldn't decide whether to laugh or cry. 'Dingus? Not—he's a Basset Hound, right?'

I nodded. 'Yes. Why?'

'I told you that I went looking for old colleagues; well Dingus *was* one of my colleagues. At least the human one was.' He stood there, shaking his head. 'Well I never... did he say what he wanted?'

I started telling him the tale. I was barely half way through when he began nodding.

'He knows, Benji. He *knows.*'

'Knows what?' Then I knew. 'But he can't know. I never said a thing.'

'You wouldn't have to. At the door; was his nose twitching?'

194

PART THREE: THE COUNTRY OF THE BLIND

'It might have been, I don't know. He had his paw across his face the whole time.'

'You've forgotten that animals inherit the characteristics of the Human they were closest to. If he's anything like the Dingus I knew, he'll have known for ages. He used to play dumb, lull people into a false sense of security. And all the time he knew, dropping little hints along the way.'

I thought about the day's events—getting me to go to the morgue, the scene of the crime, then coming up here—*he'd been gauging my reaction all the time.*

'He wanted me to know that he knew,' I said.

Jimmy nodded. 'Right. He'll try and trip you up along the way. Did you bring that file?'

'What? Oh, yeah. Here.' I dug it out of my shirt and dropped it on the table. I told Jimmy I was going for a lie down.

Two hours later, I woke up. In the living room, Jimmy was reading the paperback I'd seen him with earlier.

'Did the file tell you anything?' I asked.

'Only that I need the files from Fuller's. I didn't recognise any of the other victims, and there's surprisingly few clues. It's definitely a Human though. I couldn't see an animal going to these lengths.'

'Why is Dingus trying to get to you, do you think?'

'Maybe he thinks I'm a suspect,' he said, going back to the paperback. 'Just because I was thick with his old man doesn't mean I'm not a killer in his eyes.'

We talked long into the night; about Old Times, good times, Adele, Reeky, Fido, Eddie, Dingus. After a while, none of it made much sense.

In bed, I lay in the darkness thinking that any animal with a badge could come in here at any time and haul Jimmy off to the cells. There wasn't even a lock on the door. Jimmy would make a perfect scapegoat for the Sappy murders. On top of that, I had the problem of how to get into the Rat's

THE TERROR AND THE TORTOISESHELL

offices and borrow the files. Everything was piling up on me and giving me a headache.

Needless to say I didn't sleep well that night.

26

The next morning, Taki was waiting for me. Lieutenant Dingus had called. Twice. Before I had a chance to speak, the phone trilled again.

'Third time lucky,' Taki said, putting her paw over the mouthpiece. I went next door to take the call.

'Yes, Spriteman.'

'Hello, Benji? I just got the report through from Clancy on the latest victim. Would you like to hear it?'

'Certainly would. Shoot.'

Dingus gave me a physical description of the man: hair colour, eyes, height. I made noises in what I felt were the right places.

'There's one other thing though that puzzles me. Those things we found in his back, made to look like quills? They were broom handles; ordinary broom handles, sharpened at each end. Can you believe that?' I told him I could not.

'You know what I think, Benji? I think it's a suspect we've completely overlooked. And they've put all these others in the frame—Reeky, Eddie, yourself—to take the heat off themselves.'

I struggled for something to say. Then I managed: 'Do you have anybody in mind, Lieutenant?'

'Dingus. I only wish I did, Benji. I only wish I did.'

'Perhaps,' I said, straight after he'd finished, 'Reeky and Eddie are clumsily trying to make it look like they're being framed, so the police won't take them seriously as suspects.' I warmed to this idea and continued with it. 'They must have plenty of enemies between them. Have you managed to talk to them yet?'

'They don't wanna be found.'

'Isn't that an admission of guilt?' I pressed on.

'It could be, but—'

'You're not convinced.'

'No.'

Dingus talked for a little while longer, mainly about his stomach complaint—he wondered if perhaps seafood didn't agree with Basset Hounds and advised me not to try clams. Then he started on about the scarcity of decent cigars in the city. 'Well, I thought I'd keep you informed on any developments,' he said at last. Ringing off, I thought that if this was an act of his it was a damn good one.

I told Taki I was going out for a while. She said that a new case had come through. Reluctantly, I told her it would have to wait. I had to get some fresh air.

I wandered the streets knowing that I had to do something. That Dingus knew about Jimmy couldn't be gainsaid. A part of me thought that if Dingus was as good as everybody said he was, then he'd know that Jimmy wasn't the killer. But supposing they were all wrong? Supposing the police didn't care who they pulled in? But Jimmy himself was pretty sure it was a Sappy. I wasn't sure I had his belief. And then there was Reeky and Eddie, hiding out somewhere. And the attempt at framing them *was* pretty clumsy...

I had to find them, even if they had nothing to do with it. If I did, it might stop Dingus from sniffing around Jimmy for a while if nothing else. In the meantime, hopefully something else would come up.

There was one creature who might know their whereabouts. I made my way over to Ronson Towers but Arnie wasn't there. Next I tried Quaffers, but he wasn't

PART THREE: THE COUNTRY OF THE BLIND

there either. Then I tried a few other places still with no success. I was getting jumpy, realising how much stock I was putting into finding M^{C}Stink. I decided to try Arnie's apartment again. When I heard his familiar grumbling on the other side of the door, I could've cheered.

When he opened the door it was a shock to see him wearing clothes. 'Nice threads, Arnie. I've been looking for you everywhere,' I told him as I sat on his sofa.

'I've been a busy little Tortoise today, haven't I?' he snapped. 'Whaddya want?'

'You seem a little on edge today, Arnie.'

'I won't ask you again,' he warned.

'Okay, have it your way. I need to see Reeky M^{C}Stink.'

Arnie stared at a stain on the carpet in from of him. 'I don't know him,' he muttered.

'Sure you do, Arnie. You know everyone.'

'What would I want to know *him* for?' He laughed unpleasantly. 'He's bad news.'

'What about the Porcupine, is he bad news too?'

'They both are. Rotten to the core, the pair of them.'

I decided to try it another way. 'You say that about everyone, Arnie. Maybe I'd find they were a swell couple of guys.'

He stuck his head in chest and grumbled. Then he brightened up.

'Yeah, why not?' He turned from the window, eyes sparkling. 'You really wanna see them? Okay, I'll see what I can do. Give me a day or so.' He went to the door and opened it for me. 'Be seeing ya around, Spriteman.' Closing the door after me, I heard Arnie mumble a name and then a few choice curses.

'Our mutual friend was here while you were out,' Jimmy told me when I got back to the apartment. 'I could hear him from in here, talking to your neighbours. You know he sounds just like the human Dingus? It's uncanny.'

THE TERROR AND THE TORTOISESHELL

'What was he asking?'
'If any of them had seen any new tenants around here the past couple of days. Someone told him to shove off.' I laughed at that.
'Benji, we have to get those files.'
'I know.'
Phoning the office, I told Taki I was working on something. She reminded me of the case that'd come in earlier. I asked her for the details and told her I'd call back. After thinking about it for a while, I rang her again and asked for Ma Spayley's number.

She answered on the first ring. 'I'll get him for you,' she yelled above the squeals of baby rodents.

'Yeah, Mr. Spriteman?' said Number One, breathless as usual.

'How do you fancy doing a bit of surveillance work for me?'

After about a hundred yesses and thank yous I gave him the details. 'You think you can handle it?' He said he could.

'He never even asked about money,' I said when he hung up.

I phoned Taki and told her to expect the Mouse at some point. She sounded a bit taken aback. So did Jimmy.

'You've got a Mouse taking on your caseload?' he said when I hung up.

'It's a strange world we're living in, chum. Want some coffee?'

'I'll make it,' he said, rising. 'Yes, it's a strange world all right.'

The rest of the day we spent planning. We'd both been in Fuller's before; Jimmy had been there dozens of times picking Adele up from work, so he knew the general layout and where the files should be. The place hadn't changed much by the sound of things.

PART THREE: THE COUNTRY OF THE BLIND

'You'll probably need a set of skeleton keys. I used to have a set—ah good.' He grinned when I put them on the table.

When the details had been sorted out as well as they could, I went to bed, setting my alarm for two o'clock; no beauty sleep for me tonight. Before I dropped off the perch, I wondered how the Mouse would get on.

27

At two a.m. I'd been having a dream about Fuller. He'd been drunk as usual, and somehow he'd staggered head first through the paper's printing press, which had bleached his body white but also covered him with the print for a new edition of the paper. When he came out the other side, a bunch of equally inebriated news-hounds stood around the Rat and began to read him from head-to-foot.

'I see those murders are still going on,' one of the journalists said, pointing a filthy claw at the print running across the Rat's body. 'It makes you wonder.'

'Makes you wonder what?' another journalist asked.

I never found out what that Rat was wondering, thanks to that alarm clock. Battering it into submission I sat up, wondering what the dream could signify. As I splashed cold water on my face in the bathroom, I decided it was best not to know.

Taking the coffee Jimmy had made, I stood by the window. Parting the blinds, the rain-streaked glass showed a black city, block-upon-block of heavy charcoal shadow. It looked unreal. I didn't want to go out into it.

While I'd slept, Jimmy had sorted through his wardrobe for black clothes. When I was done up head-to-foot he handed me a flashlight. He asked me if I had the skeleton

PART THREE: THE COUNTRY OF THE BLIND

keys. I nodded. He wished me good luck. I told him I'd need it.

Outside, the rain was heavier than it looked on the fourteenth floor, the sidewalks full of puddles. When a drop of rain got under my hood it felt like ice. But I couldn't turn up the collars because they'd bend my whiskers, and I had a funny feeling I might need them tonight. Setting my chin against the rising wind, I made my way through the empty streets.

In the half-hour walk to the paper's offices, I passed only four animals: two Dogs, a Cat and a Bird. If the singing was anything to go by, the Cat and the Bird were drunk. One of the Mutts asked me if I had a light. A handful of cars went by. Way off in the distance a siren wailed and then it went quiet. That was all.

A few minutes later, I was standing in a nook between the paper's office and the building next door. I looked around to check the streets were clear. Then, remembering Jimmy's instructions, I headed for the back of the offices and the underground parking lot. Finding the flight of stairs leading up through it, I was soon at the rear of the ground floor.

Fuller's office was on the fifth, but I couldn't risk being cornered in the elevator. The stairs took a while; at one point my whiskers started to twitch, and I had to duck into an alcove to avoid an elderly Cat with a bucket and a mop muttering about furniture polish. Outside, I saw the rain was still coming down proverbially.

I was standing at the doors outside the office on the fifth floor. I waited a while to see if anything occurred. When nothing did, I slowly opened one of the doors.

Fuller News is situated in a large open-plan office divided into sections by brown, shoulder-high screens. I couldn't see anybody. I listened, but heard nothing. Ducking down, I let the door close slowly behind me. In the Old Days, Jimmy said the place had been a hive of activity, day and night.

THE TERROR AND THE TORTOISESHELL

That was when the papers were daily; now it depended on how drunk Fuller and the other Rats were.

I gave it a few more seconds before making my move. Shuffling along on all fours again felt strange, but I couldn't be certain the place was empty. Keeping as close to the screens as I could, the first couple of desks I passed I saw nothing except piles of candy wrappers and empty soda bottles on tables, every bin overflowing. Beyond the third screen I heard a low muffled noise.

Reluctantly, I shuffled forward a little more and raised my head, just enough to see above the edge of the desk. Immediately, the heel of a shoe blocked my vision. I panicked and was on the brink of saying something when I figured it out.

Following the shoe upwards, I saw the splayed Rodent dozing at the other end of it, its body draped across the chair like crumpled laundry, its other leg balanced on top of the full trash-can. When the Rat snored and its chest rose, I could see the remnants of its dinner splashed across its tie.

The next work space was empty. The one after that contained another comatose Rat. I got a whiff of bourbon and nearly gagged. I crawled away quickly, towards the centre of the room. Straight ahead would take me to the window. To the left were more work spaces. To the right, a room marked EDITOR. Next to that was the room Jimmy said should be the filing office. Deciding to play it safe—a right turn and I'd run a greater risk of being spotted—I headed for the window so I could sneak back along it behind the furthest work screens, then crawl past Fuller's door to the filing office.

Suddenly the room exploded into brilliant whiteness. I reeled back, bumping into the radiator under the window. There was a rumble outside, and the after-effects of the lighting blast stung my eyes. Behind me one the Rats grunted. The gap between the row of partitions and the radiators was

204

PART THREE: THE COUNTRY OF THE BLIND

only perhaps a couple of feet. I crawled my way along it, trying not to bang into the partitions. At the other end I'd be only a few feet from Fuller's office. When I reached the end of it, it felt like I'd run a marathon.

At the door to Fuller's office I raised my head to peer through the glass panel. At first I couldn't see the Rat, only the light from a small *anglepoise* lamp on his desk. Then I saw him, slumped into his under-sized chair as if somebody had squashed him into it. The bottle on the table next to the lamp was two-thirds empty.

I still felt I'd be safer if I shuffled past Fuller's office. While I was kneeling before the door of the filing room, I fished the skeleton keys out of my pocket. Taking one last look back, the office was as quiet as the grave.

I turned the key in the lock slowly. When the tumblers clicked, the noise seemed louder than the clap of thunder that preceded it. Pushing the door softly, I shuffled into the darkness beyond.

As the door closed, I got the flashlight from my other pocket. All of a sudden my whiskers caught a strong smell of furniture polish. I thought I'd caught a waft of it outside too, but in here it was overpowering. Had I wandered into the cleaner's cupboard by mistake? Now that the door was closed, I went to click on my flashlight.

Before I had a chance the room lit up, temporarily blinding me. Instinctively I backed away, shielding my eyes until I fell back against the door. But the light remained, its powerful beam shining right into my eyes. Suddenly a gravelly voice said:

'Ah, skeleton keys, Sir. Aren't they a wonderful thing?'

I stood up slowly, my heart bouncing around inside me. I realised then why the smell of furniture spray was so pungent: it was to disguise the smell of cheap cigars.

28

'Is this what you were looking for, Sir?'
When the after-images from the light left my eyes, I saw Dingus sitting in a chair opposite me, his paw full of papers. When he moved to close the filing cabinet drawer, the light from the *anglepoise* lamp was blotted out.

'How did you know, Dingus?' I asked, awed. 'How *could* you know?'

'We'll talk about that outside, Sir, on the drive to Shefton Heights. But I suggest we get out of here before somebody finds us.'

Before I had a chance to reply, Dingus was standing in the office and I was standing next to him.

'I imagine you crawled round, the same as me,' I whispered to him. 'I think we should—'

The Lieutenant, shaking his head, reached over my shoulder and clicked the light switch, plunging the office into almost total darkness.

'Let's just go,' he said.

He was half-way across the room before I moved. When he turned to see where I was, his eyes lit up like opals in the darkness. To my right, a Rat grunted and I nearly jumped out of my fur. The whole thing was like some bizarre nightmare.

Before stepping into the corridor, Dingus took a can of furniture polish from one of his pockets and gently placed it on a desk.

PART THREE: THE COUNTRY OF THE BLIND

'How did you get the can of polish off the cleaner?' I asked.

'She turned for a second. I forgot until that moment that I'd *need* to mask my smell. I mean, I don't know if I have a distinctive odour or not, but—'

'Oh you do, Dingus, you do. You've started calling me 'Sir' again.'

He gave me one of his earnest, cross-eyed looks. 'I wasn't sure how you'd react to this, Benji.'

He took the five flights of stairs quicker than I would've imagined. It wasn't until we reached the underground parking lot that he finally stopped and bent over, gulping in the damp night air. Together we must've sounded like the makings of an asthmatics' convention.

Out in the open, the rain was still lashing down. I followed Dingus through two empty side streets, and about four hundred puddles which he splashed right through. He'd parked his car at the end of a *cul-de-sac* behind a decent-sized truck. I doubted that had I even been looking for his car I would've spotted it. After wrestling with the lock for a few seconds, the door finally opened and he got in. Leaning across the seat, he released a catch on the passenger door. I got in with a squelch and slammed the door shut. I didn't even give him a chance to get the engine running, firing question-after-question at him.

'Have you finished?' he said when I stopped. I nodded. 'Yes.'

'Okay, first things first. We have to go to your apartment now. I need to speak to Mr. Spriteman.' Dingus revved the engine, and eventually we wobbled out onto the road.

'How long have you known?' I asked.

'About Mr. Spriteman being alive? Ever since the day he came looking for Mr. Dingus.'

'Jimmy said he never found anybody he'd looked for.'

THE TERROR AND THE TORTOISESHELL

'I was there. Me and Mrs. Dingus heard the door being tried in the middle of the night. When we looked down we saw him outside in the back yard. I was of two minds whether to show myself, but I saw that he was raving, talking to himself. If he hadn't been I might have said hello.'

'What happened to Mr. Dingus?'

'Attacked by a mob from the Zoo in the street. I saw it happen. There wasn't a damn thing I could do about it.' He shrugged. Outside, the wipers struggled vainly to sweep rain from the windshield.

'He's in much better condition now, Lieutenant. Jimmy I mean. Had a haircut and everything.'

'Not all the humans were bad,' he carried on, as if I wasn't there. 'I suppose that's why I have to know about these murders. Nobody else seemed interested. To most of the guys in the station it was just a few Sappies. But then Bootsy was killed and it all changed.'

'But how did you know that Jimmy would come to me?'

'He came to me so I figured he'd go to you. Maybe he'd already been to you. When your name appeared in the paper alongside Bootsy's, I thought it was as good a time as any.'

'He called me a few times on the phone. Once he said he even hung around outside Shefton Heights, presumably at night.'

Dingus turned to look at me. 'I've been watching you on and off for days. I never saw him.' So if the bundle of clothes I'd seen in the distance wasn't Jimmy... I laughed so hard I nearly coughed up a fur-ball.

'You never phoned me though. Or did you?' I asked when I'd stopped coughing.

He looked confused. 'No.' So I still had that mystery.

'Jimmy didn't kill those people, Dingus,' I said as the rain bounced off the car's fabric roofing. 'I'd bet my life on that.'

'So would I.'

'You would?'

PART THREE: THE COUNTRY OF THE BLIND

'Certainly. At first I had him in mind as a suspect; there was this strange smell around a few of the crime scenes. It was like somebody was trying to hide something. It got me thinking about what a human would have to do to survive these days. That last time I caught it I smelled really hard. And underneath the other odours, there was a faint trace of Mr. Spriteman.' Dingus's sense of smell was as impressive as everyone said it was. 'In the Old Days he used to come round to us, so I already knew what he smelled like. I still wondered if it might be him, but I began to pick up an older smell at the crime scenes, similar but much denser. As few of the bodies have been found straight away, I thought this older scent was maybe the murderer's.'

To my surprise we were pulling up outside Shefton Heights. Switching off the engine, Dingus carried on talking.

'But that left the question: if he *wasn't* the murderer, what was he doing at the crime scenes? Well, maybe he just wanted to know about the killings so he could protect himself. But I thought no, he's a detective; always will be. He must have his own reason for looking into the murders. And when Bootsy was killed and you were implicated, this strengthened my belief that we were all working on the same case. If so, we needed to pool our resources.'

This seemed like a good time to tell him about Adele and everything else.

'Adele... you know, I remember an Adele being mentioned one day. Don't ever remember seeing her though.' He tapped his mouth. 'So, Mr. Spriteman thinks that all these murders are part of the same thing? Wow.'

That set the cogs in the detective's mind whirring, which became infectious: the little cogs in my brain began spinning as well. Between us, we could have milled flour.

'I think we should go up and see Mr. Spriteman now,' the Lieutenant said eventually.

'In a second. You said you thought Jimmy was alive. But you didn't have him as a suspect.'

Dingus smiled. 'Correct.'

'Which means that—'

'I wanted you to think that *you* were a suspect. That way I could get closer to both of you.'

'So when Bootsy was murdered you had the same idea as Jimmy: to pay me a visit.'

'Unfortunately for Mr. Bootsy, yes.'

'So that business at the morgue was just to see how I would react.'

The Basset Hound smiled. 'Shall we go up now?'

'Hang on. One final question: How did you know I'd be at Fuller's?'

'To be honest, that was luck. As I said, I've been watching you for a while. Mrs. Dingus isn't best pleased with me, I have to say, staying out all hours. When I smelled Mr. Spriteman at your apartment, I decided to keep a permanent watch on you, because if he was wrapped up in this you'd take extra care not to get caught. I saw you heading in the general direction of Fuller's, so I took a chance and a few short-cuts to get there ahead of you. I'd been wanting to have a look in there myself.'

'But you're the Police,' I said. 'Why not go straight in and ask?'

'Because I'm largely playing a hunch. I'd seen that article in the paper about one of the victims working there, and wondered if there was some connection or other. But I didn't want Fuller putting my visit in his rag the next day and messing things up. If the lead led nowhere, Fuller would still make a big deal of it, and I didn't want word getting back to the police what I was up to.'

We left the warmth of Dingus's car for the warmth of the elevator. On the fourteenth floor, I started whistling. Dingus nodded. I opened the door.

PART THREE: THE COUNTRY OF THE BLIND

Jimmy was on the sofa. 'Did you get the files?' he asked as I popped my head around the door.

'No,' I told him. 'But luckily for us, someone else did.'

I moved aside to reveal Dingus with the files in his paw. After the initial shock, Jimmy threw back his head and laughed.

'Son of a gun!' he said.

29

Two hours later, Dingus and Jimmy's reminiscences showed no signs of slowing. I didn't begrudge them their memories, but I began to feel like a fifth wheel. When Jimmy asked what had become of Dingus Senior, I took that as my cue to go to bed. It had been a long and stressful day.

The sun was shining when I woke up, but Jimmy and Dingus were still yapping. I stopped around long enough for a glass of milk and a wash and went out to see if Arnie had had any luck arranging a meet with Reeky McStink. I wasn't sure how it important it was now that Jimmy was in the clear, but decided to go anyway.

It took Arnie even longer than usual to answer.

'What's the matter, Spriteman, you wet the bed?' he said with his usual good grace. 'Wipe your paws before you come in.'

'Still wearing the threads, I see. This your new image, Arnie?'

'Listen,' he said, his eyes like flint, 'they're maybe not as hot as yours, but I wasn't left with the riches you were.'

'What's chafing your hide?' I asked him, remembering my last visit.

' "What's chafing my hide..." ' Arnie shook his wrinkled head. 'I suppose you're here to see if I've found McStink for

PART THREE: THE COUNTRY OF THE BLIND

you. That's all anybody comes by here for; take, take, take.' He swatted a fly that landed on the arm of his chair.

I wasn't in the mood for Arnie's self-pity and was just about to say so when he stared me straight in the eye.

'Since that botched raid of yours on the HFC place, the Skunk and the Porcupine have been laying low. Maybe getting a little culture. You like museums, Spriteman?'

The question took me back. 'Museums?'

'Yeah, museums—old dusty places full of stuffed animals that nobody gives a damn about. Me, I don't see the point. Why have a monument to a past as awful as that? Perhaps *that's* the reason nobody bothers with them much. There's two museums in the city, you know that, Spriteman? There's the new one, full of gadgets and flashing lights which was supposed to keep the kids interested; and then there's the old museum, the dusty one, the one that nobody gave a second glance to even in the Old Days—what such a place must be like now! I mean, who wants to look at stuffed animals when the real thing is walking the streets?'

'Thanks, Arnie,' I said, reaching into my wallet. He stopped me.

'This one's on the house.'

At first I thought he was joking, but his expression told me he wasn't.

'Get out of here before I change my mind.'

So I did. Partly because I found myself in the peculiar situation of being intimidated by a grumpy reptile in a fluffy sweater. Heading back home, I wondered if the two detectives would still be on their nostalgia trip.

I found them both sitting at the coffee table in the living room, which like the floor was covered with reams of paper.

'So,' I asked, 'any developments?'

'Certainly are,' Jimmy said, pouring me a coffee.

'Here's what we know: three of the eight victims were journalists. That's including Adele, who's *definitely* part of this. And thanks to Dingus here, we now have info on three other victims.'

'Two of them I found in the old criminal records at the station,' Dingus said. 'Both for wrecking animal testing labs. They worked together.'

'How long ago?'

'A while ago, admittedly. Then nothing. Perhaps they went further underground, or into some other area of sabotage. My guess is the former.'

'What about the other victim?'

'Now this is an interesting one. After the HFC raid, the officers had a look around. They found some old photographs and old employee records. One of the victims had been an employee when the place was known as 'The Gourmet Club'. He was the assistant manager.'

'Let me guess: he was the victim found outside the HFC.'

'Right. So we have six of the eight victims accounted for. The link is an involvement with animals, albeit in different ways: two trying to save them, the other involved with the carcasses. Then there's the three journalists who all knew each other.'

'But there's no link between the three journalists and the other three victims,' I said. 'That means there might be two separate killers.'

'Possible,' Jimmy put in, 'but unlikely. We think the two journalists must've been working together on some story. Adele was working on 'something big' when she was killed, remember. When she died, perhaps the story was passed to them.'

I wasn't convinced. 'Is there anything in the files to suggest this?'

They both shook their heads. 'Nothing. We went through all that for nothing.'

'So what about Bootsy?' I said. 'Why was I set up?'

PART THREE: THE COUNTRY OF THE BLIND

'Because one or both of you were onto something. Or they thought you were. And then there's Reeky McStink', Jimmy added.

'First of all, there's the body found outside the HFC, which he owns. Then there's the Fido murder. Also, the last victim was done up like a Porcupine.'

'I don't think Reeky McStink has anything to do with this,' I told them. 'I think that whoever *is* responsible is going to a lot of trouble to implicate others.'

Jimmy nodded. 'So do we. But they seem to be spending more time trying to frame Reeky than anyone else.'

'Someone told me he has friends in high places.' Jimmy looked surprised. Dingus did not.

'Wouldn't it be great,' I said, leaning back on the sofa, 'if we could talk to Reeky right now?'

They both looked at me for a few seconds without comprehension. 'He's at the old museum downtown, hiding. I just found out.'

'Son of a gun,' Dingus said around an unlit cigar.

'I used to spend hours in there as a child,' Jimmy said. 'I didn't even know it still existed.'

'A perfect hidey-hole then,' I said.

'Son of a gun,' Dingus repeated.

30

While Jimmy and I talked, Dingus made a few calls to secure backup for our visit to the museum. We all now felt that Reeky could well be the key to the whole thing. At the least he may know who was framing him.

'To be on the safe side, I've kept details of the raid on a strict need-to-know basis,' Dingus said when he got off the phone. 'If we pull Reeky or Eddie it'll be on some minor offence, to begin with. Detective Scragg will be coming along. He's a bit rough round the edges, but a good officer. If we get them to the station, I'll get him out of the way somehow and we can question them properly.'

The day dragged into late afternoon. I went out and got takeaway. On the way, I called in at the office to see if Taki had heard from the Mouse.

'He's sorted everything out,' she told me. 'Mr. Stroheim says he's a natural. Oh, and another surveillance case just came in.'

'The Mouse has sorted what out?' I asked. 'Who is Mr. Stroheim?'

She explained, as if to a little kitten, that he was the client she'd told me about. She handed me a couple of sheets of paper. 'His report,' she said.

'His *what?*' I sat on the edge of Taki's desk and read through the Mouse's 'report'.

PART THREE: THE COUNTRY OF THE BLIND

'He's better at this than I am,' I muttered. Taki, the soul of discretion, carried on typing. 'And you say there's another one come in?'

'Just. Mr. Stroheim put a colleague of his onto us, thanks to the Mouse.'

After phoning the Spayley's and giving Number One Mouse the details of his new assignment, I went and got the food. On the way home, sections of the Mouse's report flashed before my eyes.

Late afternoon dragged into early, then late-evening. We ate, played cards and talked about the case. Long after midnight, the phone rang. Answering it, I passed it onto the Lieutenant.

'It's all set,' he told us.

I'd put off talking to Jimmy until the last minute. It was pretty obvious that he couldn't come along, but the look on his face told us he wasn't too happy about it.

'It'd be madness,' I said.

'I know it would. So, I'll stay put in this coop like a good little Hen.' He sighed.

'You should try and get some sleep,' I told him.

'Too much coffee. Good luck.' He offered me his hand and I offered him my paw. His palm was red hot. For a second, my head spun.

The Municipal Museum is perhaps the most innocuous building the city has to offer. Grey, weather-beaten and set well away from the roadside, it's the kind of building you could walk past every day of your life and only notice when it wasn't there anymore. Ergo: the perfect hiding place.

As soon as we pulled up, a Labrador in uniform came over to Dingus's car. 'I got the plans for you, Lieutenant,' the Dog said.

Dingus unrolled the large sheet of laminated card across his lap, nodded once or twice, then got out of the car, going over towards a small knot of officers who pointed at the building when Dingus spoke to them.

THE TERROR AND THE TORTOISESHELL

'Would you believe the doors are *open?*' he said when he came back to the car.

'What?'

'The boys have been up and had a look. Every door is unlocked.'

'If Arnie's leading me a merry dance—'

'I don't think so. I'd say they'll definitely be in there, just not where anybody would think of looking.'

Dingus slouched up to the entrance in his usual manner. At the door he turned.

'Come on, Benji. It's perfectly safe.'

Behind me, several officers with guns took a few paces forward. I looked back at Dingus.

'Are you crazy?' I hissed.

'The officers have already been in and had a look around. Apart from the exhibits, there's nobody there.'

'So why are we going in?'

The Lieutenant grabbed my ear. 'Because,' he whispered, 'my guess is the vault isn't empty.'

'But—' I grabbed one of Dingus's oversized lugholes. It was like holding a large hairy lettuce leaf. 'If that's the case, they'll probably be armed.'

'I know,' Dingus said, still holding my ear. 'That's why we've got three officers in the main part of the building and five more covering the back stairs outside the vault. Also,' letting go of my ear, he removed something from one of his depthless coat pockets and handed it to me, 'we're armed too.'

I looked stupidly down at the gun and let go of his ear, which slapped back against his face like a wet towel. Since the Ed Mahoney thing, I'd gone off guns.

'Let's go,' Dingus said.

Inside, the lobby was dark and cold, the only welcome coming from several million dust particles swirling in the air around us. Despite this, the place had a definite odour of

PART THREE: THE COUNTRY OF THE BLIND

furniture polish and disinfectant, and a musty smell like the paperbacks at my apartment, but much worse. To our left, a wood and metal staircase spiralled up through the ceiling. At the top of it, a Bloodhound crouched with a rifle.

Ahead was a door which must've been twelve feet high, all dark wood and brass fittings. With a bit of squeezing, we got through without raising any squeaks from it. Immediately I inhaled another mouthful of dust; Dingus sneezed into his raincoat. He wiped his wet black nose into an off-white handkerchief he pulled from another of his unseen pockets.

The main exhibit room was at a guess fifty feet long, although with nearly every available space packed solid I could be way off the mark. The only light came from a series of tiny rectangular windows set high into the walls. We both had flashlights but were reluctant to use them. From the walls, glass eyes embedded in large, disembodied, moth-eaten heads gazed across to the heads on the opposite side of the room. Beneath each head a small brass plaque informed you what type of animal the head had belonged to—a Moose with wilting antlers here, an Elephant with a broken tusk that looked like an enormous chipped tooth there—both affronts no doubt perpetrated by the same individuals responsible for tipping several large display cases off their tables, littering the floor with shards of glass that glittered in the moonlight.

Dingus moved forward, so I did the same. I watched him step over the puddles of glass fragments, the stuffed Panda that looked like it'd tried to break free of its glass case, ancient stuffing oozing from the hole in its back like foam from a gutter.

The gaps between the remaining upstanding tables and exhibits were so narrow we had to walk single file, squeezing past suits of dull, unpolished armour, splintered tables and waist-high boxes inexplicably covered with cloth. When Dingus pulled up with a cry, I went crashing into the back

THE TERROR AND THE TORTOISESHELL

of him. Before I could ask, his flashlight clicked on and I saw him trying to extricate one of his scuffed shoes from a Crocodile's mouth. Pulling it free, he carried on, killing the light. Warily, I kept my distance.

I was looking at a pile of cannonballs on the floor and wondering where the cannon had got to, when I heard snuffling noises. Ahead, I saw Dingus with his nose pressed up against a torn poster on the wall, an ancient piece of yellow paper informing patrons where to meet in case of fire. Tentatively, he began to lift a corner of the poster, and nodded as he lifted. Then, with a sudden movement, he yanked the poster away from the wall to reveal a small door underneath.

'You smelled them out?' I said. 'Through a locked door?'

'I know someone who met Reeky once,' Dingus whispered. 'He said he wasn't called Reeky for nothing. Apparently the Porcupine isn't much better.' He turned back and cast his flashlight across the room. 'You know, this place is perfect—anyone could come in here, do what they liked and they wouldn't know what was below.'

'What exactly is below?'

'The crypt, or vault. It's full of redundant exhibits or stuff that was being repaired.' As he spoke, his nose began to quiver.

'Move back,' he whispered. 'The smell's getting stronger.'

Before we had a chance to move the handle of the small door began to drop and the door eased open.

'This is the Police,' Dingus called out.

'We know it's the Police,' a low, starchy voice said on the other side of the door. 'We've been waiting for you.'

When the door swung open, there was nobody in the doorway. Small steps pattered back down into the gloom. 'It's okay, we ain't gonna shoot you,' the voice called back up.

'I've heard Reeky can be quite volatile,' Dingus told me, 'so let me do the talking.'

PART THREE: THE COUNTRY OF THE BLIND

'Fine by me. Lead the way,' I told him.
Before going down, he waved a paw in the air. As if by magic, an armed Bulldog appeared from behind a human skeleton. Turning, I saw Dingus swallowed up in the black maw of the doorway, his feet clapping down on the stone steps. I followed. Immediately, something unpleasant wafted up towards me. Hearing voices below, I stopped.
'What's all this about, Dingus?' A new voice said.
'Well, Sir, we need to speak to you about a few things, and—'
'What sort of things?'
'We could start with the Human Food Club, if you'd like.'
'Oh, that. Okay, grab a pew.'
Going down the rest of the stairs, their conversation seemed to be drowned out by the smell coming from below. It was rank. I took a deep breath and stepped into the room beyond.
'Hey, who's this?'
The smell was so strong I was sure they'd be closer, but Reeky McStink and Eddie the Quill where both a good ten, twelve feet away. Dingus was standing roughly six feet from Eddie. I wondered how that powerful hooter of his could stand it.
Eddie the Quill was about six-and-a-half feet tall, and so filthy that even standing still he looked like he was moving. Among the varying lengths of his black and white quills, small blue eggs nestled, looking like they could hatch on request. To complete the effect, an assortment of small ticks and parasites scuttled around and over them. His snub nose was full of whiskers like plucked guitar strings, and his eyes were small and black, as was the rest of his head. I thought I saw something leap from him to the floor, but when I looked there was nothing. For such a large animal he had surprisingly small feet.
Reeky McStink was slightly shorter, just under six feet. His fur, which was short, bristly and mainly black, was

broken up by the series of vivid white blotches and hoops that ran up and across his body. The one between his eyes resembled a target; so did the pair under each ear. Between his legs was a tail thicker than a witch's broom.

Dingus ignored Eddie's question. 'I'd much rather we had this conversation downtown, Reeky.'

'I'm sure you would,' Reeky replied. 'Me, I'd rather stay here, among the exhibits.' He waved a paw tipped with five vicious-looking claws around him. 'You should see what they got in the next room, Dingus; looks like a dinosaur in kit form—Hey! What the Hell was that?'

Outside there was a loud bang, then another, and another. Reeky glared at Dingus.

'I asked you a question: What was that?'

'I don't know, Sir.' Dingus told him. The Skunk did not look impressed.

'Well, Lieutenant,' the atmosphere changed, the Skunk's mood becoming ugly, 'if you wanted me to go downtown that much, you should've said.'

'That's nothing to do with us, Reeky. It's just kids with firecrackers, or—'

Dingus's words were drowned out as a large chunk of plaster dropped from a nearby wall, rapidly followed by a pane of glass above an outer door. '*What on earth do you think you are doing, Officer?*' a voice outside yelled.

Reeky turned to face us. 'You brought Scragg *here?*' The Skunk started to turn its back. From the corner of my eye, I saw Dingus putting a large handkerchief to his face.

'Benji, get up the stairs,' he said as he backed away towards the staircase. Just as a face appeared in the doorway above, Reeky began to stamp his paws furiously.

Eddie's reaction to this was immediate. As Reeky raised his tail in our direction he shot past us into one of the vault's side rooms. Then Reeky lifted one of his legs, and sprayed.

Before my eyes stung with tears, I saw the spray of liquid shoot across the eight or nine feet between us. I just had

PART THREE: THE COUNTRY OF THE BLIND

time enough to side step it, watching as it splatted against the wall, the pale green paint bubbling on impact as if it had been blow-torched. Then the smell kicked in, a smell to which no words could ever do justice. I stuck both paws over my mouth, fearing the stench might corrode my gullet like the spray was corroding the paint on the wall. Stumbling backwards, I bumped against the bottom step of the vault. Virtually blinded, I crawled my way up. I was near the top of the stairs when somebody grabbed my paws and yanked me through the door, slamming it shut behind me. I lay with my back against the door, coughing and wiping my eyes. When my vision cleared, I could make out Dingus doing the same.

'You didn't get any on you?' he asked between splutters.

'The wall got my share,' I told him.

While we both sat on the floor hacking away like a couple of codgers, I heard the racket below; gunshots, screams, noises like heavy furniture being thrown about. An officer came over and asked us if we were okay. Dingus asked him what had happened. The officer said all he knew was that one of the other officers thought he saw something and started firing, and after that everybody joined in. He also told us that one officer had been spiked by Eddie the Quill, but he'd live.

As we went outside, Scragg was bundling Reeky and Eddie into the back of a van. Seconds later, an ambulance pulled up. Not overly keen on the sight of blood at the best of times, I suggested to Dingus we follow Scragg back to the station.

Dingus nodded and we left without saying a word.

31

When we arrived at the station, the first thing Dingus did was ask for tomato juice.

'Tomato juice, Sir?' The desk sergeant said.

'Tomato juice, yes. As much of it as you can get. Oh, and a paint gun. Let me know when you get them. I'll be in my office.'

Puzzled, the sergeant went to look for tomato juice.

Dingus ushered me into an office nearly as small and shabby as his car. The walls were painted battleship grey, there were cigar stains on the ceiling, paper everywhere. Finding me a chair he told me to sit down.

'*That*,' he said, 'did not go as planned.' Opening a desk drawer he pulled out an almost comically thick cigar and set fire to it. The smell was even more horrific than his usual cigars, but in comparison to the smell that emerged from under the Skunk's tail, it was like a flower garden.

'Reeky really didn't want to be brought in, did he? Any particular reason, you think?'

'To do with the murders? I just don't think he liked being surprised.'

There was a knock at the door.

'Yes!' Dingus shouted out.

'Sir, we found some tomato juice.'

'Really? How much?'

PART THREE: THE COUNTRY OF THE BLIND

'There's a barrel in the canteen, sir. But I think it's been there a long while.'

'It doesn't matter.' Dingus shouted again at the closed door. 'Which room is Reeky being held in?'

'Interview room six, Lieutenant.'

'Okay. Take it there. Tell Detective Scragg I'll be along in a minute.'

In the corridor I asked the obvious question.

'You don't know about tomato juice? Tomato juice and Skunks?' I shook my head. 'Well of course I haven't tried it out, but apparently tomato juice neutralises the odour that Skunks produce.'

'How on earth did somebody find that out?'

'I don't know. Ah, here we are.'

Ahead of us, two officers were awkwardly rolling a barrel down the corridor. Stopping at interview room six, one of them knocked on the door. When he opened it, Scragg looked incredulously at the officers, down at the large container of juice, then back at the officers again.

'It's okay, Scragg,' Dingus called out. 'Let them in.' With some reluctance, Scragg held the door open.

'Are you expecting Reeky to try anything?' I asked.

'We can't be too careful after what just happened,' Dingus said. 'I think we'll pay Eddie a visit first. Where is he, Detective Scragg?'

Eddie was in interview room nine, the room I'd been questioned in about a million years ago. Inside, I saw that the room had been significantly altered to accommodate the new prisoner.

Eddie the Quill, a vicious killer under normal circumstances, looked strangely child-like sitting behind the large Perspex screen that divided the room in two. This was due in no small part to the huge piece of rubber sheeting that had been wound several times round his body and then fastened with cuffs on either side. He now looked like a swiss roll whose filling had gone bad.

THE TERROR AND THE TORTOISESHELL

'What's this, Benton?' Dingus asked the officer in the room, pointing towards the glass.

'It's all we had at such short notice, sir. But you can hear every word he says.'

'I meant the rubber sheet—where did you get it from?'

'Er, from the gymnasium, sir.'

'*You wrapped Eddie the Quill in a crash-mat?*' I remarked, pointing needlessly.

'We've never had to deal with anything like this before,' the officer said defensively, looking to Dingus for approval.

'Okay, okay. It doesn't matter. Well done, Benton.' The officer relaxed slightly.

Dingus walked over to the screen and looked down at the Porcupine. 'You nearly killed an officer in the museum, Eddie.'

'I could get outta this any time I wanted,' the Porcupine said, his voice slightly muffled through the Perspex.

'Now what I'm wanting to know,' Dingus began to fidget with the huge cigar, 'is why you and Reeky would go to such lengths to avoid talking to me.'

'It's only made of rubber, you know,' Eddie said, looking down at himself. 'If I flexed a bit—' as Eddie did so, dozens of quill points pressed through from the other side of the rubber. 'See?' Dingus, unimpressed, re-lit his cigar.

'You see, the way it looks now, Eddie, you have more to hide than what went on at the Human Food Club.'

'I think when I get outta here I'm going to make a complaint. You know it took three of your clowns to pull that cop off my back? He was stuck like glue. I lost a lotta quills.'

Dingus took the cigar from his mouth, looked at it thoughtfully and stubbed it out on the edge of the table. 'Okay, have it your way. See you later, Eddie.'

'I think he only knows what Reeky tells him,' the Lieutenant said as we headed for interview room six. I was inclined to agree.

PART THREE: THE COUNTRY OF THE BLIND

'He was probably right about that crash-mat though.'

'Yes,' Dingus replied cheerfully. 'He probably was.'

Approaching interview room six, we heard raised voices inside. After seeing Eddie, I wondered how Reeky could have been pacified.

It was a surprise to see Reeky M^{C}Stink sat in a chair opposite Detective Scragg, with no plastic sheet between them; but not that surprising when you actually saw what Reeky was wearing.

At some point during his brief stay at police headquarters, Reeky M^{C}Stink, the cities' greatest villain, its most shadowy and enigmatic figure, had been put, to all intents and purposes, in a diaper; several large white sheets had been wound and fastened through and over his legs, then stretched across his midriff. To complete the indignity, several large safety pins had been clipped to the sheets to keep them in place. I looked over at Dingus with more admiration than I could express.

'You sly old Dog,' I muttered out of the corner of my mouth.

Across from Reeky, Scragg looked as if he was ready to blow a gasket. Evidently, he was getting nowhere. Just behind the door, a bored-looking officer stood next to the open barrel of tomato juice, waving a paint gun (presumably filled with juice) in Reeky's general direction.

'I was just asking the Skunk here about the Human Food Club,' Scragg said. 'Asking where he got all that meat from, isn't that right, Reeky?'

'Is this "good cop, bad cop" I see before me?' the Skunk replied with as much dignity as he could muster. 'Now I've heard about Dingus and I know he couldn't *possibly* be the bad cop.' He turned his eyes to Scragg. 'So that means—'

'*I'm warning you, M^{C}Stink!*' Scragg stuck his face right into the Skunk's. 'I still haven't forgotten what I ended up covered in at that restaurant of yours.'

THE TERROR AND THE TORTOISESHELL

'Looks to me like you've brought a vat of it along with you,' Reeky replied, nodding at the barrel.

'Why you—' Scragg lunged at Reeky, who I'd only just noticed was cuffed to the table. Again he went eyeball to eyeball with McStink. Beside me, the officer waved the gun full of tomato juice.

'Scragg here just threatened to shoot me if I sprayed him, Lieutenant,' Reeky told Dingus. 'And I don't think he meant with the contents of that drum.'

Scragg held his position next to Reeky, his eyes starting from his head. Dingus went over and patted him on the back, whispered in his ear. 'Be back in a minute,' Dingus told me as they both left the room.

When he returned he was alone, the cigar once more alight. Taking the seat that Scragg had just vacated, he took the cigar from his mouth and placed it in the ashtray on the table.

'I don't have to ask you what you've been discussing with Detective Scragg. I was wondering if perhaps we could go back a bit further.'

'It's your party, Lieutenant. Any particular period in time interest you?'

'Well... there are lot of things we could talk about. I mean, you've become very successful since everything changed.'

'That's true,' Reeky said affably.

'And, I would imagine that kind of success must bring jealousy—by this I mean business rivals, that kind of thing.'

This time the Skunk was less cocky when he replied. 'Go on.'

'Well, let's take an example. I'm sure you heard about the tragic death of Fido the Fisherman. I believe you and he were quite close, at one stage?'

'It's an interesting theory, Lieutenant. Go on.'

'The things is, Mr. McStink, that Fido the Fisherman happened to be a suspect in these Sappy killings. That was

PART THREE: THE COUNTRY OF THE BLIND

until we found him full of holes, holes identical to the ones received by an Officer of ours just now. *Then,* we find another Sappy victim. As you'll no doubt know, these poor Humans have been made to look like animals. Well, this one, he's been made to look like an animal with sharp quills... It's as though the two things are related. So I looked for a common factor in these events, and guess what I came up with? You. You are the common factor.'

McStink tried leaning back in his chair but the cuffs stopped him. 'I wondered what the real reason was for all this.'

Dingus leaned across the table. 'Did you or someone in your organisation kill those Sappies, Reeky?'

'No. Definitely not.'

'So somebody is trying to set you up. Any ideas who that might be?'

'I've heard the law are pretty good at that sort of thing,' Reeky deadpanned.

'Not if you're in as deep with them as I think you are.' Dingus rose and walked slowly around the room, chewing on his cigar. It took nearly another five minutes before Reeky eventually spoke.

'Okay, Dingus, I'll level with you. Sure, I've got enemies, but nobody who would go to that trouble.'

'Not even if you were looking for the Sappy killer yourself?'

'Why would I want to look for the Sappy killer?'

'Because you have friends in high places. Because there could be something in it for you.'

Reeky shook his head. 'Uh-huh. I'll admit I'm interested who the killer is *now,* but that's only because they're trying to set me up.'

'Did you know any of the victims?'

'Nope. How could I?'

'Detective Bootsy?'

THE TERROR AND THE TORTOISESHELL

'Nope again.'

I decided to have a go. 'After the HFC raid somebody took a few pot-shots at me, then tried to flatten me with a car. Know anything about that?'

'If you don't mind me asking, who the hell *are you?*'

'This, Reeky, is Benji Spriteman. He's a private investigator. And like you, somebody tried to frame him for the murders.'

'Looks to me, Lieutenant, like somebody is going to a lot of trouble to cover their tracks.' Reeky tried leaning back again, but the cuffs stopped him. 'Are these things really necessary?' he asked.

Dingus carried on, ignoring the question. 'Did you know that the body found outside the HFC was a former, pre-Terror employee?'

That surprised him. 'No.'

'And that evening nobody who works for you heard or saw anything strange?'

'Me, I wasn't there. I was hiding out in the museum with Eddie. You can check that out with him. The restaurant was closed that night, we always shut midweek. Next morning a member of staff told me what they'd found—I said to leave it where it was and for everyone to get the hell out of there to be on the safe side. I knew you guys were waiting for an excuse to get me. Then I heard that some Old Cat started rummaging round the bins, made a lot of noise. When somebody went over to see what all the fuss was, that's when they found him.'

Dingus leaned back in his chair and nodded. 'So let's get back to Fido. Did you consider him a rival?'

'Hell, no.'

'Perhaps he considered himself one.' Dingus suggested. 'Perhaps he had to be taught a lesson.'

Reeky leaned as far forward as the cuffs would allow, his voice low. 'We're all capable of getting above ourselves,

PART THREE: THE COUNTRY OF THE BLIND

Lieutenant. In any business—any world even—there has to be a pecking order. If somebody in that business were to forget their place, they would have to be dealt with in an appropriate fashion.'

Dingus, finishing his comedy-sized cigar, took one of his regulars from his raincoat. Undoing the cellophane wrapper, he continued. 'Let's get back to these murders. Why would whoever's killing these Humes go to the trouble of setting you up, Reeky?'

Reeky changed and we got a brief glimpse of his temper. 'Because they're insane! Who cares? It's only a few dead Sappies, right? What possible good would it do me to hunt them down; go to that kind of trouble to kill them? Look Dingus, I've helped you all I can. Am I free to leave now? As far as I can see, all you have me on is breaking and entering the museum.'

Dingus appeared to think about it. 'Detective Scragg will be back soon, I'll let him decide. Goodbye, Reeky.' Dingus headed for the door. With his paw on the handle, he turned and faced the Skunk one final time. 'Oh, just one more thing: What would somebody have to do to warrant a visit from Eddie? Theoretically speaking, of course.'

Reeky, realising he was in the clear, warmed to the subject. 'Of course. Well, theoretically... I'll give you an example. Recently I had dealings with someone who... how can I put this... said they could acquire for me certain information in exchange for a cash payment. Let's call them Animal A for the sake of things. But Animal A reneged on the deal; such a situation would require a visit from Eddie. So Eddie goes to see Animal A. Animal A then tells Eddie that he has information which could prove useful to me, if he's treated leniently. Another individual in my employ—let's call him Animal B—is on the take behind my back... well, I'm faced with a dilemma: whose crime is the worst? I have to make a decision. I decide that because Animal A gave me some interesting information on Animal B, he would now get a lighter punishment than the one Eddie may have originally intended; instead, *that* punishment would be transferred to Animal B, who has nothing interesting to tell me. You know, Lieutenant,' the Skunk said, grinning, 'I can't see me requiring Mr. Quill's services any longer. He has an awful temper, you know. And the smell gets to you after a while.'

Dingus chuckled. 'Be seeing you around, Reeky.'

'Not if I can help it, Lieutenant.' Reeky said as I closed the door.

In interview room nine, we found Scragg working on the Porcupine. In the corridor, Dingus told Scragg to charge Eddie the Quill with the murder of Fido the Fisherman, and to release Reeky M^{C}Stink.

'Are you crazy?' Scragg said, beginning to simmer. 'Every villain in the city will think we're a soft touch. He'll tell all his associates that we—'

'He'll tell them nothing, because he knows that word would get around that while in police custody we had him chained to a desk wearing a nappy. Pictures can be taken, Scragg. In fact, perhaps you could do just that after you've charged Eddie? And then, perhaps, you could question Mr. M^{C}Stink in your own inimitable way. I don't believe there'd be any need to rush...' Scragg dashed down the corridor with a dirty grin on his face, first to give Eddie the good news, and then presumably to get a camera. As Dingus and I walked back to his office, he noticed the smirk on my face.

'You know, Dingus, Reeky *is* interested in the murders. But he has nothing whatever to do with them.' I started to laugh.

'Oh? What's so funny about that?'

'What's funny Dingus, is the fact that for once I know something you don't.'

32

I KEPT DINGUS IN SUSPENSE all through lunch and then crashed out in one of the cells for a few hours while he attended to something else. By the time we met up and went to Dingus's car, it was already dusk.

'Okay, the suspense is killing me. What is this thing you know?'

We were heading through town and I was surprised that he hadn't figured it out. I told him to keep driving. I'd let him know when we got there. It was nice to be holding the aces for a while. As we neared Ronson Towers, I told him to pull into the parking lot.

I was out of the car and halfway to the lobby before Dingus had secured the boneshaker.

'Let me do the talking,' I told him in the elevator.

I hammered Arnie's door like a plain full of Buffalo wanted in. Not surprisingly, Arnie appeared at the door quicker than usual.

I didn't give him a chance to speak. As soon as the door opened I barged inside and grabbed him by the jersey.

'What kind of deal were you doing with McStink, Arnie?' I said, pulling up his grubby sweater.

Sure enough, his scrawny little body was covered in bruises. Dingus stepped in, closed the door.

'Hello, Arnie,' he said.

THE TERROR AND THE TORTOISESHELL

'You two know each other?' I said with a paw full of wool. Again, I felt like my thunder had been stolen.

'Everybody knows Arnie, Benji. Even Reeky McStink, apparently.' Dingus turned to me, his squint worse than usual.

'You must've upset Reeky pretty bad for him to do that to you,' I said. 'We've just been talking to him. When he said somebody welched on a deal with him I thought of you straight away. He also said he didn't know who was setting him up for the Sappy killings. Did you do that, Arnie? Is that why he got rough?'

'No!' Arnie's voice went up a notch. 'I never did that!'

'I think you've been playing both ends off the middle, Arnie: passing information to McStink and selling the dirt on him too. When he found out, he sent the Porcupine round to sort you out. But you gave him some hogwash about Fido and that took the heat off you. So you're implicated in Fido's murder, Arnie. Unless you start talking.'

'Okay, okay!' he whined. He flattened the jersey back over his scaly body. When he spoke, his voice had lost its usual snarl.

'Okay—I did go back on a deal with Reeky—or at least he thinks I did. In truth, there wasn't a deal there in the first place. I just made him think there was. I told him I knew who the killer was.'

I looked at Dingus and he looked back at me. 'What?'

'But I didn't know, honestly. Reeky was so desperate for any kind of information; well, he told me it would be worth my while. He even gave me money in advance. I got greedy. It would get him in even thicker with the big boys down at the cop-shop if he told them who the killer was.'

'So you didn't know anything about the killer?'

'I knew some things, but my contact ran out on me. I realised he was stringing me along the way I was stringing Reeky along. Then Reeky tumbled me. I offered to give

PART THREE: THE COUNTRY OF THE BLIND

the money back, but it was too late for that. I'd made a fool of him.'

'So you ratted on Fido.'

Arnie gulped. 'I felt bad about that, because I was dealing with him as well. Hey, don't look at me like that! I had to do something!'

'What was this information on the killer you thought you had?'

Arnie smiled a crooked little smile and shook his head. 'I went into the wrong business, I see that now. If I'd gone over to your side... Well, let's just say I'm a natural at this kind of thing.'

'You're waffling, Arnie.'

'I got the idea after that murder on the seventh.' He talked as if we weren't there. 'You lot didn't seem to be getting anywhere, so I thought: What if I found this sicko myself? It must be worth something to somebody. So I kept my ears open. I was pretty well in with Reeky at that point; a bit of information here, a bit there... I thought I could find whoever it was, no problem. Boy, what a dummy.' He shook his shrivelled head, laughed a bit more, then carried on.

'I went to Fuller, see if he was interested. The only thing he was interested in was making the Police look foolish; as long as it was only Sappies buying it, it didn't matter.

'But when Bootsy got it, things changed. I went back to Fuller and suggested that perhaps the supply of Sappies had run dry and the killer had taken to killing animals. Suddenly he was interested. But then the other Sappy got iced and Fuller said that Bootsy's killing was just a copycat job.' He stopped, appeared to think about something, then carried on. 'Well, it's not down to me any more, so I may as well tell you: that latest victim worked in the lab, the same lab as the other two.'

He started jabbering about how the game was over for him when I pulled him back. 'Hang on, Arnie; what lab?'

THE TERROR AND THE TORTOISESHELL

'You don't even know about the lab?' Arnie roared, his tiny head wobbling around like it was on a spring. 'Hell, the money I coulda made from you two! Three of the victims were animal rights protesters. They infiltrated the lab to try and stop what was going on there.'

'Arnie, *what* lab? Not the one by the canal?'

'I don't think so. That's where my source let me down. He told me I'd find the killer in this lab. When I asked where the lab was and what went on there, he got all coy on me. That's why Reeky gave me the going over: I thought I'd be able to get the information out of my source, but he didn't cough up. I arranged to meet him, but he stood me up.'

'Suppose you tell us who this source is,' I said.

'Suppose you cross my palm with silver first,' he replied, a glint in his eye like the Arnie I knew.

We both dug in and gave the Tortoise the cash. Shoving it under his sofa he looked up, smiled. For once, Arnie was enjoying himself.

'You know Spriteman, it's interesting to see you palling up with Dingus here. And me your mutual friend; not that either of you knew about that. But Dingus isn't our only mutual friend. Now; how about you two sit back, because I'm gonna tell you a story.'

33

'So, describe this Flipper to me.'

As Dingus spoke, an oncoming car honked for us to get out of the middle of the road. When it passed us, a large black and white head screamed something out of the window.

'He's a crazy old coot who lives by the river. A few times I've wondered if he really is as crazy as he makes out. If he isn't, it's a good act. He—oh God.'

Dingus glanced over at me. 'What?'

I didn't want to, but I told him anyway. 'Whenever I saw him I used to tell him what was going on—you know, the SPCH, the murders, the whole bit. He'd shake his head and say how terrible it all sounded. But he already *knew!* And then the night I was... I told him everything.' How much use everything I knew was to him I didn't know, but I should've kept it shut nonetheless. 'He has this trick of knowing you're there without looking up. He's interesting, funny, *unpolluted*, in a way, like some Old Cat who just happens to be standing on two legs.'

It sounded like Arnie had felt the same way; at first. He said he'd been sniffing around one of the crime scenes when this 'crazy old dude with a bad odour' turned up, and they'd got talking. They were both interested in the murders, only in Flipper's case it was more curiosity than anything. Every once in a while he'd throw things into the conversation that gave the impression he knew a lot more than Arnie did. And Arnie, not being one to miss a trick, began piecing these things together.

'Then he told me he not only knew *who* the murderer was, but *where* he was,' Arnie had said. 'Reckoned he was in some lab or other. I asked if he meant the lab by the canal that did the surgery, but he shook his head. He said he'd tell me next time we met up and arranged a meeting. In the meantime I asked around, see if anybody knew of this lab. Apart from the one at the canal, I drew a blank. I wondered if he'd been bluffing me the whole time. He never even showed up for our meeting.'

I'd asked Arnie why he thought Flipper was so willing to divulge information if he wasn't getting anything from it himself.

'I thought about that for a while and came to the conclusion *who cares?* All I could think about was the money. But when he talked about it he was more animated. My guess is he was enjoying himself, like it was all some kinda game.'

They'd arrange to meet by the river. 'Always by the river'—the same place I met him.

"...he was enjoying himself, like it was all some kinda game."

Dingus looked across again. 'Pardon me?'

'I was just thinking about what Arnie said, about Flipper treating it all like a game. Do you think Flipper knew who Arnie was, and what he did?'

'Looks that way. And think about this, Benji: *What if he knew that you knew Arnie?*'

At that moment, a giant idea shifted from the back of my head to the front: *And that everything Arnie said would get back to me?*

Suddenly it made sense: the silent calls, being framed for Bootsy's murder. Something else occurred to me.

PART THREE: THE COUNTRY OF THE BLIND

'Flipper's owner,' I said quietly. 'And they live in the middle of nowhere.'

'What?'

'Flipper mentioned his owner a few times. I assumed he'd been killed or run off or something like that. But *Flipper* never said that; he'd have no reason to run. Which means that Jimmy's right after all: the killer has to be a Human.'

'So Flipper's owner is the killer,' Dingus said, almost chewing his unlit cigar in half, 'and Flipper's his accomplice, helping his owner by trying to pin the murders on others: you, Reeky—no doubt he'd have got round to Arnie at some point. But he made sure that you found out, Benji. Why?'

At first it wouldn't come, and then I had it. 'Adele,' I said. 'Jimmy said the murders started pre-Terror with Adele as the first victim. Which means Flipper's owner knew I was Jimmy's cat.'

'But why not leave things as they were?'

'Because Flipper's owner is crazy. He has to be to do all this. It's all part of the game.'

'You don't think that—no, no, no. Forget it.'

'What?'

'Well, suppose that Flipper's owner knows that Jimmy's still alive?'

A chill went through me. 'But how?'

'I don't know. Did you say you've been in this Flipper's house?'

'That was the night I told him everything I knew. Bootsy had just been killed and I got drunk down at Minsky's. Then I went for a walk by the river and ended up at Flipper's.'

'You were drunk? I thought Cat's couldn't drink.'

'As a rule, they can't. When I got there, Flipper opened a bottle of scotch and put some in my tea. Evidently it doesn't have the same effect on all of us.'

'What was the house like?'

THE TERROR AND THE TORTOISESHELL

'A mess. The whole place was like a library, books everywhere. But I didn't notice what any of them were about.'

'No lab? No sign of Flipper's owner? No smell?'

'Not where I ended up. But there could've been a spaceship parked in back and I wouldn't have noticed. That's how far gone I was. I paid for it though.'

'How?'

I told him about the crazy dream I'd had, the animals stretching, the whole bit. As I told it, Dingus finally managed to bite through his cigar, which unfortunately for him was now lit. With speed worthy of an Old Cat, he swept the lit end from his lap and out of the window.

'Doesn't that dream sound familiar to you, Benji?'

I told him it didn't. Neither did I want it to.

'All those animals growing so quickly? Benji, it sounds like The Terror.'

Again, I had goose-bumps all over me.

'Are you sure it was a dream?' he said eventually.

'What do you mean?'

'Well, I don't know a lot about alcohol; me and Mrs. Dingus have been tipsy a few times but nothing like that ever happened. Are you sure it was just whisky he put in your tea?'

'I can't be certain. You think he spiked my drink?'

'It's possible. If that was a dream you had, it was incredibly vivid. Maybe it wasn't a dream.' He went quiet for a while. 'Do you think that there's a lab at Flipper's place?'

'Must be,' I said. 'And if not there, somewhere close by. Flipper's owner couldn't risk going too far, and that place is pretty isolated.'

Dingus pulled up sharply at the side of the road. 'Look, there's a phone booth. We should phone Jimmy and tell him what's happening. He might even be able to tell us who this guy is.'

PART THREE: THE COUNTRY OF THE BLIND

'He won't answer it in case it's somebody else.' I told him. 'We'll have to go up there instead. It'll only take a few minutes.'

I managed to get the pair of snooty Persians to hold the elevator while Dingus caught up. When they saw him coming towards them with his cigar and dirty Trench Coat, they took the stairs instead. There was a ghost in the place that night pressing buttons, because the elevator stopped and opened its door at every other floor, but nobody got in. Finally, we arrived on the fourteenth.

Opening the door to the apartment, I heard the shrill ring of the telephone. For some inexplicable reason I had the feeling it had been ringing for some time. Something began to crawl in my stomach. I opened the door to the living room. Jimmy wasn't there; he was probably in the bathroom or lying down. I went over to the phone, picked up the receiver.

'*I did think about Dennings Lane again but that would've been predictable*', the distorted voice said. '*Then I thought, why not take them back to the scene of the last crime? I remembered seeing a charming old office building quite close to the funfair that seemed appropriate. The things you find in these empty office blocks...*'

Before I had a chance to speak the line went dead.

Dropping the phone to the floor I raced into the bathroom, hoping to find him there. He wasn't. I tried the bedroom, the kitchen, even the closets with increasing desperation. There was no sign of Jimmy anywhere. Dingus was behind me asking what was wrong but I couldn't tell him; half formed thoughts flitted through my brain, each one worse than the last.

'Jimmy,' I managed eventually. 'They've got Jimmy.'

34

THE DRIVE TO THAT office block was the longest drive of my entire life. Neither of us spoke, instead we listened to the protesting roar of Dingus's engine and the sound of each other's heavy breathing.

We were quite close to the midway when I spotted the first squad car. By the time we reached it, I'd spotted several more, along with the usual ghouls and rubberneckers clogging the sidewalk like thick slime. Again, they'd called the cops as well as me. The voice on the phone hadn't said exactly where to look, but no doubt they'd told the police.

The throng of cops and assorted ambulance chasers was thickest outside an old redbrick building with a flat roof and shuttered windows. A young cop saw Dingus' car and waved a hole through the animals for us. We pulled up directly outside the door.

'Sir, you wouldn't believe what we've got in there this time—'

We kept walking as the rookie kept talking. Trudging up the building's worn front steps, we went inside.

To find what we were looking for, all we had to do was follow the voices. Talking a left, then a right along a dusty corridor stacked full of chairs, we were able to put faces to voices. We were in the doorway of a room, the eye of the storm.

PART THREE: THE COUNTRY OF THE BLIND

The first thing I saw wasn't the body, but the writing on the wall. *In the country of the blind the one-eyed man is king*, it said in shaky red letters. On the floor below the writing was something that didn't make a lot of sense. My eyes were moving away from it toward something nearer that also didn't make sense. But at least it was recognisable.

Jimmy had been shot in the back of the head. His body was facing the other atrocity in the room. Knowing that the last thing Jimmy Spriteman saw in his life was the heavily mutilated body lying on its back on the far side of the room made me feel sick. While Jimmy looked at this awful thing, the killer had stuck a gun to the back of his head and fired.

I looked away from Jimmy's body and back to the horror lying at the far end of the room. Then I got angry with myself. The reason for this anger was that I found myself strangely grateful the other man had been killed first, and it was his blood and not Jimmy's which had been used to daub the message on the wall.

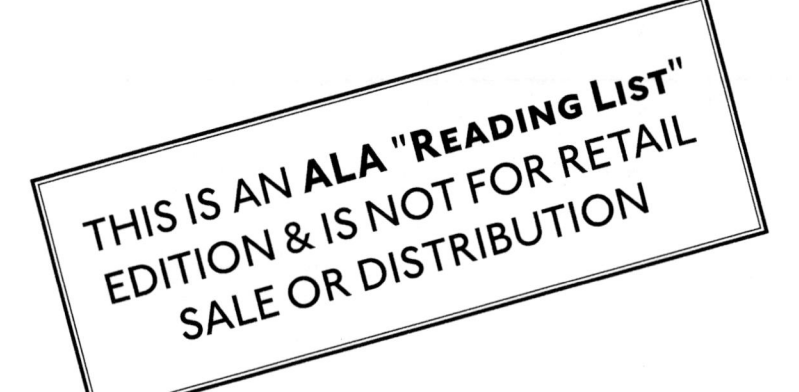

THIS IS AN **ALA "Reading List"** EDITION & IS NOT FOR RETAIL SALE OR DISTRIBUTION

Part Four
—
Last Sappy Standing

35

'I've heard of a body in a locked room,' a voice was saying nearby, 'but never the other way round.'

The voice could've come from anyone; I was paralysed. My eyes were open, but I didn't see anything. I was a useless mass of fur that others had to walk around. A part of my brain was screaming at me, a reaction to the shock. *Think about something. Anything.*

Okay, what possessed Jimmy to leave Shefton Heights?

That was easy: he must've received a phone call.

What was the call about? Why did he answer it?

The caller probably told him I was in trouble in this God-forsaken hole. Maybe they said they had some vital information.

Perhaps. But why did he answer the phone in the first place?

I don't know! Maybe it was cabin fever; he'd been holed up alone in that run down office block for months. He'd wanted to come with us even though he knew it would be dangerous, remember?

'Will you hurry up and take those damned pictures so we can get it out of there?' another voice said, its tone like the crack of a whip. I blinked.

I looked around to find I was in a different place from when I'd entered; somebody must've moved me into the

THE TERROR AND THE TORTOISESHELL

corner, out of the way. I looked down to where Jimmy's body had been, but it was gone. An image of popping flashbulbs came back to me, a long black bag being carried out of the room.

'He's... gone.' I said. 'He's *really* gone now. They'd known all along.'

A heavy paw slapped my shoulder. 'We took him... away as soon as possible.' Dingus's eyes were blurred. 'Benji, do you want a lift back home? No, I didn't think you would.' He slapped me on the shoulder again. Another wave of sadness came towards me, straight out of Dingus's eyes. I wished there was a button at the back of my head I could press to get rid of the hurt.

'That writing,' I pointed at the blood on the wall. 'What's it supposed to mean?'

'It's from a story by H.G. Wells,' Dingus replied. '"The Country of the Blind".'

'Let me guess. And the one-eyed man is king.' I curled my paws into fists, claws digging into my pads. 'Arnie said he liked playing games. The bastard's enjoying himself. He's *taunting* us Dingus, he's treating us like—' At that I let out a feeble laugh.

'Sir.'

We both turned to see an elderly Alsatian with a large camera standing by the door. 'It's all yours, Lieutenant,' he said.

I followed Dingus over to the second body. It was only then I noticed Clancy standing solemnly next to it. Without the histrionics he was a different Dog. He waved his paws in front of me and offered his condolences. As soon as the words reached my ears their sentiment seemed to evaporate.

'What happened here, Clancy?' Dingus asked.

'Exactly, I don't know yet. What I can tell you is that this man has been dead for quite some time.'

'Days?'

PART FOUR: LAST SAPPY STANDING

'Maybe. Maybe longer. I'll know later. It appears that the centre of the torso has been removed so that this, this *house* could be placed in the empty cavity. Does—does this mean *anything* to either of you?'

'It's the house by the river,' I said quietly, leaning forward to get a better look.

It was an old dolls' house that had been altered to resemble Flipper's house; the walls were covered with weeds, the door looked ready to cave in—parts of the roof had even been painted black so it looked like the slates were missing. Although I hadn't really noticed these things on my one visit there. I was still pretty sure it was Flipper's place.

Looking through the tiny upstairs windows, I saw nothing except empty rooms. I bent down close to the corpse so I could see through the ground floor windows. Inside, the front room was filled with tiny oblongs.

'Books,' I said turning to Dingus and Clancy. 'Just like the real thing.'

'Benji,' Clancy's voice was low. 'If we move the house out of the body, it'll be easier to look at.'

I looked up stupidly. 'Uh? Yes. Of course.'

Moving out of the coroner's way, Clancy took one side of the house and Dingus the other. They put it on a dusty table at the other side of the room. Then Clancy went outside and came back with another Dog carrying a black bag. The body was fastened inside it and taken out. A few minutes later, Clancy came back. We were the only ones left in the room.

The three of us stared at the bizarre object on the table like it was some grotesque art exhibit, crouching on our haunches so we could squint through the windows, walking around it so we could look at it from different angles. Clancy said what we had all been thinking.

'What's wrong with it? There's something not right.'

I lowered myself and looked through the windows again. And then I saw it.

THE TERROR AND THE TORTOISESHELL

'The ground floor: it's too high.'

Dingus and Clancy bent to take a look. 'You're right,' Dingus said. 'The floor is only a couple of inches below the ground floor windows.'

'The colour doesn't match either,' I added. 'It looks like a sheet of cardboard.'

I ran my paws along the front of the house and found the hinge on the left hand side. Popping the catch, I motioned for them to stand back.

Pulling the front of the house away from the rooms, a gap of several inches revealed itself beneath the cardboard. Grabbing the false floor at either end, I slid it out and placed it on the floor.

The real floor was littered with tiny plastic animals: Dogs, Cats and Birds, along with a few human figures and half a dozen tiny beakers and test tubes. Behind all this jumble, right at the back of the floor space, was a key. A real key. I laughed despite myself. 'Son of a bitch has a laboratory after all. It's in the basement.'

'But why leave you the key to it?' Clancy asked. 'I don't understand.'

'Because he's been building up to this all along,' I told him. 'He thinks he's invincible.'

'It sounds like he's insane.'

'He is. This is a big game to him. He's like a Cat with a ball of wool. Guess which we are.'

'I think it's about time I got things organised,' Dingus said.

36

STANDING AT A WINDOW in another room, I watched as Dingus marshalled his officers. Behind him, Clancy was waving his paws at a couple of sad-faced mutts who looked like they wanted to go home. The night had turned cold; the headlights from squad cars and the meat wagon looked like laser beams cutting into the concrete. Thankfully, all the sightseers had gone. There was nothing left to see, but usually that didn't stop them. But the cold might.

Alone in the room I felt like I was in a bubble, protected from the madness and the grief. I'd just started to think what the Old me would normally have been doing about now—curled up on the floor in the agency no doubt, glad to have the place to myself—when Dingus popped his long face around the door.

'Okay, Benji,' he told me. 'We're ready.'

A dozen or so officers would be going with us. Outside, an officer was holding open the door to a squad car. 'I thought it would be wise to go in a car that didn't make a lot of noise, Lieutenant.' He looked over at Dingus's jalopy.

'You be careful with that,' the Lieutenant called out to the rookie climbing into it. 'It's a delicate piece of machinery.' I climbed into the back of the squad car. Dingus got in the front beside the officer.

THE TERROR AND THE TORTOISESHELL

'A few cars should be at the river by the time we arrive,' Dingus said. 'I've told them to wait by the road near the towpath. Scragg will be in charge of the officers.'

'He's finished with Reeky?'

'I just spoke to him on the radio. He said he had a very satisfactory talk with him. My guess is he'll go straight to Bachman. He's probably making a complaint as we speak.'

Dingus was uncharacteristically quiet on the way to the river, the only sounds he made were when he tapped his claws against the car door or on the dash; even the cigar in his mouth went out. At one point, he raised both paws in the air and then clamped them down on his scalp and began shaking his head. The officer driving glanced over at him but said nothing. Perhaps this was how the Lieutenant usually behaved when he wasn't allowed to drive.

We were in the city now. I was surprised to see the streets busy, but remembered that it wasn't even nine o'clock yet. Nightclubs and restaurants flashed their neon lights across the pavements, turning all the Dogs, Cats and Birds who passed them a fleshy pink for a few seconds before darkness swallowed them up again. Dogs with three colours of fur wore shirts with four colours; black Cats wore white shirts and for an evening became Penguins. We passed the all-night market with its endless overhead light bulbs and stalls full of fake this and counterfeit that, mouldy food, rain-damaged electrical appliances, hamburger vans; God, how I wished we could swap places. The small worm of tension in my stomach was turning into a cobra, curling through my ribcage, rib to rib; Jimmy's face kept jumping up before me, his living face; I never saw his face in that building, just the back of his head. Was I angry, or grateful, or both? Another cobra, this one grief, was trying to crush me from the inside; I imagined the tension snake eating it. Grief would have to wait.

PART FOUR: LAST SAPPY STANDING

The alternative was to imagine what might happen at that battered old house by the river. It would be just me and Dingus going in, the other officers backing us up outside. It was risky, but it was the only way we'd learn anything. And even if we did end up buying the harp farm, at least *he* wouldn't get away. And before it got to that stage he'd tell us *why*. At least we'd know, even if it was the last thing we ever learned. Everything hinged on *why*.

When the car pulled up beside the riverbank, the two squad cars were already parked. While I waited in the car, Dingus went over to a couple of uniforms and chewed the cud. Slapping one of them on the back he came over, shaking his head; but I got the impression it wasn't because something was wrong.

'Ready?' he asked.

'As I'll ever be, Lieutenant.'

Dropping down from the raised surface of the bank onto the muddy towpath, the river's unbroken surface looked like a huge oblong sheet of smoked glass. Above us, the moon glowed behind thin clouds.

With the mud sucking at our paws, we trudged forward, side-by-side. When the path widened, Dingus went on ahead, seemingly lost in whatever thoughts were spinning around his head. I tried not to think about anything. After a couple of minutes we passed the spot where Flipper and I had found the kittens. Beyond that, the path became less accessible; a tangle of weeds, rubbish and mud. Slender branches from weeping willows jabbed spindly fingers into our heads and over the black water. To the right, the riverbank started to build, shutting us in. If we needed to escape now, the river was our only hope. Looking back to the noise I heard, I spotted the first of the officers bringing up the rear. When the packed earth path began to rise, it felt like we were standing on the belly of a fat man sleeping off his dinner. Dingus stopped and looked straight ahead.

THE TERROR AND THE TORTOISESHELL

'That's it?' he said. He sounded incredulous. 'That farmhouse?'

From this vantage point, with the moon's rays highlighting the sagging roof with its missing tiles, I saw what he meant. We were looking at a quaint old cottage beside the river that had seen better days; snapshots of some old dear living there filled the mind, wondering if she was ever going to get enough money together to fix the roof; it wasn't the kind of place you imagined would be home to two lunatics. I went cold all over.

'You okay?' Dingus asked.

'Someone just walked over my grave,' I told him. 'Come on, let's get this over with.'

Stepping down off the fat man's belly, Dingus spoke again.

'You noticed all the lights were off?' I said I had. 'Do you think they'll be sitting there in the dark, watching us?'

I thought about it. 'I think they'll be down in the laboratory, waiting for us.' Approaching the bridge, I began to slow.

'At least I hope they are,' I continued. 'Because we're going to be very exposed on this bridge—*Dingus!*' I hissed.

Showing the same disregard for safety he'd shown in Fuller's offices, Dingus clopped up the steps of the bridge, stopping at the top to lean against the rail.

'Come on up,' he told me. 'It's a nice view up here.'

'*For God's sake, get down!*' I hissed, hitting the ground.

He gave me a strange look, my eyes peering out of the long grass. 'What are you doing down there?'

'Trying not to get shot,' I told him.

'We won't get shot,' Dingus said. 'You said yourself there'd be nobody upstairs.'

As Dingus continued across the bridge, I stuck to my original plan of slithering along the boards like a snake,

PART FOUR: LAST SAPPY STANDING

only rising once I got to the steps on the far side. Behind me the other officers took my lead, sliding across the boards.

Dingus was waiting for me outside the house. One of his paws was glowing where the flashlight beam shone through his fur.

'Switch yours on too, Benji. They have a loud click. I think you should go ahead of me. You've been here before.' Despite my reluctance, I did just that.

Like last time, the door was open. Stepping over the threshold we were met by a welcoming party of Old Cats who threaded themselves between our legs and made yamming noises. Dingus, ever the innocent, bent down and began petting them.

The air smelled worse than I remembered, mostly Cat fæces and urine, but also of greasy water and unwashed dishes. Shining the beam around the kitchen, nothing had changed. I stepped into the living room, with its combined aromas of dust and old books. The light from the flashlight made some of the piles of books glow, while others looked like they were crouching, ready to pounce, or topple, at any second. Dingus was scenting the air; his eyes were like green fire glowing in the darkness. He bent over and picked up one of the books, took in its cover, turned over a few pages, then set it back down on the pile.

Ahead was a door I hadn't noticed last time. Dingus pointed to it with his beam of light.

That door was open too, but only slightly. I stood before it holding my breath for a few seconds, but all I could hear was the beating of my heart. Pulling the handle towards me, I expected a noise like the opening of a crypt, but to my surprise it opened silently. Stepping over the threshold, I found myself back in my nightmare.

Again, darkness, the only light coming from a small box on a table in front of me, a mote-filled beam scything across the room. On either side of the beam were row upon row of seats, all of them occupied. It hadn't been a dream after all. My heart turned into a hammer in my chest, threatening to break through my ribcage.

Dingus was moving along the rows. When I saw him smiling I thought I'd slipped back into my nightmare. There was nothing humorous about this place.

'It's okay, come and look.'

Moving past the back row of seats, I waited for sharp claws to grab at me, but none did. Slowly, I turned to look at the occupants. It took me a second or two to get the words out.

'*Stuffed toys?*'

'It's the same in every seat,' Dingus whispered back.

When I checked, I found he was right: every seat, perhaps fifty in total, occupied by a furry toy of some description.

'Animals,' I said. 'Every one is an animal.'

The Lieutenant wasn't listening. He was picking up the toys one by one and holding them up to his large, wet nose. He did this several times, picking a different row for each toy. He was nodding furiously. 'Oh, by the way,' he said as he sniffed, 'there's a door to the left of that screen. Is this the same film you saw last time?'

'Er, yes, I think so.' I looked over to the left and noticed the door. I could still hear Dingus sniffing at the toys in the darkness.

'Well,' he said when he'd finished, 'whaddya know...'

Knowing he'd tell me in his own time, I headed for the door, my furry shadow distorting the screen as I crossed it. I had a strange fear that someone would shout for me to get out the way. Thankfully, it didn't happen.

This time, the door was closed. We listened for noises on the other side, but there was nothing. I tried the handle. As before, there was no creak or groan. There was also no movement. Dingus fished through his pockets. After pulling

PART FOUR: LAST SAPPY STANDING

out bundles of tissues, cigar wrappers, used notepads and old candy bars, he produced the key.

'Fits perfectly,' he said, putting it in the lock. Then he turned it.

Slowly, very slowly, he opened the door.

37

It was a good thing we hadn't barged through that door, as it led straight onto a narrow stone staircase. At the bottom was another door, the kind without handles which you could push through dramatically and leave opening and closing in your wake. As soon as the door of the projection room closed behind us, we both felt the drop in temperature. In single file, we descended the stairs in the dark, using the wall for support, the touch of the cold stone chilling my pads. At the bottom, I let out a sigh of relief.

'Okay, Dingus,' I said, my paw on the swing door, 'here goes.'

Easing the door open, I looked through the crack. 'We won't need the flashlights for this,' I whispered out of the corner of my mouth.

I opened the door a little further so Dingus could see the long, empty whitewashed corridor lit with fluorescent tubes. On each side were five doors, all with handles, all closed. Stepping through the door, we let it close softly behind us. At the far end of the corridor was another swing door.

'What now?' I asked Dingus.

'Probably along to the bottom there. But I think we should check these other rooms out first.'

'All of them?' My heart sank. Dingus was already opening the first one, disappearing into darkness. When he flicked on his flashlight, I followed him in.

PART FOUR: LAST SAPPY STANDING

The room was perhaps six by eight, and crammed with cardboard boxes the way the living room above was crammed with books. Against the far wall was a small cupboard which Dingus opened, revealing row upon row of canned food.

'Peaches,' he said, handing me one can after another. 'Corned beef. Tinned stew. Evaporated milk. Fruit salad. Look at the state of these tins, Benji. They're rusted to hell.'

I turned one upside down. When I saw the use-by date, I wondered what would come out of the can if it was opened. It certainly wouldn't be tinned peaches anymore.

From there we went to the room opposite. As with the other, it had no lock. None of the doors did. Inside we found more cardboard boxes and mouldering cans.

The next room was more interesting; amid the general clutter of ancient bedsteads and piled-up mattresses, we found a pile of brooms, minus handles, pushed under one of the bedsteads. The handles had evidently been used for some other purpose, such as turning a grown man into a Porcupine. The next two rooms contained nothing except old paperback novels, more cardboard boxes and various odds and ends, along with a few clothes. Going through these dank, windowless rooms was like exploring some abandoned jailhouse; then, when you stepped out into the corridor, you were walking around in a deserted hospital.

Of the other five rooms, three were empty. One, the last room on the left, had a damp wall. Shining our lights onto it, we saw the cracks running down the bottom half and the water seeping through. You could also hear the river sloshing against it outside.

The remaining rooms, the two on the right, were far from empty. One room was full of dead things floating in jars stacked against the walls, an array of surgical equipment laid out on a table nearby. The last room was by far the largest. Despite being full of equipment, it must've been at least twice the size of the others.

THE TERROR AND THE TORTOISESHELL

The first thing we noticed in there though, was the smell; a smell I'd had to get used to lately.

'Benji, over here.'

Dingus's flashlight beam passed over a long marble slab in the centre of the room.

'It's a dissecting table,' he told me. 'See the drains there, along the edges? That's so they can—'

'Let's just go, Lieutenant,' I said. 'Get this over with.'

After the last two rooms it was almost a pleasure to open the next set of swing doors and finding nothing more threatening than another corridor. It was half the length of the previous one and painted a grimy grey. Even better, there were no side rooms to look into. There was just the one straight in front of us. With a handle.

I'd been about to try it when I heard a voice from the room beyond. Whoever was in there, they were having one hell of an argument.

38

'It sounds like Flipper,' I said.

'*Yes! Yes, he was useless! That's why we're doing this, remember? Now—*' It suddenly went quiet. My paw was still hovering above the handle when the shouting began again.

'*No! I won't let you talk like that in here, do you understand?*'

Dingus and I looked at each other. His face was impassive.

'Got your gun ready?' he asked. I nodded.

'*We'll discuss this later. I have to go upstairs—*'

We nearly leapt out of our furs when the door creaked open. Flattening ourselves against either side of the wall, five long seconds passed. Ten. Nobody appeared. Flipper's voice started up again, on the left hand side of the room. I was positioned to the right of the door. If I moved forward slightly, I'd be able to see inside. I inched towards the open door.

Flipper's voice continued to rise and fall at the other side of it. As it rose again I crept into the open space. Immediately I saw Flipper's broad back blocking my view of the room.

Without further thought, I kicked the door in and leapt into the room, pointing the gun over to my left to cover Flipper and his owner. But all I saw was Flipper looking startled.

THE TERROR AND THE TORTOISESHELL

'Okay, where did he go?' I pointed the gun at Flipper's head while my eyes searched the room for another door or a closet, anything that he could've hidden in. But apart from a couple of chairs, the room was empty. Flipper began to regain his composure.

'I said: where did he go?'

'*He* killed him, Benji,' Dingus said as he walked in. His whiskers were positively *twanging*. 'At least that's what he thinks he believes.'

I wasn't sure what Dingus was driving at, but evidently Flipper was. His eyes blazed. He started to come towards us until we waved our guns at him.

'It was something you said earlier,' Dingus told me, 'about Cat's not being able to drink. Remember I told you about the strange smell at a few of the crime scenes? It was a mixed smell, like Jimmy's was, but it was stronger; and different somehow. In the car I figured out what that difference was: alcohol. Cats *can't* drink, Benji. And that—' he pointed at Flipper with his gun, 'that ain't no Cat. Look at him, Benji. Look at his *eyes*.'

As I did, I realised it was the first time I'd ever really held his gaze; Flipper rarely made eye contact. But when he had I'd noticed that his eyes *were* strange; to me, it'd just been another odd feature of an odd Cat. But as I looked now, I saw it. Immediately my spine turned into a Popsicle. When I opened my mouth to speak, 'Flipper' beat me to it.

'I'm more of a Cat than you'll ever be.' He was holding my gaze now, all right. The voice had changed too; gone were the rough but friendly tones, replaced by a smoother, more cultured, arrogant voice.

'So who are you?' I said. 'Where's your owner?'

There was a long pause before he answered. 'All you need to know is that *he* was one of *them*. And you two—', he pointed at us, ignoring the guns levelled at him, 'are no better than he was, doing *their* work.'

PART FOUR: LAST SAPPY STANDING

Dingus coughed, then spoke. 'Mr. Carlin, you are under arrest for the murders of nine human beings and one feline. You do not have to say anything—'

This was too much. I turned to Dingus. 'Dingus, what the Hell is going on here? What are you talking about?'

'Benji—look out!'

But I was too slow. I was still eyeballing Dingus when the gun was snatched from my paw. As Dingus pointed his gun at 'Flipper', 'Flipper' pointed my gun at me.

'Now,' Flipper/Carlin said, aiming the gun at my head, 'we can stand like this all night. But if he fires at me, Benji, I fire at you.'

My gaze went over to the Lieutenant. Reluctantly, he dropped the gun to the floor.

'What did you do that for?' I asked.

'Because Mr. Carlin knows he's not going anywhere. Besides, he's desperate to tell his story to someone, and I don't know about you, Benji, but I'd quite like to hear it.' Flipper/Carlin grabbed the gun off the floor while still pointing my gun at me.

'Okay, both of you. Into those chairs.'

We manœuvred in a semi-circle around the room until we reached the two chairs and sat down.

'First things, first,' I said. 'What's all this 'Mr. Carlin' stuff?'

'I got uniform to check who owned this place before The Terror. When we arrived at the river, I found out it had belonged to an Edward Carlin, a brilliant but erratic scientist who'd been thrown out of every organisation in the country due to his, shall we say, unorthodox ideas and practices. I didn't get all the details, but I'm sure that Mr. Carlin here will fill us in—'

'*That's enough!*'

Dingus shut up as the bullet flew over our heads into the wall.

THE TERROR AND THE TORTOISESHELL

'Who's telling this story, you or me?' He pointed one of the guns at his chest. 'I am. Now listen. You see this crumbly little wall I just put the bullet into? Well it, like you two, isn't going to last much longer. Sometimes, in the middle of the night, you can hear the water lapping against the stone. I want you both so quiet that you can hear it for yourselves.'

'Or else what? You'll shoot us?'

'It's that, or I fill the wall full of lead and you drown. Us Cats, we're not great swimmers, are we?' He chuckled to himself. 'Either way, when I leave here you'll just be two more dead animals, and with the evidence for the murders ultimately pointing to a human being... but first, would you like to hear my story?'

Thinking about that filthy black river out there, I decided that I would like to hear his story very much. It might well be the last story I ever heard.

39

CARLIN, HIS VOICE SLOW and cultured, the total opposite of Flipper's, took a long time to say very little. While he droned on I took the opportunity to study the speaker.

His 'fur' certainly appeared to be Cat fur; presumably glued on, it meant patchy sections were matted together in great clumps, which I'd taken for poor hygiene. Through which, sallow patches of dough-like flesh were visible, along with various cuts and bruises. I wondered if these marks were because of how the fur had been fastened to the skin. The 'paws', along with the eyes, were the biggest give-away if I'd bothered to look properly. Carlin's 'paws' were too blunt, bunched together and covered with fur. The nails were quite long though, and had been sharpened to small, claw-like points. The 'ears' appeared to be little more than tufted lumps stuck on the top of the head, his real ears presumably covered with thick wads of fur; but no matter how I hard I looked, I couldn't see them.

The nose appeared to be correct: snubbed, with a pink blotch at the front and whiskers on each side. Some kind of extremely painful plastic surgery must have flattened out his real nose. The lips were easily covered with fur, but the teeth were quite startling; they weren't needle-sharp like they should have been, but some effort had apparently been made to chisel them into points. Then there were those eyes: tomb-grey and surrounded by fur, eyes which had always avoided close inspection—until now. And of course there was the smell—his *true* smell—blocked, whenever I saw him, in part by that damned onion he used for fishing... all in all the transformation wasn't perfect, but it was good enough for Carlin to have survived this long.

'Incidentally,' he said, turning to me, 'most of the things you told me in our little heart-to-hearts were hardly revelatory. I trust you got home safely, the night you were here last? You seemed to be rather the worse for wear, as I recall.'

'Only because you spiked my drink. What was in it, Carlin?'

'Flipper. What does it matter?'

'I thought maybe it was to numb the effect of the film you made me sit through.'

'I noticed that you didn't seem too enamoured of it,' he said, stroking his chin to reveal another piece of dough-coloured flesh. 'A shame really, as apart from me, you are the only one to have seen it and lived to tell the tale. You didn't seem to truly *understand* what the film was about, if I may be so bold. But never mind, we'll get to that later.

'Going back to what I was saying a few minutes ago: Yes, I've been watching you. Quite funny, really: the hunter and the hunted, but in reverse. And you didn't suspect a thing. Telling me all about the escapades of the SPCH; I had to bite my tongue a few times, I can tell you. *Who did you think was responsible for starting all that in the first place?*'

Before Dingus or I had a chance to digest that bombshell, Carlin carried on.

'After The Terror struck, it was obvious that something had to be done. As the only one who could see exactly what had happened, it fell to me to take responsibility. The solution was pretty obvious: what little remained of humanity had to

PART FOUR: LAST SAPPY STANDING

be destroyed; if it meant a few animals dying in the process, then that was the price worth paying. All it took were a few anonymous letters to the press suggesting that 'the people' were planning a revolt of some kind. So the few traces of humanity that did remain were being taken care of for me, without me having to lift a—' he looked down at his "paw" and laughed softly.

'You make it sound like a war.' Carlin shrugged.

'So,' I said, trying to sound calm, 'here you are. The Last Sappy Standing. In the country of the blind, the one-eyed man is king.'

Carlin idly shook one of the guns at me. 'One more crack like that...' the gun wobbled in his hairy mitt, but the real threat came from his eyes.

A brief lull in his speech made me aware of the sound of the river. Then, my whiskers began to twitch. When Carlin started to talk again, this time addressing Dingus, I slowly moved my paws behind my back and touched the wall. It was cold and wet, river water dribbling down the plaster.

I was giving Carlin my full attention when he turned back to me. 'So, Benji. You must be wondering: why you? What have you ever done to me?'

'It certainly crossed my mind.'

'Well, the truth of it is that until recently you'd done nothing to me. Can I ask—have you ever heard of the term 'ancestral guilt'?'

'I can't say that I have.'

'Okay. Let's put it like this. If somebody hurt you, you would want to hurt them in return. Agreed?'

To keep the peace, I nodded.

'Good. Now sometimes, that revenge can be easily administered; the perpetrator can be hunted down and the deed accomplished. But sometimes it isn't as simple as that, and the emphasis of blame can move so that others are left with the burden of revenge. In effect, they inherit the problem.'

Taking a deep breath through what remained of his nose, Carlin leaned into me and pressed the gun into my ribs.

'Do you know what that journalist had the nerve to say about me, about my theories of evolution? As for her intention to circulate those opinions in that foul newspaper—she had to be stopped. It was as simple as that.'

'So you killed Adele because of what she might have written in the paper?' I said as he backed away. 'Do you think the vast majority of people would've paid any attention?'

'What she *might* have written? I could see it in her face, her opinion of me. I told her, you have to experiment if you want progress. It's in the nature of things. Sacrifices have to be made. Sometimes, the lowly do suffer.'

'So you carried out experiments on animals,' Dingus said. 'Lots of people did that.'

'Just because a creature happens to be born in a human skin, it doesn't mean that they're not an animal, Lieutenant.'

'*You're saying you were experimenting on humans too?*' a shocked Dingus almost yelled.

'We have to move forward, it's as simple as that. Anyway, we're getting off the point. She died, that's all that matters. But then it struck me—what if she'd told others?

'Then there was this article in the paper about how her boyfriend was a failed Policeman, and her car had only been serviced a few days earlier... and when those other fools showed up, claiming to be doing an article on local characters... did they think I was stupid? I decided that if they wanted character, they should come and see the film I'd made.'

'So you killed them too?' I put in.

'Naturally. As well as the two lab assistants I'd hired who seemed to have a problem with some of my ideas.'

'They were animal rights activists, trying to expose you. You were a very popular individual, Carlin.'

PART FOUR: LAST SAPPY STANDING

'*Flipper.* I won't tell you again. But it all turned out for the best. Things generally do when higher powers are involved.' I wondered what that meant, but kept quiet.

'Of course, I've had my doubts along the way,' he carried on as though we knew what he meant. 'Work as important as mine, as *vital,* is bound to attract doubts. But then *It* happened!' He threw his 'paws' into the air. 'Can you imagine what that moment was like, seeing all those laboratory specimens expanding in their cages, *talking* to me through the wire? They proved to be a much tougher group to dispose of than their so-called human counterparts—they were on the threshold of a new existence, after all.

'But as I was despatching them, I saw—*I truly saw*—what was happening. This basement, or I should say, this *bunker,*' he gestured with a furry arm, 'was originally designed to withstand a nuclear blast; a Terror of some kind, if you will. Somehow though, I doubt that the powers that be could have forseen this eventuality.'

'I hate to point this out to you, Carlin, but you really are insane.'

'If you define insanity in such basic terms, then I daresay you're correct. But *you* are the ones who cannot see, which to my mind makes *you* the crazy ones. *You* are the ones that are acting like Human Beings, despite the freedom which has been thrust upon you: evolution speeded up to a wonderful, horrifying, beautiful degree. Being at the forefront of it, by playing my part, I was destined to see these changes and survive. Those Machenites, or whatever they call themselves, aren't that far off the mark: an uprising *was* underway and humanity has at last paid for its ignorance. Yet, I've survived.' He paused to catch his breath.

I wondered how far gone Carlin must've been before everything changed? The Terror was probably just the cherry on top as far as this fruitcake was concerned.

'So you're saying you're part of God's Divine Plan, something like that?'

THE TERROR AND THE TORTOISESHELL

'I wouldn't go that far,' he said with complete seriousness. 'But I definitely had a responsibility. Somebody had to be in charge. But to undertake my duties, I saw that I had to change and adapt too.'

By sticking a load of Old Cat fur on your body and dousing yourself in heaven-knows-what, I thought.

'Over the years, all kinds of hormones and scents have been invented which I knew would aid my cause—there's no point going into details, you wouldn't understand. It took a while, but I got there in the end. That day, I looked in the mirror and saw who I was destined to be; that I too had evolved: "*Now then, Benji, are you well? What's goin' on out there in the big, bad world?*"' Hearing Flipper's voice again just as I was getting used to Carlin's made me jump.

As we stared at each other, I could hear that the dribble of water behind me was becoming a substantial trickle. I looked over at Dingus out of the corner of my eye and saw his whiskers twitching. Carlin started to speak once more.

'So I began to venture outdoors, to see if anybody would find me out. Of course, nobody did. They, like you Benji, only saw a mangy old Cat who talked to himself.

'I prowled the streets and the alleys, waiting for a sign. For a long time, nothing happened. Would you believe I started to doubt again? The only thing of note that happened was a certain Tortoiseshell Cat began taking his walks along the river I fished in...

'Then one night, a few weeks later, I was making my way back here. I was in a cut-through at the back of a grocery store, and there, among the shadows on the opposite side of the street, I saw him. At first I couldn't believe my eyes; I watched him scavenging around in the trash, but I couldn't move. When he began to move away, I knew I had to follow him. He went to what looked like an abandoned office block on the outskirts of the city. I still didn't know what to do, only that fate yet again was intervening. I kept watch over

PART FOUR: LAST SAPPY STANDING

him night after night. Over time I could see what it all meant; we were the last two, both adapting to our environments in order to survive. But it also went back to ancestral guilt; the punishment for the lies of the journalist had not been fully meted out; the guilt had simply passed like a flea, from one animal to another. It was the sign I was looking for. But I couldn't kill him; with you now on the scene, I had to decide who was most guilty: Benji or Jimmy? So, the best thing I could do would be to bring the pair of you together.'

'So you burned down the building Jimmy was staying in,' Dingus said.

'With the aid of a few strays egging me on, yes. I mean, where on *earth* could he go next?'

'Okay,' I said, wanting to change the subject, 'what about Bootsy and Arnie? The restaurant worker?'

'Another example of fate, destiny, everything fitting into place. On one of my trawls through the city, I visited various apartment blocks, checking for humanity. There was always the chance that I'd find somebody or something that would prove to be of some use. I knew someone who had lived in Ronson Towers, and worked at the Gourmet Club. If I got caught breaking into his property, I could say that I used to be his Cat...

'His apartment was on the seventh floor. The door was locked but I soon took care of that. Inside the apartment there was a *terrible* stench. When I opened the door to the living room it was a bit of a shock to find him still in there.

'He was a raving lunatic, of course; been holed up in there since The Terror, living on whatever he'd had left in his cupboards. He was practically drooling. I started talking to him. I made the mistake of telling him who I was, or rather, had been. He laughed, he actually *laughed* at me, at my progress, that's how mad he was. Such an imbecile could not be allowed to live.'

Dingus and I gave each other a quick look—two victims from the HFC.

THE TERROR AND THE TORTOISESHELL

'What about the other Gourmet Club employee?' I asked. 'The one that was found outside the restaurant?'

'Oh him. You know, I forgot all about him... he just turned up here one day, completely out of the blue.' Carlin smiled.

'You expect us to be believe that?'

'He came here looking for sanctuary—he knew I was secluded. Unfortunately, when I took him into one of my rooms along the corridor there...' he shrugged.

'You must've had quite a collection by that time.'

'As you say. And it presented a problem. They were beginning to stink the place out. What could I do with them?'

Carlin's eyes glazed over. I took the opportunity to reach back and touch the damp wall. When I ran a claw along the plaster, it soon became snagged. That gave me an idea.

I turned to find Dingus looking down at what I was doing. He nodded. I began to rub at the plaster. Small chunks of it started dropping into my paw. When Carlin began speaking again, I almost dropped the plaster I'd collected.

'Those bodies were of no use to me anymore; just relics from a bygone age. But perhaps our re-formed Police Force could get some use out of them?'

'What I want to know is this, Sir,' Dingus said, raising his voice. He rubbed at one of his ears as though he was trying to get something loose. I smiled to myself and scratched at the wall even harder. 'How did you get those bodies to the locations unseen?' the Lieutenant shouted. 'It must've been quite a job.'

'On the other side of river is an old car dealership,' Carlin said, raising his voice to match Dingus's. 'The keys are still hanging on pegs in the cabin. On my nocturnal journeys I'd always drive the cars back. When I'd been trailing the Human, I found several suitable locations to exhibit the bodies. It was surprisingly easy. Fun, too.'

PART FOUR: LAST SAPPY STANDING

'But why do it at all, Sir?' Dingus said, turning up the volume a bit more.

'Because, you stupid mutt, they were symbols of what I'd been trying to achieve—I was advancing civilisation.' As the conversation became steadily louder so did my scratching; great lumps of plaster were now coming away from the wall. River water trickled over my paws.

'Almost like sacrifices, in a way!' Dingus shouted.

'Sacrifices, offerings, warnings—call them what you like.' I felt like I was witnessing a conversation between two profoundly deaf creatures, each trying to outdo the other in volume. Dingus, not for the first time, played the dumb guy to the hilt.

'Mr. Carlin, I mean, Flipper—I really don't understand any of this.' He looked over at me quickly before turning back. 'You're going to have to explain it to me in layman's terms. I'm afraid me and Mr. Spriteman here are not as bright as you.' I now had a paw full of plaster and dust.

Carlin shook his head pitifully. 'Lieutenant,' he shouted back, 'you disappoint me. Really.'

'Okay, we'll leave that for a while. What about Bootsy?'

'There was this Tortoise, Arnie, who kept turning up at crime scenes. He lives in Ronson Towers—you see how fate keeps intervening, Lieutenant? He'd tell me little things and I'd tell him even more. In the course of our conversations, various names—Reeky McStink for instance—kept cropping up. Now there sounded like the kind of guy who would appreciate a bit of fun, I thought.

'Anyway, the name Bootsy came up. He said that Mr. Spriteman here was thick with him. Call me an old ham, but I've always loved old crime novels—the plots, the sub-plots, the and twists and turns—so when the opportunity presented itself, I decided to create my own little mysteries.'

Carlin turned to smile at me. My paws were still behind my back, one full, the other almost full. Thankfully, he was so oblivious to everything but the sound of his own voice that he hadn't noticed.

'So!' he said, as if he'd just produced a Rabbit from a top hat, 'that's how it all happened. *Everything* fell into place. Destiny. The end of my story. The only thing left to do now,' he clicked the triggers on the guns, 'is to add a couple of full stops.'

I realised the time to take a coughing fit had arrived. Out of the corner of my eye I caught Dingus's nod, and proceeded to hack myself into oblivion.

'Sorry, I have an allergy,' I told Carlin when I stopped. 'Ducks. Do you have any round here, Carlin? Any *Ducks*?'

'You know, I think I saw some *Ducks* on the way here,' Dingus said.

Carlin waved the guns at Dingus, then at me, then back at Dingus.

While he was still staring at Dingus, I took my chance, hurling both pawfuls of plaster into Carlin's face. Dingus diving on the floor a split second before Carlin fired blindly at him. With a quickness I hadn't known I still possessed, I managed to wrestle Carlin to the floor. I growled and spat, my claws were out, and I was tearing at his face. My fur bristled as a bullet sailed over my back into the wall, the noise deafening. I looked up to see Carlin standing above me, pointing both guns at my head. Before he had a chance to fire Dingus smashed a chair across the back of his head, knocking him to the floor. One of the guns slipped from his paw into the corridor; amazingly he managed to keep hold of the other one. Before we had a chance to grab him, he was out of the door, only stopping to pick up the dropped gun. With Cat-like speed he turned and fired twice, but both shots missed us by a mile, the bullets lodging in the wall. He fled down the corridor, firing at us several times, before slipping out of the door at the far end. With the echoes scudding across the room, I turned to find Dingus holding a chair in front of him, a Lion-tamer without a Lion.

PART FOUR: LAST SAPPY STANDING

'What are you doing?'
'Using it as a shield,' he said, going out into the corridor.
'You're going after him?'
'I'm not staying down here.' He was looking past me. Turning, I saw the floor was swimming with river water. We could probably have chanced it down there for a while, but as I can't swim and we had no other exit, I decided it was best to follow him. Grabbing the other chair, I followed Dingus along the corridor. We got to the far end of it before two sharp *pwangs!* from the top of the stairs halted us.

'You okay?' I asked Dingus as I huddled behind my chair.
'Think so. I don't think he's aiming for us specifically, just trying to slow us down.'
'You still want to go on?' I snapped.
'It's that or wait for the wall to collapse,' he told me.

I followed him as he opened the door on the dark stairwell, slowly clattering our way to the top of the stairs like infirm metallic insects. Dingus grasped the door's handle. *One,* he mouthed, *Two, Three*—

Dingus half-shoved, half-kicked the door so hard it banged against the wall as loud as a gunshot. After a few seconds crouching on the cold floor in the darkness, the only thing we could hear was the film projector clacking away over to our right, the room turned black and white by the projector's beam.

'I can smell him,' I whispered.
'So can I.'

I looked up from behind my chair, and row upon row of glassy dolls eyes stared back at me. On the fourth row, one of the dolls was twice the size of the ones surrounding it. No sooner had I spotted it than the air was bright with gun flares, one bullet hitting the wall while another ripped through the cinema screen. In the confusion, footsteps scrambled out into the living room.

'You go left and I'll go right,' I told Dingus.

THE TERROR AND THE TORTOISESHELL

I went on all fours past each row, still using my chair as a shield, the dozens of blank faces staring at the picture on the screen, half of which was flapping down to the floor as if bowing. As I got closer to the living room door, I could hear some of the Old Cats *miaowing*. A creak from there drowned them out.

'He's going into the kitchen,' I whispered to Dingus who was on the other side of the doorframe now. Slowly I opened the door.

The gap wasn't wide enough to get a paw through when a bullet whistled through the doorway. Acting on reaction alone, half fear and half anger, I threw the door open and heaved the chair into the living room, sending hundreds of books toppling to the floor. Dingus moved in ahead of me, scanning the room, but Carlin had already gone.

'What do we do now?'

'Wait,' Dingus said. 'He wouldn't dare come back in here. And if he goes outside the others are waiting for him.'

In the stillness that followed, several pairs of bright green eyes came towards us out of the darkness. Bending, I petted the head of the nearest Cat. I looked over to see Dingus doing the same. For a minute or so the only noises we heard were the Cat's contented purring.

What happened next happened quickly and caught both of us off guard. Around us, the Cats suddenly stopped purring. Then a white light appeared under the door; he was leaving the kitchen and going outside. Rising, we climbed over the spilled books towards the door. My paw was shaking as I gripped the handle, turned it. I half closed my eyes against the glare of light pouring into the kitchen. When my eyes had fully adjusted, I saw the kitchen was empty.

'*Okay, now drop the gun!*' a voice outside said. Then, '*Good. Now move forward. Slowly.*'

Standing at the door we saw Carlin inch forward in the spotlight, furry hands in the air, the officers with their

PART FOUR: LAST SAPPY STANDING

guns trained on him. One shouted for him to stand still. But he kept walking.

'Something's not right, Benji,' Dingus said as we crept outside.

'I won't tell you again to stand still!' but Carlin kept going slowly over to the right. One of his hands looked strangely enlarged; together, we both realised why.

'HE'S STILL GOT A GUN!' Dingus shouted. 'He only dropped ONE!'

I knew then where he was going; the path to the right dropped away, straight down into the river.

'Take one more step and I'll—'

By the time they fired, Carlin was already gone. From behind him, we saw the flash of his pistol and his fur-covered body falling into the black water below. The volley of shots that followed was too late, his body quickly swept away by the strong current further downstream.

'All that,' Dingus said, shaking his head, 'and he gets away.'

'He just shot himself in the head!' I said.

'No. That's what he wanted us to believe. It was a trick. He aimed too high.' When I began to protest, Dingus got the flashlight from his pocket, shining it on the spot where Carlin had stood. 'Look, check the ground for yourself—no bloodstains.'

'But he was firing from left to right,' I argued. 'The blood would've gone into the river.'

Dingus shrugged. 'Perhaps.' He began walking away.

'Hang on a minute,' I said, catching him up, 'you think he decided to take his chances with the river?'

'Look at all the other things he managed to get away with. Why not that too?'

'Next you'll be saying he was responsible for The Terror and not just some madman.'

THE TERROR AND THE TORTOISESHELL

Dingus held up a paw and let it fall. Without replying, he headed back along the bridge.

Inside the squad car I said it again.

'Okay, maybe he's not responsible for The Terror,' he said after lighting a cigar. 'But you have to admit, crazy or not, he's a remarkable person.'

'You're talking like he's still alive out there.'

Dingus answered by blowing out a great plume of blue cigar smoke.

'I think he's dead,' I told him. 'That ridiculous body of his'll probably wash up somewhere in a couple of weeks' time. Bloated and dead.'

Dingus continued to smoke his cigar as if he didn't have a care in the world.

'Yes, that's what'll happen,' I said. 'You just watch.'

Epilogue
—
(Another) New Beginning

THIS IS AN **ALA "Reading List"** EDITION & IS NOT FOR RETAIL SALE OR DISTRIBUTION

I suppose we were a strange-looking bunch standing there in the graveyard dark, our paws and claws dug into our overcoats, breathing milky coloured air into each other's faces as we chatted. It was mid-December now, a month since the excitement at Carlin's/Flipper's place, and winter was well and truly upon us.

I had to admit I was surprised by the turnout, considering that besides myself and Dingus nobody had known him. Scragg and Clancy had turned up, Taki had called in at Number One Mouse's, and he'd brought Ma Spayley along with him. Inky from the Heights had showed up, as had Tigger and Shove Off. Even Ms Galbraith was there. We'd been standing for nearly half an hour, but nobody complained.

'Benji?' Taki tapped me on the back. 'Looks like he's here.'

I turned to see a shabbily dressed Beagle coming towards me, the tail of his overcoat flapping behind him, his dog-collar barely visible, his face tucked into the collar of his coat. In his paws, the Reverend 'Snoopy' Smith carried a small wooden box.

I'd got the idea after Jimmy told me what happened at that deserted office block he'd been holed up in. Seeing the place go up in flames like that, he'd said that if you had to go, that was the way to do it.

'Which of you is Benji Spriteman?' Snoopy asked.

I stepped forward and introduced myself.

'Can I ask you, Mr. Spriteman, if you're absolutely sure about this. It's highly irregular.'

THE TERROR AND THE TORTOISESHELL

I told him yes, I was sure.

'You are aware that this is a *Pet* cemetery?' He looked doubtful.

'I know that,' I said. 'Jimmy loved animals.' *Probably more than people,* I realised. And as most of the Sappy cemeteries had been vandalised by Street Cats, this seemed the best option.

'I would imagine, then, that the desecration of the, er, *human* burial sites is the reason you wish this service to be conducted in darkness?'

'I don't want the whole world knowing about it,' I agreed.

The vicar inclined his smooth, white head. 'Very wise,' he told me. 'In light of recent events.'

It took a few days for the truth about Carlin and the murders to get into Fuller's rag. Jimmy got a brief mention, being one of the victims, but that was all. I got my own badly spelled paragraph too, as did Dingus.

Straight away, the recriminations started. Sammy Bachman was ousted as Chief of Police when his links with Reeky McStink were discovered, and he soon joined Reeky and Eddie in the slammer, where I gather life is no picnic.

The evening's events were inevitably covered in lurid detail by the Rat ('THE LAS SAPY SANDING—AN HE WAS BARKING—IN A MANER OF SPEKKING!'), who took great pains to point out that a lot of the credit should go to him for letting the police know about the former employees who'd become victims. The article read like it had been passed (literally) through about four other animals before it got to the Rat, which was all the better for us. There was even a juicy bit claiming that Carlin/Flipper had shouted something to the police just before he pulled the trigger. But if he did shout something, nobody who was there that night heard it. But the officers did all agree on one thing: that Carlin/Flipper had a huge grin on his face as he fired the gun. Unfortunately, none of them could say if

EPILOGUE: (ANOTHER) NEW BEGINNING

the bullet actually hit its target, because he seemed to fall the second the shot was fired. Milking the story for all it was worth, Fuller offered a reward to anyone who could find him alive. But there were no takers; the common belief being that if Carlin wasn't dead when he hit the water, he would be by now.

Me, I wasn't so sure any more.

The whole thing seemed to trouble Dingus, too; not just the absence of a body, but the claims Carlin had made that night, and the way everything seemed to revolve around him, then fall into place. It gave us both a few sleepless nights. Most of what he told us was so much rubbish, true, but other things... thankfully, these doubts were soon forgotten when Fuller broke the news of the explorers.

'Would you like me to say a few words, before we—?' Snoopy looked down into the hole.

'Yes. Yes, that would be nice.' I wasn't sure if Jimmy would've approved, but it felt like the right thing to do. I can't remember what Snoopy said. I was more aware of Ma Spayley's sniffing somewhere behind me. I felt oddly detached from it all. I supposed it would hit me later.

When he'd finished, Snoopy passed me the box containing Jimmy's ashes. Bending, I placed the box into the hole, pleased to see that there was still plenty of room.

'I've brought you something,' I said, looking down at the box. 'Well, actually, I'm returning something to your keeping. Take good care of it.' Reaching into my pocket, I removed the book and placed it on top of the ashes.

'Well. This is it. So long, Jimmy.' Wiping the soil from the bottom of my coat, I went and stood back beside the vicar. I wondered if anybody had heard what I'd said. I felt kind of embarrassed. Snoopy glanced over at the pile of earth next to the grave. Taking a pawful, I gently sprinkled it on top of the book and the box as Snoopy said a few more words.

We all stood back and watched as the hole was filled in, the light from the lamps Inky and Tigger held never wavering. I was surprised to see Snoopy filling in the hole himself. Later, he told me it was his pleasure.

When the grave was filled and smoothed over, I invited everyone back to the apartment for a few drinks and snacks. It was a cold night and everyone walked briskly, pairing off and talking, while I kept to myself at the front. Taki caught up with me after a while and asked me how I was. I told her I was fine. Smiling, she fell back, leaving me to my thoughts.

The town was fairly quiet; it was midweek so the only trade was for the restaurants and bars. Stuck to a wall beside a bar was last week's newspaper headline: EXPLORERS—«WE FOUND CIVILISAYSHUN».

I smiled when I thought of Dingus, phoning to ask if I'd read the paper. When I said I hadn't, he told me what to expect. I let out a sigh of relief so great it blew all the loose papers off my desk.

After all those weeks without contact, the explorers had arrived back in the city. The Terror, they told us, *had* happened everywhere; it was a world-wide phenomenon. Before Dingus could carry on, I interrupted him.

'If it's true, how come we haven't had contact from anyone else?'

'Because by the sound of things there have been some pretty serious battles in the rest of the country—the Humans actually held onto several cities for a while after The Terror. Apparently, everyone thought we were one of those cities. And with us being on the east coast, meaning there was only one way in, nobody wanted to go on a suicide mission. And with all our phone lines down except local ones—'

Like the story Carlin spun us, it didn't tie up somehow, but I don't suppose *anything* ever really ties up one hundred per cent. For the good of my health, I decided to let it drop; life was too short. I don't suppose any of us would know the whole truth of it, any more than we'll ever know how and why humanity evolved from the seas.

EPILOGUE: (ANOTHER) NEW BEGINNING

Within a few days, the city felt like a different place. Animals arrived from different towns and cities, curious to see the city that had been shut off from the world for so long, animals with strange clothes and even stranger accents, telling us how wonderful it was back where they came from (which begged the question: why leave?). The tales from these new lands lured many animals away, including my favourite reptile pal, Arnie. After snitching on everyone he knew and a fair few he didn't, he realised that his luck had finally run out. When the police turned up at his apartment to ask him about his dealings with Reeky and Eddie, they found an empty apartment with a sign on the door saying SO LONG SUCKERS! For all his faults, I couldn't help admiring the little guy's pluck.

In the same week Arnie did his moonlight flit, Lieutenant Dingus (still a Lieutenant despite an offer of promotion; he said he preferred it that way), Chief of Police Scragg (now head of the force much to Fuller's chagrin), and myself went back to Carlin's farmhouse to see what we could see. Apart from an ancient underground nuclear shelter floating down river, an unstable house full of books, and a dozen or so Old Cats crying for food, we found nothing of interest. The whole place was demolished soon after. We found good homes for the Cats: Shove Off took a couple and Tigger has one. Some nights I can hear them yamming out in the corridors.

About half a mile from Shefton Heights, Taki hurried me home so we could sort out the little spread we were having for the wake. As wakes go, I suppose it was a success; the apartment was full, we played music. Mostly though, we talked. Clancy and Shove Off had an interesting (and noisy) argument about whether it was possible to strangle yourself. Entertaining? You could've sold tickets.

After an hour or two, I began to flag. As if she somehow knew, Ms Galbraith said she'd stayed well beyond her

THE TERROR AND THE TORTOISESHELL

bedtime, gave me a hug and said goodbye. A steady trickle of departures followed, which meant that the air in the room became breathable again.

'Make sure he's up good and early,' I told Ma Spayley when she and Number One came to say goodbye. 'I get the impression Mrs. Collinson won't be satisfied unless the job's done thoroughly.'

Number One told me it might be a big job. He asked if he could take a few of his siblings along with him. I said that if it would help, he could take all his brothers and sisters along—providing Ma Spayley was agreeable.

'You'll be like the Baker Street Irregulars,' Ma Spayley said, smiling proudly. Number One scowled, not sure what she meant.

'What was that book you put in Mr. Spriteman's grave?' he asked me. Ma Spayley began to apologise for him. I stopped her.

'I'll tell you if you do a good job tomorrow.'

Ten minutes later, the flat was almost empty. Dingus patted me on the back, and Scragg left slightly the worse for wear a few minutes later. Shove Off waddled over, said it was a good send-off. I thanked him for coming.

That left Taki and me. She opened her mouth to speak but I got there first.

'I'm okay,' I told her. 'And I know where you are if I'm not.' Nodding, she kissed me on the cheek and left. I locked the door.

A quick glance round told me the place needed tidying up. I decided it could wait. Instead, I went over to the window and thought about the changes going on below; the Human Food Club, closing its doors and re-opening as a bowling alley. I wouldn't be going, that's for sure. To me it would always be a meat market. The ground where the Zoo had been was now an official meeting place of sorts for the Machenites. Of all the similar groups that sprung up following The Terror, the Machenites were the only

EPILOGUE: (ANOTHER) NEW BEGINNING

ones who'd prospered. In other places, The Terror had been known by other names, but our name for it seemed to catch on everywhere after a while. It was certainly better than the glum name and prophecies of the Orwellians—the last thing potential followers wanted to hear was that the world was even *worse* than they feared. And I suppose The Terror is as good a name for it as any.

The Agency had started to take off too; the publicity from the murders, along with Dingus passing on cases that an overburdened Police Force couldn't handle, meant that I'd had to take on more staff, Number One Mouse becoming my leading operative—besides myself, that is.

As for Sappies, I haven't seen any since the night we found Jimmy and that other guy in the building near the fairground. And Carlin too, of course. Sappies had become a bit like flying saucers—plenty saw them but nobody had definite proof. Every so often, I'd spot a mangy-looking Cat walking along the street and wonder if that was all it was. I'd hate to think that lunatic was still out there, waiting his chance to start over again.

Turning away from the window, I walked past the scattered chairs and dirty plates that littered the room. I looked at the bookshelf, now minus its copy of *The Devil You Know*, Jimmy's favourite book, and decided it was time to go to bed.

I had my claw on the light switch when I heard a *miaow* out in the corridor. Going to the door, I looked through the spy-hole. One of Shove Off's Cat's was looking up at the door. Through the distorted view of the spy-hole, he looked much bigger than any Old Cat should look; an Old Cat who for a second looked more like a—

It had never occurred to me that Old animals might eventually change too. But *we* had. For some strange reason, it wasn't a very pleasant thought.

With a shiver, I turned off the light and went to bed.

The End

About the Author

JOHN TRAVIS HAS HAD over 60 stories published in various books, magazines and journals in the UK, United States and Canada, most recently in *British Invasion* (Cemetery Dance) and *At Ease with the Dead* (Ash Tree Press). In the *Humdrumming Books of Horror Stories*, his story in the second volume, "The Tobacconist's Concession" reached the year's shortlist of the British Fantasy Awards for "Best Short Story". His first collection of short fiction, *Mostly Monochrome Stories*, has recently been published by The Exaggerated Press. His work has been praised by Ted Klein and David Renwick among others.

The Terror and the Tortoiseshell is part of an ongoing series featuring the feline Private Eye, Benji Spriteman. The second novel, *The Designated Coconut*, has just been completed, and two short adventures can be found in *Mostly Monochrome Stories*. He finds writing in the third person like this very odd indeed.

ATOMIC FEZ

Here's some we
made earlier...

TWISTHORN BELLOW
A novel by Rhys Hughes

Rhys Hughes once again foists his mad tale-spinning ability upon the world with this brand-new novel of monsters attacking all that is bad (musicians, Frenchmen... you know, *those* sort of people), tipping his hat in the direction of both '**Hellboy**' and **Philip José Farmer** in the process. when this author describes something as "this is the maddest thing I've ever written", you know you're in for something special.

It may come as no surprise that France wants to take over the world again. But this time they plan to go much further and gain control of the spiritual dimensions too, making French the official language of the afterlife! Twisthorn Bellow is a freshly baked golem who has fallen into a vat of nitroglycerin, turning him into a living stick of dynamite. As well as battling against monsters and rock musicians, he's the only thing that can preserve and protect the glorious British Empire and prevent the French-ification of the entire cosmos. But considering the French have all the best ideas and tunes, he doesn't stand a soufflé in Hell's chance!

Few living fictioneers approach this chef's sardonic confections, certainly not in English.
—Michael Moorcock

Rhys Hughes is more fun than one of those barrels of monkeys people talk about, and you're probably going to have a good time with his book.
—Peter Tennant; *Black Static*

Just beginning to read: saliva already forming on chin.
—Brian Aldiss

Paperback: $19^{99}/£11^{99} ‡ ISBN: 978-0-9811597-1-3
E-Book: $9^{99}/£4^{99} ‡ ISBN: 978-0-9811597-5-1

THE BEAUTIFUL RED
A collection by JAMES COOPER
Forward by CHRISTOPHER FOWLER

Red...
The colour that surrounds us as we enter the world;
the colour that consumes us when we die.

Red...
The colour of life and everything in it.

Red...
The colour we produce when we scream...

The Beautiful Red
12 extraordinary tales of madness and dysfunction,
dissecting the red world, where only the
sound of our violence can be heard...

A brand-new collection of twelve horror tales from **James Cooper**. This, his second collection, comes complete with a foreword from the Award-Winning Master of Urban Horror: **Christopher Fowler**.

The quality of [James Cooper's] *output so far easily matches that of the best-known talents in contemporary horror.*
—Carl Hays; *Booklist*

It's been quite a while since I've encountered stories like this, tales that ignore topical tastes in favour of a strange view of humanity that's timeless, classical, and mysteriously sad.
—Christopher Fowler (from his foreword)

[James Cooper is] *one of the most promising writers to emerge from the small press pack in recent years.*
—Peter Tennant; *Black Static*

Paperback: $19.99/£11.99 ‡ ISBN: 978-0-9811597-0-6
E-Book: $9.99/£4.99 ‡ ISBN: 978-0-9811597-6-8

WICKED DELIGHTS
A collection by JOHN LLEWELLYN PROBERT

Wicked...
The book that sucks the blood from children
...Delights
The film that turns people into self-destructive sadomasochistic obsessives
Wicked...
The lunatic asylum that steals souls
...Delights
The art exhibition of mutilated humanity...
where the exhibits are still alive!

John Llewellyn Probert's latest short story collection – containing 18 delicious selections across 352 delectable pages – mixes the cruel with the carnal, the sadistic with the sexual, the erotic with the outrageous, to bring you tales of a cuckolded husband's terrible revenge, the television channel where you can pay off your debts but at the worst price imaginable, the man willing to do anything to improve his chances of success with the ladies, a marriage guidance counsellor who goes to bloody extremes to prove her point, the woman who will do anything to keep her family, and a city made entirely from human bone. All of this, and the last Christmas ever, just to make things even *more* cheery.

★ *Vividly creepy images... are all the more compelling when rendered in Probert's breezy style.*
—**Publishers Weekly**

There's dark humour here, and unexpected poignancy—indeed, the book is as full of surprises as the man himself. Horror is lucky to have him.
—**Ramsey Campbell**

Jacket-less Hardback: $39^{99}/£22^{99} † ISBN: 978-0-9811597-2-0
E-Book: $9^{99}/£4^{99} † ISBN: 978-0-9811597-7-5

ATOMIC FEZ PUBLISHING

Selecting Only the Finest of Experts' Made-Up Stuff

www.AtomicFez.com